'Fraidy cats . . .

I shoved the tulip key into the slot. For a moment I feared that the key was stuck, but it engaged with unseen metal fixtures, and the wall suddenly seemed to give.

I stepped back, worried that the earthquake earlier that day had weakened the structure of the building. Carefully, I crept back up to the wall, put my hands against it, and gave it a nudge. A four-foot-wide section started to swing, and the outline of a door emerged from the pattern of bricks. Now, I gave it a proper shove. The whole thing creaked and swung open into the basement, rotating on a hidden, interior hinge.

I leveled my flashlight into a pitch-black corridor.

Isabella leaned into the tunnel, ears pricked, nose crinkling. She walked through the opening, and I fell in line behind her. Rupert sat on the basement floor, looking apprehensive. He wanted nothing to do with this murky, gaping hole in the wall.

"It's okay," I assured him. "You can stay here—in the cold, dark basement—without the flashlight."

Rupert gave me a nasty look and cautiously followed us through the opening in the bricks.

Titles by Rebecca M. Hale

HOW TO WASH A CAT

NINE LIVES LAST FOREVER

HOW TO MOON A CAT

ADRIFT ON ST. JOHN

HOW TO WASH A CAT

REBECCA M. HALE

BERKLEY PRIME CRIME, NEW YORK

THE BERKLEY PUBLISHING GROUP
Published by the Penguin Group
Penguin Group (USA) Inc.
375 Hudson Street, New York, New York 10014, USA

Penguin Group (Canada), 90 Eglinton Avenue East, Suite 700, Toronto, Ontario M4P 2Y3, Canada
(a division of Pearson Penguin Canada Inc.) • Penguin Books Ltd., 80 Strand, London WC2R 0RL,
England • Penguin Group Ireland, 25 St. Stephen's Green, Dublin 2, Ireland (a division of Penguin
Books Ltd.) • Penguin Group (Australia), 250 Camberwell Road, Camberwell, Victoria 3124, Australia
(a division of Pearson Australia Group Pty. Ltd.) • Penguin Books India Pvt. Ltd., 11 Community
Centre, Panchsheel Park, New Delhi—110 017, India • Penguin Group (NZ), 67 Apollo Drive,
Rosedale, Auckland 0632, New Zealand (a division of Pearson New Zealand Ltd.) • Penguin Books
(South Africa) (Pty.) Ltd., 24 Sturdee Avenue, Rosebank, Johannesburg 2196, South Africa

Penguin Books Ltd., Registered Offices: 80 Strand, London WC2R 0RL, England

This is a work of fiction. Names, characters, places, and incidents either are the product of the author's
imagination or are used fictitiously, and any resemblance to actual persons, living or dead, business
establishments, events, or locales is entirely coincidental. The publisher does not have any control over
and does not assume any responsibility for author or third-party websites or their content.

HOW TO WASH A CAT

A Berkley Prime Crime Book / published by arrangement with the author

PRINTING HISTORY
Green Vase Publishing hardcover edition / February 2008
Berkley Prime Crime mass-market edition / January 2010
Read Humane edition / May 2012

Copyright © 2008 by Rebecca M. Hale.
Cover illustration by Mary Ann Lasher.
Cover design by Diana Kolsky.
Interior text design by Kristin del Rosario.

ISBN: 978-0-425-24851-5

BERKLEY® PRIME CRIME
Berkley Prime Crime Books are published by The Berkley Publishing Group,
a division of Penguin Group (USA) Inc.,
375 Hudson Street, New York, New York 10014.
BERKLEY® PRIME CRIME and the PRIME CRIME logo are trademarks of
Penguin Group (USA) Inc.

PRINTED IN THE UNITED STATES OF AMERICA

10 9 8 7 6 5 4 3 2

ALWAYS LEARNING   PEARSON

For my grandfather, Bill

Prologue

I FOLLOWED A trail of paw prints, clumped up litter, and splattered flecks of soap up the stairs and down the hall to my bedroom. Sticky wet spots covered the floors, the walls, a rolltop desk, a wicker laundry basket, and a half dozen scattered books. A miserable wet lump of fur huddled in the middle of my bed.

"This is for your own good," I said, stealthily creeping towards him as I clutched the corners of a large beach towel. The lump glared back at me incredulously.

"We're almost done. We can't turn back now," I argued, slowly moving closer to the corner of the bed. The lump continued to stare at me suspiciously.

I glanced down at my arms and legs, grimly surveying the map of fresh scratches. Sighing, I gripped the towel and moved into position. The quivering lump dug his claws into the bedspread, anticipating my next move.

I lunged forward, the towel unfolding as my arms spread wide. My target tried to jump out of the way, but the billowing beach towel swallowed him whole. I felt a twinge of guilt as the sheet came down over his disappointed face;

then I carried my struggling wet fugitive back downstairs to the kitchen sink.

THE DAY HAD begun with a sense of foreboding, filled with apprehension of the task that lay ahead of me. Yawning in a reluctant gulp of crisp spring air, I wiggled my toes to rouse the two slumbering cats entwined at the foot of the bed—a mass of white fur tinged with peachy, buff-colored highlights.

One of them stood up, her back arching in a full body stretch before her slender figure leapt nimbly to the floor. Isabella issued a commanding look in my direction and sauntered out of the bedroom.

I swung my feet down to the hardwood floor, unearthing the second of my feline foot warmers. The more portly of the pair, he hit the ground beside the bed with a squawking grunt and waddled sleepily across the room to his inclined scratching post.

I splashed a basin full of cold water on my face and plodded slowly down the flight of stairs to the kitchen. Isabella greeted me with an impatient chirp and looked pointedly at her empty food bowl. Her imperious gaze followed me through the dark kitchen as I groped for the light switch and stumbled towards the coffee machine. Together, we watched as the first promising drops of brew began to plink into the glass receptacle. Isabella sat down on the floor in front of me, her wand of a tail waving back and forth, while I siphoned off the first precious ounces of the dark, steaming liquid. Coffee in hand, I dribbled a cup of dry cat food into the small white bowls on the floor underneath the kitchen table.

Upstairs, heavy feet padded towards the litter box, creaking the floorboards above my head. Seconds later, the unmistakable sounds of spastic, frenzied digging shook the ceiling, snowing the kitchen table with a light covering of dust. Isabella and I listened as the litter box—a shiny, red contraption complete with a covered hood—began to rock to a lively mambo beat. Thousands of sandy particles pattered against its plastic walls as the commotion above us increased in intensity.

I ran a caffeine-coated tongue over my top lip, waiting for the inevitable culmination of the boisterous goings-on inside the bouncing red igloo. Isabella trilled expectantly as a violent eruption launched the energetic digger out of the litter box and propelled him down the stairs. His fluffy, white blur careened around the corner and skidded through the entrance to the kitchen. He was covered from head to toe with a fine dusting of cat litter.

I greeted him casually. "Good morning, Rupert."

He blinked innocently up at me, grains of litter scattering from his furry eyebrows to the kitchen floor.

As a species, cats are generally known for their cleanliness. For Rupert, however, that objective couldn't quite compete with his love of litter box dancing. Despite his best efforts to remove it, stray pieces of litter clung to his white coat like persistent black fleas.

I had put this off as long as possible. A rank, unpleasant odor had begun to follow him around. It was time to give him a bath.

Biting down on my bottom lip, I strolled over to the sink and pulled out a couple of worn beach towels from a nearby drawer.

"Nothing special going on here," I said breezily, discreetly reaching my hand up to the shelf that held the cat shampoo.

My fingers flailed about in an unexpected vacuum. I risked an obvious glance to the empty shelf, and then down to the smug, satisfied cat sitting on the kitchen floor, munching on his breakfast. He paused, sensing my stare, and beamed triumphantly up at me.

Twenty minutes later, I finally found the shampoo bottle—shoved into a crevice between the refrigerator and the wall, alongside several toy mice and a bouncing ball. Rupert monitored my search from a series of defensive positions in the hallway, under the table, and behind the kitchen curtains. He crept commando style through the kitchen, sliding across the floor on his furry, round belly, eying me warily as I gripped the bottle around its neck and tapped it on the palm of my hand.

"Clever," I said, tapping furiously.

Rupert flashed me an impish grin and slowly began to back away. I reached out to grab him, but caught only air as he spun around and raced down the stairs that led to the first floor. That pudgy, white fur ball could be amazingly fast when motivated. The chase was on.

Rupert's long, feathery tail popped up, bouncing like a pogo stick as he hopped down the steps. He rounded the corner at the bottom of the stairs, spinning out as his claws scrambled on the slick wood floor. I dashed down after him, and, seconds later, stood in the middle of the open room that spanned the commercial, street level of the building. Pivoting slowly, I scanned my dusty surroundings for a hint to his hiding spot.

I was standing in the middle of my Uncle Oscar's antiques shop, the Green Vase. At least, I still thought of it as Uncle Oscar's. I had recently inherited his antiques business along with the three-story building it occupied.

Rupert's fuzzy, white reflection in the storefront glass revealed his location, hunched behind the edge of the adjacent counter that housed my uncle's antique cash register. I didn't want him to know that he had been discovered, so I continued the pretext of looking under cracked display cases and behind dusty bookshelves, gradually making my way over to the front door. I saw him tense up as I drew nearer.

Easing forward, I inched towards the counter and stepped surreptitiously into position. Rupert held his breath, trying to hold every hair perfectly still.

A small bird landed on the pavement outside. Overwhelmed by his feline instincts, Rupert couldn't help but glance out the window at it. Seizing the opportunity, I swooped around the counter and caught him by the long hairs on the back of his neck. Rupert made a peeved, squelching sound as my fingers locked around his wide midsection, and I hoisted him up.

"Let's get this over with," I said, lugging my captive back upstairs.

Isabella had watched the chase scene from a perch on the top of a bookcase in the showroom. She trailed a safe distance behind as I trudged up the stairs with my despondent cargo.

Rupert's furry face looked up at me woefully.

"It's not that bad," I said soothingly. He shot me a livid look that conveyed his obvious disagreement.

Back in the kitchen, I scrambled to turn on the water and adjust the temperature without losing my grip on the increasingly agitated Rupert. When I finally managed to lower him into the sink, he splayed his back legs out, catching the rim. After a flurry of skin-gouging scratches, I succeeded in positioning him in front of the running faucet. Vengeful, vicious mutterings emitted from the basin as I dunked him under the stream of running water and began to lather him up.

To wash a large, uncooperative cat is to take on a seemingly impossible and sure to be thankless task. I was just about to start the rinse cycle when his slippery, struggling body broke free. With lightening speed, his soapy, white blur jumped out of the sink, streaked across the kitchen, and sprinted up the stairs. I heard him scamper through the litter box and dart into my bedroom, a shower of damp litter spraying out behind him.

Cursing under my breath, I grabbed a large beach towel and raced after him.

Chapter 1

THE QUIRKY LITTLE flat above my Uncle Oscar's antiques shop had been subjected to over twenty years of his erratic remodeling efforts. The result was a series of irregularly shaped, mismatched rooms spliced together into a gerrymandered floor plan. To pass from the living room to the bedrooms above was like navigating a three-dimensional jigsaw puzzle.

The kitchen featured faded wallpaper that clung limply to its drywall with the improvised help of unconventional construction materials such as paperclips, staples, and sticky tape. It was also home to a temperamental dishwasher that was prone to sporadic, mid-cycle eruptions. A stray piece of food hidden on the backside of a plate or wedged between the tines of a fork could cause offense. The first sobbing bubbles of self-pity would quickly escalate into a heaving regurgitation of the machine's entire liquid contents, sending several frothy gallons spewing down its front and out onto the mosaic of chipped and uneven floor tiles below.

But already, the Green Vase felt more like home than any

place I'd ever lived. Uncle Oscar's familiar spirit lingered around every cobbled-together corner. His haunting presence was warm and welcoming from the moment I carried my first box of belongings across the threshold downstairs.

At the time, all I knew was that I had traded in the quiet, predictable solitude of my previous life for an uncertain future in a vaguely defined self-employment. Fate had kicked open a door and punted me through. Dusting myself off on the other side, I had no inkling of the inscrutable eyes that were following my every move.

MY OLD APARTMENT had been a short drive away from Oscar's antiques store. Stacked like a pancake into an art deco building on a busy street up in the center of San Francisco, my living quarters were economical, if not luxurious. After a week spent hunched over my desk, silently crunching numbers, I would load the cats into my trusty Corolla and escape down the hill for one of Oscar's decadent, high calorie feasts.

Uncle Oscar loved to cook for us, and we loved his cooking. His specialty was fried chicken, a dish rarely prepared in this health-conscious city. You could always tell when Oscar was working in his kitchen; succulent smells wafted out the living room window and percolated down to the street below. My mouth would start watering as soon as I pulled up to the curb outside.

I can still remember our last visit. I let myself in through the store entrance on the ground level with my spare key and released the cats from their carriers. Rupert and Isabella bounded up the stairs to the kitchen, knowing they would find tasty appetizers waiting in their dinner bowls.

I brought up the rear, winding my way through the labyrinth of Oscar's store. It occupied a long, cavernous room that took up the entire first floor. Or at least it would have felt cavernous if it hadn't been so completely jammed with Oscar's collections.

The floor, where visible, was made up of dark, hardwood planks that made pleasant creaking sounds as I walked across them. Dusty molding trimmed the edges of the walls and gathered cobwebs on the ceiling.

I stumbled through the room, late afternoon sunlight flickering on the many gold-infused objects that cluttered the store. A stale, musty smell hung in the air, mixing with the fried chicken fragrances coming from the kitchen above.

When I finally reached the stairs at the back of the room, they were partially blocked by a massive wooden crate propped up against the stairwell. Each time I visited, it seemed more and more shipping containers were stacked inside the store.

My sweater snagged on the rough exterior of the crate as I squeezed through the narrow opening between it and the wall. By the time I untangled myself and ascended the rest of the way to the kitchen, both cats were smacking up chunks of sautéed chicken liver from saucers underneath the table. Rupert gave me a reproachful look for my tardiness.

"You've spoiled them," I complained, giving my uncle a hug. "They refuse to eat regular cat food now."

He was a scruffy old guy. He had thick, bushy, gray eyebrows with several wild, straw-like quills poking out of them at odd angles. A couple of days' stubble studded his rounded cheeks and scratched against me as I wrapped my arms around his short round shoulders. His navy blue collared shirt was spotted with ingredients from tonight's menu.

"They told me you were starving them again," my uncle responded with a wink towards Rupert, who was squirming at our feet anticipating the next course.

Uncle Oscar's antiques store was called the Green Vase, although a passerby could be forgiven for failing to see the faded gold lettering on the front door announcing this information. The windows were dingy and cracked in places, and everything inside was coated with a thick layer of con-

gealed dust. Items were randomly grouped together in piles
or stuffed into deteriorating cardboard boxes, sometimes
with no clear rationale for their association.

Oscar had a 'true believer' theory about antiquing.
Worthy shoppers, he felt, should appreciate the chal-
lenge of digging through his haystack piles in the hopes
of finding a single, precious needle of antiquity. If they
were not up for this task, he would grumpily direct them
to one of the many well-lit, neatly arranged stores down
the street.

"Amateurs," he would harrumph with derision at the
end of this oft-repeated rant. To my untrained eye, the
Green Vase showroom looked a lot more like a flea market
than an antiques store, but I kept this opinion to myself.

The Green Vase sat in a quiet corner of downtown San
Francisco, just to the north of the financial district, in a
neighborhood called Jackson Square. Tucked behind the
city's signature Transamerica Pyramid Building, this area
was mostly forgotten by both local San Franciscans and
the city's crowds of tennis shoe tourists. Only a few pe-
destrians and the occasional delivery truck shadowed its
sidewalks. A sophisticated hush blanketed the (mostly)
high-end antiques stores that filled the shady, tree-lined
streets.

Amid this placid, sanitized atmosphere, it was hard to
imagine what the scene had been like during the raucous
days of the Gold Rush. But in the warm, comfortable
kitchen above the Green Vase, Oscar's stories brought the
colorful characters from that time to life.

According to Oscar, gold was first discovered in the
Sierra foothills in the spring of 1848. As more and
more nuggets began rolling into San Francisco, rumors of
the California El Dorado circled the globe, escalating in
scale on each re-telling. Reports of miraculous riches,
sparkling in the riverbeds for anyone to scoop up, spurred
many to hitch a ride west by any means possible.

Before long, a desperate mass of humanity had inundated San Francisco. This eternally optimistic crowd had

convinced themselves that they were but one day away from hitting the mother lode. While they waited for that eventuality, they spent their meager vials of painfully collected gold dust in this 'anything goes' corner of the city.

Saloons were crammed into every spare foot of available space—in ramshackle buildings, lean-to shacks, and leaky canvas tents. These establishments offered patrons far more than a good stiff drink. Gambling, prostitution, and tawdry sideshows were the norm. Blatant criminal activity carried on unhindered by any police deterrent. The unwary were quick to lose their shirts, if not their lives.

Nowadays, the historic Jackson Square neighborhood contains some of the only buildings to have survived the infamous 1906 earthquake and the subsequent firestorm that swept through the rest of the city. Three story red brick structures predominate, with many having undergone extensive renovations. Elaborate ornamental trimmings frame the windows, eaves, and gutters of several of the storefronts.

Uncle Oscar couldn't have cared less about such architectural details. He was far more interested in the people who had calculated, connived, and caroused their way through this corner of the city. He knew everything there was to know about everyone who had come to San Francisco during the Gold Rush.

Oscar had read countless books on the topic, studied every historical map he could find, interviewed local historians, and sifted through the remains of endless estate sales. He was well known at the San Francisco library, where he had combed through their entire historical documents section. His knowledge on the Gold Rush period was encyclopedic.

After dinner, Oscar would dig around downstairs in the store, bring up a recently acquired item, and entertain us with a lively narrative about its past and the people who might have used it.

I am sure that the ghosts of the free-spirited characters from Oscar's stories still wander other parts of the city, but they have long been expelled from Jackson Square.

A collection of high-end art galleries and antiques stores have moved into this once derelict, now dressed up, neighborhood. Rows of pretentious storefronts line the streets, displaying a range of high-priced settees, credenzas, vases, maps, prints, engravings, pewter pieces, and historic trinkets.

Uncle Oscar had blatantly ignored this trend. Plopped down in the middle of a row of these highbrow stores, the Green Vase could not have been more out of place. The bright and shiny storefronts on either side blushed with embarrassment at its faded awning, cracked glass, and crumbling brick exterior. Oscar had not cared much about appearances, his own or the store's.

While I found his cavalier spirit endearing, others did not—particularly his new next-door neighbor, Frank Napis. From the moment he moved in, Frank began filing complaints about the Green Vase with the city-appointed board responsible for ensuring the historical preservation of the buildings in the Jackson Square neighborhood.

Oscar's attorney usually represented him during these board meeting confrontations. He rarely attended.

"I don't like to give *Frank* the satisfaction," Oscar would say, spitting out the name as if it tasted bitter and unpleasant.

Even as Oscar finished preparing our dinner that last Saturday night, he was still fuming about the board meeting that had been held earlier that week.

"What a bunch of nonsense," he said bitterly, aggressively whipping a large, wooden spoon through a bowl of mashed potatoes. Oscar turned his attention to the sizzling sounds of the chicken simmering in his heavy, cast iron skillet. "This time, he's complaining about my *gutters*."

Oscar's cheeks began to flush. "Historical preservation! What do they think the gutters on this street looked like during the Gold Rush?"

I ducked as Oscar sloshed more cooking oil into the pot, creating a shower of oil-splattering sparks. Oscar's gutters were so beaten up and full of holes, they looked as if they had taken on artillery fire, but I nodded along supportively.

"My gutters are fine, thank you very much," Oscar said defensively. "They've been through a couple of rainy seasons, that's all."

Oscar had been ranting about his neighbor for months, but I had only seen my uncle's loathed antagonist once. Oscar had been out of town, and I had stopped by after work to pick up his mail.

It was early evening and the afternoon's bright sun was quickly fading to dusk. The streets of Jackson Square were quiet and abandoned, with most of the shopkeepers having gone home for the day. I stood in front of Oscar's heavy, iron-framed door, grappling with its rusty latch. As I knelt down to get a better look at the lock, I sensed a movement on the edge of my periphery. My head turned to see a man closing up the store next door.

He had a short, Napoleonic figure with a pot-bellied middle and stout, round legs. The downy, maple-brown fuzz of his thinning hair gave his head a hawk-like appearance—an effect that was further enhanced by the beaked nose that hooked out from his otherwise flat face and cast a shadow over his thin, deflated lips. Crouched on the sidewalk, the darkness closing in, I'd felt an uneasy squirming in the pit of my stomach as the man turned to stare at me.

His thin lips curved upwards in acknowledgement, followed by a strange twitch that spasmed the pale skin hiding beneath his enormous nose. I managed a weak smile in return as the lock finally submitted to the bent and twisted spare key.

I stepped inside the dark store and stooped over to pick up a couple of letters off of the floor where they had fallen through the mail slot. When I rose to leave, Napis's short, stumpy legs were already carrying him down the darkened street. I watched him disappear from my vantage point inside the Green Vase before heading back outside.

Oscar was still muttering biliously about the dispersions to his gutters, but his mood seemed to lighten as he loaded several steaming dishes onto the kitchen table, and we sat down to eat. I dove into the plate of fried chicken while the cats curled up at our feet, contentedly crunching on a mixture of tender, juicy chicken and rice. Below us, Oscar's antiques collection glimmered in the faintly lit showroom.

Unlike most of the Jackson Square antiques shops, which carried items from a wide range of time frames and geographic locations, the Green Vase's collection was narrowly focused on pieces from the Gold Rush era. Within this specific genre, however, Uncle Oscar had accumulated far more than the typical antiques fare. Artifacts from almost every aspect of life were strewn throughout the store.

For example, Oscar had an extensive collection of teeth. Successful miners had been anxious to show off the results of their labors, and gold teeth had been a favored vanity. Dentists had been called on to sacrifice countless healthy teeth in order to make space for gold replacements. Some unfortunate chops had been stripped of every last bit of enamel so that their owner could showcase a solid gold smile. Oscar's display of gold teeth was complemented by a wide array of painful-looking dental instruments as well as a Gold Rush-era dental chair.

San Franciscans had incorporated gold into every possible form of self-ornamentation: watches, cufflinks, pins, rings, seals, compasses, and chains. Gold-headed canes had been extremely popular (and useful to many given the backbreaking labor involved in mining). Gold inlays had been embedded into revolvers, knife handles, saddles, plates, dishes, and even a somewhat out of tune fiddle. The Green Vase had it all.

The peaceful silence of the dinner table was broken by a loud clanging.

"Blast!" Oscar jumped up and lumbered grouchily towards the phone.

The cats were licking up the last drops of chicken broth from their tiny bowls on the floor. Isabella looked up politely; Rupert kept slurping.

Oscar appeared to recognize the voice on the other end of the line, but I didn't pick up much more than that from his side of the conversation.

"Uh-huh." There was a long pause. Then another, somewhat more interested, "Hmm, uh-huh."

The tip of Oscar's index finger thoughtfully stroked the stubble on his chin. "Okay, I'll see you first thing tomorrow." And he hung up. He was still lost in thought when he rejoined us at the table.

One of Oscar's construction buddies, I figured, and helped myself to another drumstick.

Part of Oscar's success in the antiques world derived from his network of contacts within the local construction industry. Downtown San Francisco was undergoing a rapid building boom, and new high-rise office and residential projects were rapidly changing the skyline. To steady the structures through coming earthquakes, strict building codes mandated that the construction be fortified by metal pilings drilled deep into the earth. Each scalping pit provided the opportunity to unearth more Gold Rush-era artifacts.

Prior to the discovery of gold in the inland hills, the Golden Gate—the name given to the natural opening of the bay long before the famous bridge was built—had sheltered only a sparsely inhabited cove called Yerba Buena. The name change to San Francisco happened around the same time as the first gold discovery, and the newly named city nearly burst at the seams with the subsequent mass migration.

From an antiques perspective, San Francisco's explosive and unscripted growth during the late 1800s had left a trove of underground treasures. Situated on the tip end of a peninsula, the city had quickly exhausted the nearby supply of naturally occurring land, and the booming metropolis began swiftly sprawling out into the bay on a foundation of hastily constructed landfill. As a result, several blocks of the downtown area were built up on land that had originally been under several feet of water.

In the days before railroads spiderwebbed across the continent, there were only two ways to reach the gold fields of Northern California—stage or other cloven-hoofed transport across a hostile interior, or cramped, disease-ridden ocean passage. In the eyes of the gold-seeking masses, the quicker they got to California the better, no matter what the cost or discomfort. Desperately afraid that all of the gold would be carted away before they arrived, many of the early Gold Rush immigrants chose the faster ocean route and entered the city through its harbor.

As each ship approached San Francisco, passengers and sailors alike abandoned the vessels and headed straight to the Sierra foothills. It was impossible to find anyone to unload the cargo, much less sail the ships on to their next destination. A backlog of rotting hulls blockaded the bay. Some were converted into hotels, storefronts, and other forms of storage or residence, all of which were in short supply. Many were dismantled and the pieces used for scrap. Others were simply sunk in their moorings, drifting down into a man-made sediment of ship hulls, sand scraped off of nearby dunes, and anything else the residents of this growing shoreline wished to get rid of.

All of this debris formed the bedrock of the landfill that was now being excavated by modern day construction crews. As each new high-rise building sank its roots into the muck of this underground garbage dump, many long-discarded items were being disgorged. Most of these relics had been tossed into the mire as unwanted trash, but— every now and then—Oscar uncovered an item of far greater historical significance.

I don't know how Oscar developed his contacts in the

construction industry, but he seemed to have cornered the market. As soon as the remains of a ship or any other item of interest emerged, Oscar would receive a discreet phone call. He would meet his contact at the construction site, usually after hours or early on a Sunday morning, peruse the findings, and pay cash for any items that interested him.

Nothing in the phone call that night had seemed unusual. We had continued on with dinner in typical fashion, Uncle Oscar teasing Rupert about his insatiable appetite and ever-expanding waistline.

At the end of the evening, I cleaned up the kitchen the best I could. Oscar's living quarters were not any more organized than the store downstairs. I turned around from the sink to see Oscar cradling a well-fed Rupert in his arms.

Rupert was in a state of bliss. His eyes were closed and his legs hung limply in the air as Oscar lightly rubbed his stuffed stomach.

"I can leave that one here with you, you know," I teased.

"Hrmph," Oscar grumped unconvincingly, gently rolling Rupert into my arms. "Filthy creature needs a bath."

I carried the snoozing Rupert down the stairs, carefully sliding around the shipping crate as Isabella trotted behind us. After securing the cats in their carriers for the trip home, I turned to hug my uncle goodbye.

"See you next week?" I asked.

"Yup. I'll see you then," he replied.

I remember waving to him after I loaded the cats into the car and started the engine. He stood on the sidewalk, a faint breeze picking up a couple of strands of the gray hair on his forehead. I thought he looked a little tired, but not noticeably so. He always seemed so tough, so durable.

I guess I just somehow believed that he would go on forever.

Chapter 2

THE NEXT MORNING, he was gone.

Oscar must have been heading out the door for his Sunday morning appointment when it happened. One of his neighbors walked by and saw the body sprawled on the floor just inside the Green Vase. The paramedics broke in, but they were unable to resuscitate him. The police found my number on Oscar's refrigerator and called me late Sunday night.

By Monday afternoon, the coroner had conducted a preliminary autopsy to determine the cause of death.

"Looks like he had a stroke," the voice crackled over the phone line. I swallowed silently on the other end, still choking on the flood of emotions brought on by Oscar's sudden departure.

"Did he—," I began my question, but couldn't finish it.

"It was probably over in a couple of minutes," the voice said in a soothing tone. "I don't think he suffered much."

I spent the next couple of days marching through a numbing parade of end of life formalities. Trudging into the funeral service at the end of the week, I was emotionally drained and physically exhausted. I stared woodenly into the casket at my uncle's waxen face; then watched silently as they lowered him into the ground.

I fled the cemetery as soon as the service was over and caught a bus to the city. I sat in my seat like a stone, staring at the floor, numbly listening to the creaking frame and grinding gears as the bus wound its way down into the financial district where I was scheduled to meet Oscar's lawyer for the reading of his will.

I drug myself up the polished front steps of a high-rise office building and squeezed into a crowded elevator. My empty stomach lurched as the stifling cube zoomed skyward, finally pausing to hover at the 39th floor. My head woozing, I stepped gratefully out into the refrigerated air of an expansive lobby. A wall of windows spanned the left side of the room, framing an opulent view of the bay.

The receptionist took my name and motioned me towards a seating area, but I was drawn to the view. Looking out, I could see down past the sparkling surface of the water into the brooding, blue depths below.

I was positioned near the top of a building that sat right on the water's edge, at the farthest limit of the city's precarious crawl out into the bay. A row of piers lined the opposite side of the street. Beyond them, the bed of the bay dropped off precipitously, plunging down into deep shipping lanes.

The windowpanes were so transparent—so clear—they created a false sense of oneness with the bay below. The flip-flopping in my stomach subsided as I placed my right hand against the window, lightly touching its cool, flat surface. I could sense the twisting currents powerfully churning through the convolutions of the bay's underwater geography. The lunar forces puppeteering those swirling tides hooked into the prickling tips of my fingers, suctioning them against the glass. For a moment, the weariness inside me evaporated.

A disapproving cough summoned me back to the front

desk. The receptionist led me across an expanse of thick, sound-smothering carpet and into a maze of corridors, cubicles, and coffee stations. Several minutes later, we arrived at the prestigious office of Miranda C. Richards, Esquire.

The receptionist hesitated outside the open door, but appeared to receive a signal and ushered me forward. I stepped nervously inside the office where Oscar's attorney paced in front of another wall of equally impressive windows.

She glanced across the room at me, so I tried to introduce myself. "Hello, I'm . . ."

"Oh, it's *you*," she said irritably.

I shrugged my shoulders, speechless—before realizing that the woman was talking into a wireless device hooked over one ear.

"Cut to the point," she sniped into the headset, starting another frustrated lap in front of the windows lining the back wall of the office. "I don't have time to listen to you babble." Her voice shrilled sharply as the heels of her shoes sparked across the carpet.

I stuffed my hands into my pockets and turned to study a bright, multi-colored painting hanging on a wall near the door. A large, barn-like structure dominated the picture. It sat on the edge of a body of water, fronted by a lush row of purple flowers. An illegible smudge of handwriting in the bottom corner presumably gave the artist's name. I squinted at the blurred lines, but couldn't make out any of the words.

I peeked over my shoulder as the phone conversation continued.

"You're way out of your league. You should stay out of this." Miranda's voice silked acidly as she turned away from the window. "I don't care what my *mother* told you." She caught my look and motioned for me to take a seat in front of her desk.

I collapsed into the indicated chair. The seat cushion was rock-hard and shaped so that my shoulders were pushed against the knobby buttons protruding from the back of the chair. I shifted uncomfortably and stared at the agitated woman on the other side of the room.

Miranda Richards's forceful figure wore a bright red, closely fitted suit. The red cloth glowed a tart shade of cranberry that matched chunk-sized rubies dangling from her earlobes and around her neck. Her vigorous pacing exuded the pulse of an insuppressible internal energy.

She was in her mid-forties, I guessed from the thin lines that creased the corners of her face. A few unruly strands of gray popped out of her thick auburn hair, which was swept up into a clasp at the back of her head.

The late afternoon sun started to sink into the horizon, sending piercing rays through the wide window, focusing on my seat like a spotlight. Wincing, I raised a hand to shade my bloodshot eyes. Without breaking stride, Miranda's fingers deftly twitched a cord and the vertical slats of the blinds slapped shut. In the dimmer, artificial light of the office, I returned to the status of spectator.

She came closer to the desk and raised her index finger to indicate, I hoped, that her conversation was coming to an end. The long, claw-like nails were painted to match the pungent red tones of the rest of her outfit.

"Fine," she said, rolling her eyes. Miranda reached into one of her desk drawers and pulled out a container of lipstick. "Why don't you stop by my office tomorrow?" Her voice oozed huskily—as if she were luring an unwitting prey to her lair. "Maybe I can persuade you to change your mind."

As she began to coat her lips with a glossy layer of the red paste, the thick, floral scent of her perfume reached across the desk and almost strangled me. It seeped into my sinuses and started closing down my nasal passages. My eyes began to water. I pulled off my glasses and reached for a tissue from a box on the edge of her desk as the twitching inside my nose became unbearable.

"Ah . . . choo!" A loud, high-pitched sneeze exploded

in the office as my nose expelled the noxious perfume. Miranda's head whipped around at me, clearly annoyed.

"I have to go," she snapped testily, clicking off the device with a flick of one of her nails.

"So," she said, looking me over as she dropped into the springy, ergonomic armchair on her side of the desk. "You're Oscar's niece."

I nodded, scooting forward, trying to find a more comfortable position.

We were separated by the wide, smooth surface of her desk. It was empty except for the flat panel of her computer screen, a slim legal file, and the box of tissues.

"Miranda Richards," she said crisply, introducing herself as she flipped open the file. "You have my condolences." Her eyes flickered briefly before she rushed on. "It's lucky I could fit you in today. Did you bring some identification? We'll need to make a copy for our records."

She rolled her eyes impatiently as I fumbled through my shoulder bag for my wallet. Used tissues, a well-worn glasses case, and a collection of chewed up pens and pencils all poked out of the bag as I searched. Finally, I extracted the wallet and pulled out my driver's license. One of the red claws pressed a button whose ringing echoed in the hallway outside. A meek, colorless woman scurried into the room.

Miranda flung my license across the desk towards the assistant. "The security box, too," she said, wasting few words on her subordinate. I watched sympathetically as the woman scraped my license off of the slick surface of the desk and scampered out the door.

Miranda briefly consulted the top page of the file, clicked her tongue against the roof of her mouth, and looked up at me.

"Well, it's pretty straightforward. He left everything to you." She studied me with a casual interest, as if I were a fly she was about to swat.

"I'll handle the liquidation for you. I'm sure there will be some offers. It should bring you a nice little nest egg."

She smiled at me for the first time. "After my commission, of course."

"Um, well," I murmured.

"Yes," she replied slickly, her calculating eyes glittering as they bored into me.

"I don't know that I want to sell it, actually," I said tentatively.

Her smile slithered into a sneer. "Why wouldn't you? The Green Vase can't be of any use to you."

The nails began to click threateningly against the smooth surface of the desk. I felt as if my stomach had left the office and soared down the elevator shaft in the lobby.

"What do you know about running an antiques business?" she asked icily. She looked down at her file. "You're a—secretary or something?"

"Accountant," I replied, feeling my face flush.

Miranda rested her powdered chin on the palm of her right hand and flashed her long, manicured nails at me. "Look sweetie, that place is a pit. It needs a lot of work. Frank Napis will be all over this at the next board meeting. The new owner is going to have to make some improvements."

I tried not to blink as my weary, watery eyes met her heavily mascaraed ones. She shifted her weight, put both hands on the desk, and leaned towards me.

"You don't understand," she said condescendingly through gritted, pearly white teeth. "Oscar had a lot of clout. He was an old-timer. He'd been in the neighborhood since before they started fixing it up. The board let him get away with just about anything—with *my* help of course. But you," she twisted one side of her mouth upwards into a curl. "You, they'll eat for lunch. Sell the place and be done with it."

That settled it. "No thanks," I said firmly, mustering every available ounce of determination. "I'm going to keep it."

At that moment, I had absolutely no idea what I was

going to do with the Green Vase, but I wasn't about to share that information with the woman on the other side of the desk.

Miranda let out a harassed sigh. "Well, there'll be some money left in his accounts once the estate has been probated. Somehow, Oscar managed to do pretty well over the last couple of years." She shook her head resignedly. "You'll need to present your renovation plans to the board for their approval."

Miranda pulled open a side drawer to her desk and flipped through an index of business cards. "Here," she pulled one out and handed it to me, "talk to this guy about doing the work."

I took the card and slipped it into my shoulder bag.

"I don't see the board's schedule in here," Miranda said, halfheartedly rifling through the file. "My secretary will call you with the dates." She snapped Oscar's file shut as her assistant returned with a small metal box. Miranda eyed her reflection in the glare of the computer monitor, licked one of the red-tipped fingers, and used it to smooth down an errant strand of gray hair. She glanced over at me and nodded towards the box in an irritated, expectant manner. "Go ahead and open it. Oscar left it for you."

I reached over and grasped the flat, cold surface of the metal box. The long, rectangular lid had been painted with a shiny, black lacquer. As I stared down at it, Miranda's pushy, red figure and her stuffy, imposing office faded away. The metal box began to morph into the wooden coffin I'd buried earlier that day. I leaned forward in my chair, watching the small, black coffin drop slowly down into a deep, muddy hole. The dank, earthy smell of the cemetery seeped through my nose.

My trembling hands rattled the metal box against the polished wood surface of Miranda's desk. I gripped the edges and pushed the lip of the lid up over a single metal rib underneath. The flimsy metal top creaked open, and I willed myself to look inside. The cemetery air vanished in my lungs as Oscar's placid, frozen face stared up at me.

The assistant placed a careful hand on my shoulder, and I felt myself sway under her light touch. Miranda was clearly preparing to leave for the day, and the assistant was eager to remove me from the office before the dragon lady scorched us both with her fiery, impatient breath.

I took in a gulp of sickening, floral-infused air and my mind rejoined my body in Miranda's office, still suffering in the stiff, unrelenting chair. As my eyes refocused, I saw a thin, white envelope lying on the bottom of the metal box. I recognized the cramped handwriting that had scrawled my name across the front.

My left hand dove into the box and plucked out the package. I jumped up from the tortuous chair, grabbed my shoulder bag off the floor, and sprinted down the hall outside Miranda's office. I took one look at the swooping elevator in the lobby and opted for the stairs, gripping the envelope in my sweating fingers as I hurtled down its endless well of steps.

I didn't stop until my feet hit the sidewalk outside. Somewhere out in the bay, a steamer hooted a long, low whistle as I stared down at the envelope in my hands.

A passerby jostled my elbow, and the envelope tilted.

Something inside rustled against the paper as it slid towards the bottom corner.

Chapter 3

A WET, APRIL wind had skipped into the bay while I'd been sequestered behind the blinds in Miranda's office. The curling cape of clouds that trailed behind it chilled the intricate, stone faces of the towering downtown office buildings.

I crossed the street for the open door of a coffee shop as the first flecks of rain playfully slapped my cheeks and beaded up on my glasses—Oscar's sealed envelope riding safely inside my coat pocket.

A hissing column of steam rose up from a collection of stainless steel appliances. I stood in line, my senses swamped by the overpowering aroma of freshly ground coffee beans, waiting for a tattooed man on the opposite side of the counter to take my order.

"Cream? Sugar?" The attendant punched the words out mechanically as he slipped a cardboard sleeve around a paper cup emblazoned with the coffee shop's logo.

I shook my head and handed him the total.

I spied a wooden chair at a wobbly, three-legged table in a back corner of the room and headed towards it, threading my way through a knot of highly polished thirtysome-things. I wrestled past a bulky designer handbag and hur-dled over several Italian leather loafers before finally reaching the open seat and sliding into it.

I closed my eyes as the first invigorating sip soaked through my weary body, and the casual din of conversation filled in around me. A bevy of salon-slick urbanettes twit-tered noisily nearby, trying to assess the availability of a hunky espresso drinker at the next table. He stared brood-ingly into his laptop, seemingly oblivious to their specula-tions.

Tucked into my corner, I felt somehow isolated from the buzzing room around me. The warm comfort of the coffee seeped through me as I pulled the envelope out of my pocket, slipped a finger under a corner of the flap, and pulled down along the seam, expanding the opening the length of the package.

A long, metal key fell out of the envelope and flopped onto the sticky surface of the table. I picked it up to exam-ine it more closely, rolling it back and forth in my fingers.

The tarnished gold surface glowed warmly in the dim light of the coffee shop. The surface of the key was nicked in several places, as if it had seen regular use.

A slender, metal rod made up the trunk of the key. On one end, three dime-sized, interlocking petals formed the shape of a tulip. The opposite end had been tooled into a series of nubs and bumps. I stared at the tulip design, won-dering if the matching lock was as elaborately decorated.

Curiosity now overcoming dread, I decided to investi-gate the remaining contents of the envelope.

I took in a deep breath and pulled open the mouth of the package to reveal a single sheet of paper snuggled inside. I spread out a discarded sports section from the *Chronicle* as a shield against the day's sticky coating of spilled drinks; then I gently freed the sheet from the enve-lope and unfolded it on the table in front of me.

Just a few lines covered the top half of the page, writ-ten in Oscar's large, easily identifiable handwriting.

Don't worry your pretty head about me. I've had a
good run of it. Take good care of the Green Vase—
she's got plenty of life in her yet.
   There are so many doors left for you to open. All
you need is the right key.

The letter was signed with Oscar's characteristically
looping "O," trailed by a long, squiggling paraph.

I picked the key back up. "I bet you've got a story to
tell," I murmured, trying to imagine what Oscar meant me
to use it for.

I refolded the piece of paper and slid it and the key
back into the envelope. Memories of my uncle flooded
over me.

Oscar had been in the army during WWII and had
served as an ambulance driver during the campaign in
Europe. He'd told me several hair-raising stories of the
things he'd seen there. The experience had immutably
shaped his philosophies and beliefs.

"When your time comes," he'd say, "that's it. There
ain't nothing you can do about it, so there's no point in
worrying on it." He'd pause and look me straight in the
eye. "You have to enjoy your life while you can."

In the fog of that war he'd seen strong men cut down
while weaker ones survived. There was no rational explanation for who lived and who died. He had understood the
cruel randomness of fate, in a way that my accountant's
mind could never quite grasp hold of.

One event in particular had left its imprint on Oscar.
Midway through the war, he'd come down sick with an
unknown illness. The hospital had been overwhelmed
with casualties, and the doctors hadn't had the time or
resources to try to diagnose what afflicted him. His fever
raged for days until he finally lost consciousness. A nurse
pulled a sheet over his head and marked his body to be
carted away to the morgue.

"I was gone," he said, mouthing his dentures contempla-
tively as he reflected. "But something told me to turn back.

It just wasn't my time." He leaned across the table towards me and pulled out the misguided mortuary tag he always carried around in his wallet, waving it at me for emphasis. "I've tried to make the most out of every day since."

I sighed heavily, feeling the loss of Oscar all over again like a swift punch to the stomach. The nausea was only exacerbated by my overwhelming confusion over what to do next.

Oscar had never accepted the merits of my accounting job. He'd been trying to convince me to quit for years. He'd seen through the façade of my career for what it really was.

Hidden away in my cubicle amid the impersonal piles of balance sheets and business plans, it was easy for me to avoid the uncomfortable complications of human interaction.

Numbers were so much more reliable, so much easier to handle than the fickle transience inherent to human nature. Numbers could always be called out on a lie or a manipulation. Numerical entanglements never lasted any longer than the summation line of their equation.

When I did emerge from the dark cave of my cubicle, I walked through the city cloaked in an invisible veil of self-isolation, maintaining a careful distance from the surrounding sea of people as I navigated my way through them.

I was a shell, living vicariously off the hum of the city's ceaseless heartbeat. I could walk the constantly changing streets for hours, soaking up purpose from the lives that swirled around me.

I was a bystander, not a participant. My life was quiet and peaceful, like the deep, untroubled sleep of my cats. I had curled myself up into a ball, porcupined against the world.

I didn't realize it at the time—sitting in the crowded coffee shop, staring down at Oscar's handwriting on the crumpled white envelope—but I was slowly, subtly, being unwound from that complacent slumber.

"The right key," I repeated his phrase to myself, pondering Oscar's message.

I looked up from my table and out through the front window of the coffee shop. Misting droplets were smearing the glass, but I could just make out the street sign on the corner outside. I was only a couple of blocks over from the Green Vase.

I stuffed the envelope into my shoulder bag, squeezed myself through the maze of tables to the front door, and stepped onto the street outside.

Those people who hadn't crammed their way into the coffee shop were rushing through the increasing drip to their buses, BARTs, and ferryboats. Despite my trepidation over the possibility of taking over the Green Vase, I couldn't ignore the exuberant tingling in my toes as I turned my soggy shoes towards Jackson Square.

Somewhere in that evening's soupy fog, lurking well beyond the reach of my subconscious, there was a faint clicking sound as a door pulled shut behind me.

Chapter 4

THE STREET WAS empty as I rounded the corner and turned up the block towards the Green Vase. What meager Friday afternoon traffic had trickled through Jackson Square was now long gone.

The dripping fog had thickened into a drenching rain, rendering my glasses useless. I stumbled along, brazenly myopic, until I reached the front steps to the shop.

Even in the downpour, my nose instinctively searched for a wisp of Oscar's cooking, but only the looming ocean scent tinged the air. I stood on the sidewalk underneath the tightly shut upstairs window as cold drops of rain snuck down my collar and tried to steal the warmth from the small of my back.

The front door had been damaged by the paramedics in their efforts to reach Oscar, so the police had fashioned a temporary closure by winding several pieces of wire around the iron framing. I wrestled with the wire for several minutes before I finally disbanded it and pried open the door.

Despite its derelict condition, I had always admired the

entrance to the Green Vase. Two steps led up from the
street to a small, semicircular stone patio covered by a red
brick archway. The door was made of thick, rectangular-
shaped, glass panels mounted into a frame of curling
wrought iron strips. Even before the attempted rescue,
several sections of glass had split or cracked from years of
use. Now, one of the panes had been smashed in and the
lock hopelessly wrenched. Shards of glass were scattered
on the floor inside.

I pushed open the door and stepped into the room
where Oscar must have spent his last minutes. My heart
dropped to the floor where a dark stain spread out like an
oil slick from a sinking ship. The crimson-soaked floorboards emanated the burnt, rusting odor of Oscar's defeated red blood cells, the ghosts of whom I imagined still
hung in the dusty air of the Green Vase, searching for his
spent, expired body.

Digging into my rain spotted lenses with the cuff of my
sweater, I pushed further on into the store. The shadows
of Oscar's life floated all around me, in the cluttered piles
of antiques, the loaded, leaning bookshelves, and the vintage cash register that sat on the counter near the door.

I took in a deep, steadying breath as I approached the
stairs at the back of the showroom. Oscar had kept a
drawer full of padlocks in the kitchen upstairs, and I was
sure one of those would work on the front door until I
could get it fixed.

The wooden crate that had snagged my sweater the
night of our last dinner with Oscar still obstinately
blocked the stairwell. It glowered at me with its bulky,
bullying mass. Egged on by the turbulence of my emotions, I decided to move it to a less obnoxious location.

I sidled up to the side of the crate and gave it a nudge.
It didn't budge.

I stepped back for a moment to size up my opponent—
a squatty, solid, rectangular cube that just topped my
forehead in height. I leaned against it and gave a more
substantial shove.

Still no movement—just a rude smirk that I imagined forming in the rough grains of one of the exterior planks.

My temper rising, I crouched down and propped one foot up against the nearby wall, trying to leverage my weight against the splintery surface of the crate. Straining, I devoted all of my resources into gaining horizontal motion. The bottom edge tilted up slightly—then, suddenly, the both of us slipped backwards.

I lost my balance and hit the ground with a thud, landing painfully on a flat, metal rod that dug up into my thigh.

I eased up onto my knees and leaned over to study it more closely. A metal handle, about four inches long, poked up from an oval recess cut out of the wooden floor. My fingers worked a small lever on the inside of the opening, and the handle retracted down into the hole.

An oval-shaped cover had been propped up against a nearby wall; its surface matched that of the carved out floorboard. I positioned the cover over the hole and snapped it into place. A small, pinky-sized opening was the only evidence of its location. In the dusky light of this corner of the store, the finger hole mimicked an innocuous knot in the wood.

"A handle to what?" I wondered aloud, pulling off the cover and extending the handle.

I stood up on one side and tried to pull, but nothing happened. I walked around to position myself on the other side of the handle, realizing that the floorboards I'd been standing on were subtly more springy than the rest.

I pulled up again, and this time it yielded. There was a puff of dust and the grinding of gears as a trap door emerged from the floorboards. The door was roughly square, but the surface had been modified to fit into the grooves and striations of the planks in the flooring. Sitting back on my heels, I ran my fingers along the large, buck teeth of the open edge and peered into the dark hole. An unseen mechanism had triggered rickety stairs to unwind down into the hatch.

Cool, damp air seeped up at me as I leaned over the opening, puzzled. The stairs quickly disappeared into a pitch-black darkness.

It wasn't surprising that the building would have a basement, but it seemed odd that Oscar had never mentioned it.

I left the gaping hole unattended and sprinted up the stairs to fetch Oscar's flashlight from the top of the refrigerator. My uncle had been exceptionally proud of this heavy-duty implement. Made of a sturdy, camouflage-colored plastic, its high-powered LED issued a wide cone of darkness-obliterating rays. Gripping it confidently, I raced back down to the hatch.

I pushed a button on the handle and pointed the beam into the dark abyss.

The stairs appeared even less stable under illumination. The structure shuddered violently as I put my weight onto the top step, and I grabbed onto the trap door, nearly losing my balance. After the shaking subsided, I slowly eased my way down into the hole.

Something tickled my nose as my feet struck the concrete floor in the room below. I flashed my light up at the ceiling. It was so low I could almost touch it with the flat of my hand—an action which brought down a tangle of cobwebs that nested in my hair and glasses.

After fighting off the cobwebs, I glanced back up at the ceiling to see a single bare light bulb mounted over my head. A thin, rotting string swung back and forth beneath the bulb. I caught it with my free hand and pulled.

There was a tiny clinking sound; then the string rebounded and the light bulb came on. I dimmed my flashlight to test the bulb's wattage. It emitted a thin halo of light that barely managed to illuminate the top of my shoes. I returned my flashlight to full force and trained it into the cave-like basement.

The light carved through a dusty, black haze, revealing a room similar in size to the Green Vase showroom above.

The walls were made of the same red bricks as the exterior of the building, and the floor was a cracked, grimy concrete. Several crates like the one I'd wrestled with upstairs were stacked haphazardly up against the walls.

I continued on towards the back of the basement, shining the flashlight around in an arc. As I got farther away from the stairs, the dim light that had been contributed by the light bulb faded away. Even the broad beam of the flashlight failed to ease my growing feeling of claustrophobic panic.

As I reached the far end of the basement, there was a bump in the ceiling above my head. Startled, my knees collapsed beneath me, and I fell onto the hard floor, dropping the flashlight. It rolled away from me in a semicircle, its light bouncing wildly around the room.

A man's voice called out from above. "Hello? Is anyone there?"

Groaning, I struggled to my feet and grabbed the light.

"Hallow," the greeting echoed above me.

"Yes, yes, hello. I'm down in the basement," I called up. "Just a minute."

I began scrambling back towards the stairs. A curly-haired head dipped upside down to look at me through the hatch.

"Oh, hello there," the head shouted in my direction. "I'm Montgomery Carmichael. I run the gallery across the street. You're Oscar's niece, aren't you?"

I stumbled halfway up the stairs and shook his hand, which had followed his head over the edge. The strong, citrus smell of recently applied aftershave cut through the stale, moldy aroma of the basement.

"Nice to meet you, Montgomery," I said to the upside-down torso, my nose twitching as I tried to fight off the second sneeze of the day. I was unsuccessful.

"Bless you," he laughed as my high-pitched blast echoed off the walls of the basement. "You can call me Monty. Everyone else does."

I climbed up the rest of the stairs and back into the showroom. Blinking through my watering eyes, I tried to get a better look at my visitor.

He was a tall, skinny, stork-like man. He ambled about awkwardly on disproportionately long legs as he poked around the store. His pale green eyes stared out from under thick, curly brown hair, still damp from the rain smattering down outside. It was styled short on each side, longer in the middle, with frizzing curls that bounced wildly off the top.

A tightly wound bow tie garroted his long, stringy neck, topping off his light-colored suit and suspenders. A pair of whimsical, carrot-shaped cufflinks accented his crisply starched, button-down shirt.

I watched, perplexed, as he slid across the floor on highly polished wingtips and skid to a halt in front of me. The pores on his closely shaven face shone from the recently applied aftershave.

"So sorry about your uncle," he said, bending towards me. One of his long arms reached over to brush a cobweb from the top of my head. "It was so sudden—shocking, really."

I took a wide step backwards, dodging his gangly arm. "Yes, yes it was," I replied uneasily.

Monty turned to lean over the open hatch. "I didn't know Oscar had a basement over here," he said curiously. "How big is it? There's only a small one in my building— barely holds the water heater."

"Oh, it's big enough, I guess. It's full of shipping crates, just like up here." I gestured to the crowded room around us. "I don't know what I'm going to do with all of this."

"So, you'll be taking over the place?" he asked, jumping on my allusion. Monty, I would quickly learn, was the gossip of the neighborhood. Few comings and goings escaped his close attention.

"Yes, I suppose so," I said, feeling far less certain than I'd been in Miranda's office. I was starting to realize how much work this was going to be. "I don't know where to begin."

Monty's face lit up. "I think I can help you there," he bubbled enthusiastically. "I've consulted on the renovations for most of the places up and down the street."

It turned out Monty was inevitably a consultant on almost every renovation project in Jackson Square. His guidance was persistently offered—if rarely solicited.

I don't actually remember accepting his assistance, but, ten minutes later, we were sitting at the upstairs kitchen table, sketches of various options accumulating on its surface. Monty, whose gallery across the street was filled with a wide variety of local artwork, turned out to be a fairly decent sketch artist.

"Wow, this is really good," I said a short time later, complimenting an illustration he'd developed for one proposal we were considering.

"Oh, no, no," he gushed, soaking in the praise like a puppy. "I'm just an amateur." He picked up one of the sketches and held it towards the light, admiring it.

"You're not much like your uncle, if you don't mind me saying so." Monty's expression was masked by the sketch he was holding in front of his face.

"How do you mean?" I replied cautiously, not sure how to interpret his comment.

"Well," Monty said, grinning as he laid the sketch back down on the table. "For one thing, I've been here for nearly half an hour, and you haven't thrown me out yet. I don't think I ever made it past the two minute mark when the old . . ." He coughed unnecessarily. "I mean, your uncle, ran the place."

"You didn't get on that well then?" I asked, visualizing my grouchy uncle leading the pretentious Monty out of the store by the ear.

Monty's face confirmed my mental image. He rubbed his earlobe absentmindedly as he spluttered, "It wasn't for lack of trying, let me tell you. I stopped in several times to tell him about my ideas for the Green Vase. You know,

ways he could make improvements. He just wasn't interested."

Monty threw up his hands in disbelief as I smothered a
guffaw with my own fake coughing spell.

"I got the distinct impression that he didn't want my
help," Monty continued, shaking his head as I hid my face
behind my hands.

Monty returned to his sketches, while I tried to regain
my composure. The table was silent except for the scratching of his pencil as he filled in more details on the most
recent picture. When he looked up again, his face was
strangely serious.

"Not to put too fine a point on it," he said, fixing me intently with a penetrating stare, "but I had the impression
Oscar was hiding something over here. Like he didn't
want me nosing around."

He pointed a forefinger at his left eye and winked dramatically. "You should keep an eye out."

Chapter 5

FIRST THING THE next morning, I phoned the contractor listed on the business card Miranda had given me. The line rang several times before a static laden connection picked up. A sound like tires crunching on gravel rolled out of the earpiece as the voice on the other end cleared his throat.

"Miranda mentioned you'd be calling," he responded to my introduction. "You're Oscar's niece then?"

It felt strange to meet people who saw me through Oscar-tinted lenses. Except for my weekly dinners at the Green Vase, our worlds had never overlapped.

"He and I used to play dominoes with a group every other Thursday." The voice paused, as if considering. "Guess we'll need to find another player for this week's game." He suggested we meet at the Green Vase that afternoon.

A couple of hours later, I popped the cats into their carriers and loaded them into my car. They wouldn't have allowed me to leave them behind on a Saturday afternoon outing to Oscar's.

The rains of the previous evening had skittered away, leaving behind a city full of freshly bathed buildings. Row after row of tiered, bay windows were temporarily wiped clean of nose prints, so that the people looking out were once again clearly visible to those of us looking in.

I parked on the curb next to the front door of the Green Vase and unloaded the cats, one week to the day since our last dinner with Oscar. The cold metal of the padlock clinked against the iron framing of the door as I fed the small key into its mouth and released the teeth of the U bend.

I set the carriers down on the floor in the front of the shop and opened the doors. Somehow the cats sensed that the world was now irretrievably different. They crept slowly out into the room, their eyes wide, their whiskers twitching.

I'd tried to wipe the bloodstain from the floor, but Oscar's imprint was indelible. Isabella took one round of it; then she charged to the back of the store and up the stairs, searching the premises for the source of the blotted mark. Rupert simply sat down on the floor and looked up at me with bewildered, blue eyes. I swept him up in my arms and carried him towards the stairs at the back of the store, burying my head in the soft, fluffy fur around his neck.

The soles of my feet sprung slightly as I crossed over the trap door near the foot of the stairs, and I wondered why Oscar had kept its existence a secret. What other shrouded elephants, I wondered, lurked in the closets of the Green Vase?

Isabella circled back as I carried Rupert up the stairs to the kitchen. She dodged nervously in and around my feet, nearly tripping me in her anxiety. No small dishes of food waited under the table. No pots steamed on the stove. The kitchen was cold and empty. I flicked on the light switch and dropped down to the uneven tile floor, trying to console the furry pair of worried heads.

The shiny red litter box gleamed in the hall just outside

the kitchen. Oscar had proudly shown off his new purchase the night of our last dinner. Rupert slid towards it, sniffing loudly with obvious intent. I stepped in front of him before he could jump in and carried it up the next flight of stairs to the bathroom on the third floor. I didn't think a litter box should be visible from the kitchen, even if it was fire engine red.

After relocating the litter box, I began to wash my hands with a grimy bar of Oscar's soap. Out of the corner of my eye, I caught a glimpse of Isabella jogging past the open door carrying a shiny metal object in her mouth.

"Hey, what'ch you got there?" I called out after her as she leapt down the stairs. She didn't stop for an inspection—a sure sign she'd just snitched something.

For years, I had waged a losing battle against Isabella's acquisitive impulses. Anything that she could pull, drag, or carry off in her mouth was fair game. Once she'd squirreled away her prize, it was almost impossible to find. Over the years, I'd lost a wide array of toothbrushes, hair clips, pencils, dice, tweezers, matches, bathtub stoppers, and who knows what else to Isabella's klepto-cravings. This time, I was determined to intercept her.

I chased Isabella down the top flight of stairs and around a corner. She zoomed across the kitchen, slaloming between the legs of the kitchen table. I chased after her, nearly nabbing the tip of her tail, but she slipped past my grasp and launched down the steps to the first floor. Whatever item of Oscar's she'd latched on to was about to be lost forever in the Green Vase showroom.

I clambered headlong down the stairs after her, nearly striking my forehead on a large, splintering beam that hung low over the sixth step. My fingers raced along the uneven wallboards like piano keys as my toes gripped the slick, worn steps with less and less success.

I hit the bottom step, my feet sliding wildly. There was a flash of white fur and a bloodcurdling—human—scream.

I tried to pull up, but I'd gained too much momentum. I tumbled out into the Green Vase showroom, plowing straight into a tall, stick figure wearing a white, strangely familiar, fur cap.

"I saw you come in from across the street," Monty said, trying to straighten his bow tie as Isabella teetered back and forth on top of his head. "Thought I'd try to catch you. I came up with a few more ideas this morning."

I reached up and plucked Isabella out of the brown nest of curls. With a triumphant look, she leapt gracefully from my arms up to the top of a nearby bookcase. She'd already disposed of her trinket.

"You're just in time then," I said to the long back of Monty, who had turned to straighten his neatly pressed suit and tie in the reflection of the storefront glass. "The contractor's going to meet me here this afternoon—to take a walk through and get an idea of what we're up against."

Monty tore himself away from his reflection, clapping his hands together hungrily. "Excellent! What's this fellow's name? I might know him."

Despite Monty's efforts, an independent-minded curl near the top of his head flipped out of position and curly-cued straight up in the air.

"Um, hold on a second. I can't remember it off the top of my head." I grabbed my shoulder bag and unzipped the pouch where I'd stashed the business card. "Miranda Richards recommended him—she was Oscar's attorney."

"Oh, I know Miranda," Monty said, bobbing his head up and down to emphasize his familiarity. He leaned against the cash register counter and tilted up one of his long, wingtipped feet so that the flat, handsewn sole flashed in the afternoon sunlight.

"I've got his business card right here," I said, digging in the shoulder bag.

A shadow darkened the front door as my fingers found the card and fished it out. Monty turned to greet the entrant as I began to read the card. "His name is . . ."

"Harold Wombler," Monty gasped as if he'd been punched in the gut.

I looked up. Monty was staring at the front door, his

back stiffened, every hair bristled. Even the renegade curl springing off the top of his head seemed to register offense.

He swiveled around towards me, a look of abject horror on his face. "Noooo," he whispered hoarsely as the door swung open behind him. "Wombler?"

The shadow entered the Green Vase and stood behind Monty, blocking my view. There was an awkward silence broken only by the barely perceptible thud of Isabella's nimble feet hitting the floor in front of the bookcase. A moment later, I saw her silently circling the group, carefully studying the visitor.

Harold Wombler cleared his throat, this time channeling a clogged up carburetor. A pale look of dread iced down Monty's face. I sprung forward and vaulted around the frozen Monty to greet the contractor.

"Hello, you must be Mr. Wombler," I said, holding out my hand to the man standing in the doorway.

Harold Wombler nodded, pressing his crinkly, cracked lips firmly together.

He was a middle-aged, smaller-framed man wearing a pair of oversized overalls that looked like they'd been shredded through a lawn mower. I tried not to look too closely at the gaping holes, desperately afraid of what he might, or might not, be wearing underneath. A dingy, frayed baseball cap with an illegible message on the front covered most of his course, greasy black hair. Bushy tufts protruded from each nostril.

Monty had turned to face Harold and was now standing behind me; I could hear his teeth grinding in my right ear.

Harold finally met my extended hand and weakly engaged me in one of the most disconcerting handshakes I have ever experienced.

Harold's skin hung loosely over his entire body, as if he had recently lost a vast amount of weight. Big, hollow jowls of dermis hung from his sunken cheeks. He looked like a chipmunk that had been flattened by a steamroller and only partially re-inflated. The skin on Harold's hands was just as flaccid. It rolled beneath my fingers as I tried to grip his hand.

Harold nodded in Monty's direction. "Carmichael."

"Wombler," Monty croaked, disbelievingly.

I stepped back as the two glared at each other. Monty's fingers fidgeted with his bow and arrow ("I Left My Heart in San Francisco") cufflinks as if he might pluck them out of his sleeves and chuck them at Harold. For his part, Harold had placed one of his wrinkled hands on a hammer attached to a tool belt slung loosely across his narrow hips. He palmed it like a pistol as his shiny, black eyes stared seethingly at Monty.

Rupert wandered into the room and took a seat on the floor next to my feet, rotating slightly on his round rump as he looked back and forth between Harold and Monty. I tried to break the tense silence.

"Why don't we . . . ," I started nervously, but I was drowned out by a loud, snorkeling noise emanating from Harold's nose. Rupert slid backwards on the wood floor, looking up warily at the brushy underside of Harold's dripping orifice.

I tried again. "Why don't we go outside and start with the front of the store? That's the area that needs the most work."

Rupert was the first to move at my suggestion, bouncing nonchalantly towards the entrance. I plucked him up and secured him on the cashier counter while Monty and a still sniffling Harold filed past me out the front door.

I turned my back to the door and looked up at the ceiling, trying to summon the emotional fortitude for what promised to be a confrontational meeting.

That's when the bickering began.

"What are you up to Monkey-mery?" Harold growled under his breath.

"Don't call me that!" Monty squeaked back. "I'm not up to anything. I'm just being helpful," he said defensively.

The two combative voices permeated easily through

the broken glass of the door. I fiddled absentmindedly with Rupert's ears, listening to the harshly whispered words. He glared up at me, irritated, but my mind was focused on the conversation outside.

"Didn't you learn anything from your overnight adventure at the courthouse?" Harold's deep, baritone voice menaced through the glass.

"Look here, you know that was all a big misunderstanding," Monty sputtered, his voice rising out of its whisper. "I still can't believe you had me arrested!"

"I believe that's the proper protocol when you find someone's broken into a private residence," Harold growled.

"Do you have any idea what I went through that night?" Monty's indignant tones were now echoing through the showroom.

"A holding cell with twenty-four other miscreants from the streets of San Francisco? Yeah, I can imagine." Harold's quieter, more controlled voice chuckled. "I bet you fit right in."

Growing annoyed with my fumbling fingers, Rupert reached up and swatted at my hand. A stray claw caught my index finger, drawing a pinprick of blood.

"Always snooping around, meddling in other people's business."

I stepped back, scowling at Rupert, sucking on my wounded finger. My heel brushed against the door as Monty's voice took a hard, suspicious turn.

"You know," he paused, venom dripping from every word, "you sound just like . . ."

The pressure from my heel caused the door to creak open, interrupting Monty's sentence. A glowering silence swallowed me as I slowly turned around.

Chapter 6

"YOU GOING TO join us?"

Harold's grinding voice abraded even the hard surface of the concrete beneath his feet. The shafts of hair on the back of my neck cringed as if they'd been roughed with a piece of sandpaper.

I tried to conjure a convincingly blank expression—desperate to disguise the fact that I had been hanging on every not-so-hushed word of their bitter conversation—and joined Harold and Monty outside on the sidewalk.

"Sorry about that," I said, forcing normalcy into my voice. "I was just . . . " Distracted by the conversation I'd overheard, I thought to myself. I pointed at the window through to the counter where Rupert was inspecting his feet, grooming the feathery white hairs that poked out between his toes.

"Rupert had something in his fur," I explained lamely.

On the other side of the glass, Rupert looked up and belched obligingly.

"Hmmph." Harold stared at me with his beady, black eyes.

A light wind traipsed past us, picking up the stale scent of his breath and zesting my sensitive nasal cavity with its rank odor.

"So, what's the plan?" he demanded more than asked. "What are you going to do with this place?"

I had lost many hours of sleep the previous evening asking myself exactly that question. It was so unlike me to jump into something without thoroughly analyzing all of the angles, and I had begun to second-guess my decision. A growing seed of self-doubt was worming its way through my intestines like a parasite.

"Well," I said, feeling my throat closing up even as I began the presentation I'd rehearsed in my head earlier that day. "I'm still thinking about exactly what kind of business would be best for this location. I thought I might do some market studies, lay out a couple of business plans, and run the spread sheets for comparison."

Harold's dark, scratchy eyebrows knitted together as I spoke, increasing the paralyzing tension creeping up my spine.

"The storefront here is a bit of an eyesore, and it's visible from up and down the street." I tried not to look at Harold's increasingly sour expression. "Maybe if we could discuss some of the options and costs to fix up the bricks and front glasswork . . . then I could run the figures." I gulped, feeling awkward and completely unnerved.

"It's an antiques shop," Harold said dourly. "Why not just keep it as an antiques shop?"

I was starting to feel a little faint. A second, fractious interaction in as many days was more than my feeble, conflict-avoiding constitution could take.

I glanced back into the window. Unconcerned with my predicament, Rupert had rolled over onto his back so that the warm sun cooked his belly. An indolent paw partially covered one eye.

"Most of the other stores up and down the street are antiques shops," Harold said, agitatedly waving a wrinkled hand. I could tell he felt that we were wasting his time.

"Yes, precisely," I said, regretting my rash dismissal of Miranda's advice to sell the Green Vase. "So that's why I want to investigate some alternatives. . . ." My voice faded softer and softer.

A hissing *sfit* of air whistled out through the gap between Harold's front teeth like a deflating balloon. He turned away from me and started pacing disgustedly up and down the sidewalk.

My stomach flip-flopped as the blood drained away from my pounding forehead. I leaned against the wall behind me for support, clutching one of the exposed bricks.

It crumbled off in my hand.

Monty had been avidly watching this exchange and now swooped into the void. "You're an accountant aren't you?" he asked, the enthusiasm of a new idea infusing him. "Why don't you set up your own accounting business? There are a couple of small offices around the corner from here—people who've left big firms to go out on their own."

Harold's eyes hammered nails into Monty's skull.

"Hmm," I said thoughtfully, relieved for the momentary deflection of Harold's ire. "I hadn't really thought about that." Numbers began running through my head as I analyzed the prospect. "That's a possibility."

My equivocal assessment provided far too much encouragement. Once he'd strapped himself into the driver's seat of an idea, Monty had a precipitous tendency to steer it right over the edge.

"Of course, you've got all of this inventory, so you might as well continue the antiques shop on the side as well." He placed a long finger against his temple. "You might get some crossover business that way."

Monty crouched over, as if he were taking a seat in an imaginary chair. "*Doop tee doo*, I'm waiting to meet with my accountant to discuss my tax return." He tilted his head back and forth, arms folded together patiently. The long neck angled, as if he were looking around a corner.

"There's quite a line of people in front of me." The neck snapped back around. "Hello, what's this? A nifty antique! Something I need, I'm sure."

He stood up with a flourishing gesture. "They'll have spent their entire refund before they even leave your office."

I shook my head negatively throughout this entire routine, but Monty turned a blind eye, continuing on.

"You'll keep the shop name the same though, I imagine. Unless . . ." Monty licked his index finger and raised it, as if checking the direction of the wind. "How about 'The Green Lampshade?'"

I shook my head faster, in definite rejection.

He sighed, momentarily disappointed. "Right then." Monty hooked a finger around Harold's elbow. "Here's what I'm thinking . . ."

Harold looked at Monty as if he was about to throw him through the nearest window.

"The bricks and windows should all be replaced, of course," Monty said, motioning airily with his free hand. "And, we'll need a graphic icon that matches up with store's name."

He looked back at me over his shoulder. "The Green Vase," he intoned pompously.

Monty returned his attention to Harold, whose sour expression increasingly resembled an angry walnut.

"I see a vase with a long, slender neck. Elegant, in its simplicity, if you know what I mean." Monty arched his eyebrows dramatically. "Made out of a translucent material that will glow when the light hits it just right." He nodded his head up and down. "Yes. Yes, yes."

Monty released Harold and began prancing along the sidewalk.

"Now, we should throw out these wide windows." Monty threw his right hand up and over his shoulder, as if tossing a crumpled piece of paper. "Replace them with smaller glass pieces—say, one-foot squares—that you lay out in a crisscrossed metal frame." Monty's long legs carried him along the front of the store, the building playing the role of an immobile dance partner as he glided around it. "You see, running the length of the store."

"Then," Monty continued, nearly breathless from his exertions, "the pièce de résistance—we have a couple of the squares inlaid with the green vase icon. I know an artisan here locally who would do it for a reasonable price." He collapsed against the wall, panting as he looked up at us expectantly.

Harold grunted noncommittally, jamming his thumbs into the shoulder straps of his overalls. He wandered back and forth in front of the store, poking and prodding the building as if it were a used car.

I avoided eye contact with Monty, afraid of unintentionally giving him any further encouragement.

I peeked through the glass to check on Rupert. He had flopped over onto his side, dangerously close to the edge of the counter. The side of his chest rose slowly up and down, a metronome ticking in time to a deep, slumbering waltz.

Harold opened the broken front door and looked up at the framing, his eyes narrowing as they assessed the weaknesses in the structure. Then, having completed his inspection, he let the door go. It slammed shut with a loud, clapping sound that echoed against the sidewalk.

Rupert levitated about two inches off of the counter. There was a startled look in his eyes as his head jerked up; then he disappeared from view. I winced as I heard him thump heavily onto the floor. Lifting myself up on my tiptoes, I leaned into the glass, looking at the ground where he'd fallen.

Apparently, nothing was hurt other than his pride. Rupert's disgruntled back end stalked towards the stairs at the back of the store, the tip of his long, feathery tail kinked to express his displeasure.

Harold's guttural grunt drew my attention back to the sidewalk. "Whole place ought to be condemned," he said, "but I don't guess the board would let you get away with that."

Monty began fidgeting with his cufflinks, the pale skin on his cheeks and forehead pinkening from exposure to both the direct sun and the irascible Harold.

"You going to be around here tomorrow afternoon?" Harold asked gruffly. "Sunday?" he added, as if I might not be aware of the calendar's order of the days.

"Sure—I mean, I can be," I responded.

Monty's head popped up hopefully.

"You've got a lot of work to do to get this idea of yours dressed up into a proposal for the board," Harold said, stroking his chin thoughtfully. "I don't have time in my schedule for all that, but I can send over my assistant, Ivan."

"Great," I said, "How about two . . ."

"Ivan? Ivan Batrachos?" Monty broke in with feverish excitement.

Harold threw Monty a withering glance.

"He's one of the best craftsman in the city," Monty enthused, tapping me on the elbow authoritatively. "He's worked on almost all of the renovations in Jackson Square."

Harold sighed heavily, this time the air limply expelling from the loose, flapping skin of his cheeks.

"*The* Ivan Batrachos! Imagine that." Monty put one hand up against the wall, the other on the angular hip protruding through his unbuttoned suit jacket. He tipped up the toe of his shoe, crossing one stork-like leg over the other.

"Ivan Batrachos," Harold said, pursing his lips together and spitting on the sidewalk. "My assistant." He turned and limped off down the street, calling out crankily behind him, "Two o'clock tomorrow afternoon."

I stared at Monty, rubbing the side of my head, looking forward to Monday morning and the four, peaceful corners of my quiet cubicle.

Chapter 7

TAP, TAP, TAP. Persistent knuckles rapped on the iron framing of the door to the Green Vase.

It was Sunday afternoon. I'd seen the tapper traipsing across the street from his art studio, but pretended not to hear him as I bent down into the waist-high pile in front of me, searching for a flash of the metal piece Isabella had stolen the day before. She had stuck her head into one of the open cardboard boxes in the middle of the showroom when we'd arrived—a suspiciously furtive look on her face—but I'd rummaged through it to the bottom without success.

I looked up, reluctantly, as Monty wrapped an arm around the edge of the open door and swung himself into the room, pivoting on his planted feet like hinges.

"You're very welcome," he said, tipping his head to doff an imaginary top hat that he caught with his free hand and swept grandly across the floor.

"Thanks," I said warily, worriedly wondering what blessing had just been bestowed upon me.

"You're like a little bird," he said, fluttering his eyelashes, "that I've taken under my wing."

I bit my bottom lip skeptically as Monty pulled the door shut and leaned against the cashier counter. He coughed lightly into his flattened palm. "I've polled almost all of the members of the board about your renovation proposal."

He waved his hand in the air, dismissing the look of protest he anticipated on my face. "Don't worry, they'll be fine with either an antiques shop or an accounting office." He pumped his eyebrows up and down. "Or—a combination of the two."

I stared at him sternly, my hands on my hips, as he sauntered around the counter and hopped up on a stool.

"The thing is, it'll be best if you can get it over with at the meeting this coming Tuesday. Frank Napis—," he paused for effect, "is out of town."

I looked up at the ceiling, at a loss for words. Tuesday was only two days away.

"And, this will be the last meeting for the chairman. Gordon Bosco's about to step down. Who knows how the dynamics will change once they bring in someone new?"

A cool breeze ruffled the curls on the top of Monty's head as the front door re-opened. He whipped around, nearly falling off of the stool as he leapt up to greet the new arrival.

"Ivan Batrachos," Monty gushed, jutting his hand out, "so good to see you."

I was standing midway towards the back of the store, still hip deep in the pile I'd emptied from Isabella's box. I could just make out the solid shoulders of the man anchoring Monty's bouncing torso. I wound my way towards the front of the store to get a better look at Harold's assistant as Monty continued to pump his arm up and down.

Ivan was the physical opposite of Monty. His hulking form loomed like a giant next to Monty's slim figure.

Rich, olive skin glowed with the same confidence as his smile, which he turned in my direction as soon as I stepped out from behind Monty's springing frame. A narrow scar ran down the left side of his face, curving underneath his square jaw, the slight disfigurement only enhancing his machismo.

"Ivan Batrachos," he said in a deep, movie actor's voice, offering me the hand he had just pried loose from Monty's clinging grasp.

I shook his hand, taking in the earthy smell of new construction and freshly cut, redwood planks.

"So, I hear you're taking over the place," Ivan said, the deep, dark wells of his pupils flickering with a thinly veiled intensity. "I was so sorry to hear about Oscar's death. You're his niece aren't you?"

I nodded, surveying his brawny physique. Ivan was neatly dressed in a workingman's uniform. A clean, white T-shirt poked out of the neck of his plaid, button-down shirt. His carpenter-style work pants were constructed of a riveted—seemingly bulletproof—canvas fabric, a fitting match to his steel-toed, combat-ready, work boots.

"You know, your uncle talked about you all the time."

The comment knocked me off guard, and my throat caught, delaying my response long enough for Monty to barge back into the conversation.

"Ivan, I had no idea you worked for Harold Wombler," Monty said brightly, desperately seeking Ivan's attention. "Well, I'd heard rumblings of that, but, honestly, I refused to believe it." Monty leaned forward conspiratorially. "You're far too skilled to be indentured to that man."

Ivan chuckled good-naturedly. "Oh, I've learned a lot from Harold—and he gives me free rein on my projects. I've got no complaints."

"Perhaps I could give you a quick overview of our plans," Monty offered, flushing giddily. He pulled out some of his sketches from a parchment tube, flourished the roll proudly in the air, and took them over to the counter near the cash register.

I leaned against the dental chair, watching the amused look on Ivan's face as he followed Monty over to the counter. The turn revealed a thick mullet of golden brown, sun-licked hair that flowed over Ivan's shoulders and swished several inches down his back.

"Oscar and I had discussed some renovation ideas not long before he died," Ivan said casually as he leaned over the counter, waiting for Monty to unfurl the sketches on its surface.

Monty's shoulders stiffened like a clothes hanger had been inserted underneath his shirt. His ears turned an abashed red.

"Oh?" His voice squeaked with strain. "You don't say."

"Oscar was going to fix up the Green Vase?" I asked, incredulous.

Ivan shrugged his loose, limber shoulders, causing a temporary rapid in the waterfall of hair. "Sure. He'd asked me to come by and look at the storefront. He wanted to do something simple to make it acceptable for the board and get Napis off his back. We tossed around some ideas—drew up a couple of tentative plans. It hadn't gone very far."

Ivan turned his head to look at Monty's face, which had suddenly gone abnormally pale. "Let's see what you've got," he said encouragingly.

"Oh," Monty said as if he'd punctured a lung. His long, sweating fingers clamped down tightly on his rolls of sketches. "You put together some proposals for Oscar?" he gulped, his voice pitching higher and higher.

"Yeah, but they were preliminary really," Ivan said, flicking his hand dismissively. "Go ahead. I'm interested to see what you two have come up with."

I tilted my head, puzzled at Monty's sudden panic to show off his work.

"Look," Ivan said consolingly, "I'm no Picasso." He pulled a folded square of butcher paper out of one of his pockets and smoothed it on the counter. "Here's what we came up with from before."

I stood on my tiptoes to look over Monty's frigid shoulder and Ivan's firm, muscular one. With one glimpse I understood Monty's paralysis.

Ivan's sheet of sketches was almost identical to the ones Monty had created for me two nights earlier.

Chapter 8

"PERHAPS," **MONTY SAID** painfully, struggling to clear his throat as he turned around to face me. "I should explain."

Ivan glanced up from the sheet of sketches he'd spread out on the counter. From the quizzical expression on his face, he seemed unaware that his work had been pirated.

I sat down in the dental chair, a wave of suspicion surging over me. Monty approached me apprehensively, his face strobing blotchily from an embarrassed violet red to a colorless gray ash. He pulled a trembling hand through the curls on the top of his head.

"You see," Monty gulped, beads of sweat glistening on his forehead, "it all started at the last board meeting." He stuck a finger into the snug space between his neck and bow tie and tugged to loosen it.

"You know your neighbor, Frank Napis?" Monty tipped his head towards the southeast wall. "He's the guy who runs the shop next door."

I nodded, my expression still stoic, as Monty stepped closer to the dental chair.

"For the last several months—ever since Frank moved in there—he's been petitioning the board with complaints against the Green Vase. He brought another one at the board meeting last week."

Ivan cut in, his voice solemn. "There've been rumors that Frank was building a case to have the Green Vase condemned—so it could be seized by the city and put up for sale."

Monty waved a dismissive hand. "Oh, Miranda would never let him get away with that, I'm sure." He smiled reassuringly at my concerned expression. "Look, once you start work on the renovations, Frank won't have a leg to stand on."

I felt a worried tension winding around my shoulders. "So what happened at the last board meeting?" I asked.

"Right," Monty said, slapping his hands together. "This time, Frank was complaining about Oscar's gutters."

Monty began to circle the room, the soles of his shoes clacking softly on the wood floors. "Everyone was there—except Oscar. I've never been able to figure out why Miranda let him get away with that."

"And Gordon," Ivan piped in. "The board chairman, Gordon Bosco, wasn't there, either."

"Oh, yes, I forgot about him," Monty said, tilting his head thoughtfully. "He hasn't been to a meeting in ages—he's been too busy. I guess that's why he's stepping down."

Monty aimed a raised eyebrow towards the dental chair. "Gordon invested in a biotech start-up a while back. I think they made him CEO of the company. I hear they're about to announce progress on a huge milestone. It's all very hush, hush, of course."

Monty thumped the rubbery cartilage on the end of his nose as his eyes glassed over. "You know, I've been wondering who they're going to pick to take Gordon's place. I've been thinking about tossing my hat into the ring." His head swung hopefully back and forth between Ivan and me. "I'd make an excellent choice, don't you think?"

Ivan averted his eyes from Monty's questioning look; I

stared up at the ceiling, the corners of my mouth curling skeptically.

Monty cleared his throat and resumed his pacing. "So, Frank claimed he'd suffered water damage in one of the back rooms of his building, because the water wasn't draining properly from Oscar's gutters."

Monty streamed around a pile of boxes to give a knowing look at Ivan. "Mold. Nasty stuff—especially for old buildings."

"Mmm," Ivan hummed encouragingly, amused at the spectacle unfolding in front of him.

Monty turned back in towards the center of the room. "It was the same old song and dance—Napis whining that the Green Vase is a pit, it looks bad for the whole neighborhood, and Oscar never does anything about it."

Monty skated through the room as he spoke, skidding to a stop in front of a gold-plated saddle Oscar had mounted on a sawhorse. He swung a long leg over it as he continued.

"Nobody was really paying any attention. They'd seen it all before." Monty leaned forward in the saddle. "But not me. I keep a close eye on things." He paused dramatically, swinging his leg up high in the air as he dismounted his wooden horse. "Alert and ready for action, that's Montgomery Carmichael."

Monty picked up a gold-headed cane from a nearby display case and began swinging it in front of him like a baton. I winced as the twirling cane narrowly missed a pair of fragile glass lamps. "Frank gets this facial tic when he's worked up about something. The whole time he was speaking, his mustache kept jerking back and forth. I thought it was about to jump right off of his face."

My forehead crinkled involuntarily. I was certain Frank Napis had not had a mustache the night I'd seen him closing up his store.

"Napis has a mustache?" I asked as Monty crept around the back of the recliner.

I heard the tip of the cane punch a lever on the back of

my chair. A startled Rupert shot out from underneath as the chair kicked back. I found myself lying on my back, staring up at Monty's pale face and froth of brown curls.

"Oh, he's got a mustache," Monty assured me. "A fabulous one," he said wistfully. "It curls out on the ends and everything."

I fed my arm through the slats on the side of the chair, trying to reach the lever to right it. Monty stared off into space, absentmindedly stroking the sides of his mouth, thinking about Frank Napis's mustache.

"Moving past the mustache . . . ," Ivan prompted.

"Right," Monty said sharply, breaking out of his trance. He pushed in the lever, and the dental chair popped up, slamming me back into a seated position. "Frank left the meeting right after he made his complaint. He didn't even wait to hear the board's ruling. I thought that was kind of strange." He shrugged. "They sided with Miranda, of course."

Monty started another tour of the room as he continued. "Miranda slipped out of the boardroom not long after Frank. I had the suspicion that something was up, so I followed her outside."

Monty paused, his eyes ping-ponging back and forth between Ivan and me. "You'll never guess who was waiting for her." He licked his lips and said in a lofty voice, "Oscar."

I collapsed back in the dental chair, exhausted by Monty's antics.

"They stepped away from the boardroom and walked down a side hallway. I slid around the corner and snuck into a room that runs parallel to the corridor where they were standing." Monty's eyes were ablaze, reliving his moment of espionage. "I crept into a broom closet and climbed up on a bucket, so I could see out of a vent. I had a perfect view—I was almost right on top of them!"

I gripped the armrests tightly as Monty passed behind my chair. He glided over to the cashier counter next to Ivan and hopped up on it, crossing his legs in front of him. "That's when I heard Oscar tell Miranda that he'd found it." He paused, a jubilant expression on his face.

"Found what?" Ivan and I asked in unison.

Monty cleared his throat. "Well, Oscar didn't spell it out, exactly. But," he paused, raising his forefinger in the air. "I have a theory," he said smugly.

I sighed loudly.

"The tunnel," Monty said proudly. "I think Oscar found the entrance to the tunnel."

"Tunnel?" I asked, confused.

Ivan explained. "There've been rumors around here for years about a tunnel running underneath one of these old buildings—something dug out back in the Gold Rush days. If it exists, it's probably just an entrance to the sewer system." Ivan tilted his head in Monty's direction. "*Some* people are obsessed with the idea, but no one's ever found any trace of it."

Monty nodded furiously up and down, his top leg swinging wildly back and forth off the edge of the counter. "Oscar told Miranda he couldn't believe it had been right under his nose all this time."

Ivan shook his head in disbelief. "You think Oscar found the entrance here? In the Green Vase?"

Monty leapt down from the counter, raced to the back of the room, and hopped up and down on the closed hatch. "The Green Vase has a basement! I never knew it had a basement. It's not on any of the planning maps for Jackson Square. I checked this morning!"

Ivan raised a skeptical eyebrow at the bouncing Monty.

"Okay," Monty spluttered defensively. "Oscar didn't specifically say the word 'tunnel,' but what else could it be?"

Monty flounced his way back to the front of the room. "That's not all—while Oscar and Miranda were talking, he took something out of his pocket. It was a gold metal piece, about four or five inches long."

I eased myself up onto the edge of the chair. "Did it look like a key?" I asked softly.

Monty's eyes bulged affirmatively. "Yes. Yes, now that you mention it, I'm almost certain it was a key!" he exclaimed, nodding his head up and down. He whispered excitedly, "Probably the key that opens the entrance to the tunnel!"

I tensed in my chair, wondering if there was any truth to Monty's ridiculous story. His tale seemed as over the top as the rest of him.

Ivan looked perplexed. "What did Oscar do with the key?"

Monty's voice dropped to a more solemn tone. "Oscar took out a small, white envelope, dropped the key into it, and sealed it."

Monty's watery, green eyes stared into my bespectacled ones as he gulped and pointed at me. "The envelope had *your* name on it. Oscar told Miranda to give it to you . . . in case something happened to him."

Chapter 9

EVERYTHING WAS QUIET as the room swayed around me. Oscar's envelope burned in my pocket, the heavy, metal key weighing me down like a stone.

"Happened to him?" Ivan repeated Monty's last phrase. "What did Oscar think was going to happen to him?"

"Well," Monty stammered. "I didn't *quite* get to find out. You see, there was a disturbance . . . and then Oscar and Miranda left the building." His eyes shifted downward, studying his left cufflink.

"What kind of disturbance?" I probed sharply.

A telltale blush rose up on Monty's face. "Oh—well," he shrugged in an unconvincingly offhanded manner. "Someone may have fallen off a mop bucket . . ." he said, his voice trailing off.

Ivan chuckled, the sound puncturing the stifling vacuum that had clamped down on the room. He held up his square of butcher paper. "I don't understand what all of this has to do with my sketches."

Monty shuffled around the cashier counter, avoiding eye contact with both of us. "I haven't *completely* finished my story. You see, the last bit happened two days after the board meeting."

Monty flopped dejectedly onto the stool and sighed. "I was working in my studio that night when I saw Oscar leave for his dominoes game. He used to play every other Thursday."

Monty rested his chin on the edge of the cash register, his hound dog eyes beseeching us for understanding. "The front door to the Green Vase—it called out to me from across the street. I tried to ignore it, but it kept on tempting me."

Monty stood up from the stool, his gaze lost in the rafters. He sang out in a high, falsetto whisper, "Mon-tee, Mon-tee, the tunnel's over *here*. Come and check it out."

I rolled my eyes, but Monty seemed oblivious. He trotted around the dental chair, his voice pitching with excitement. "So, I walked across the street—just to take a look. I was only planning to peek in through the glass."

Monty placed his hand horizontally across his eyebrows as his eyes narrowed into slits. "But, when I put my head up against the door, it creaked open. It must not have latched properly when Oscar pulled it shut."

Monty pushed one of his long, bony fingers into the air as if prodding a pillow. "I poked it—gently—and it swung open!" His arms flung outward, nearly knocking the glasses off my face. "Well, then I *had* to go in to look for the entrance to the tunnel. Imagine what might be down there!"

"Rats," Ivan answered, ticking off a list on his fingers. "All kinds of insects, spiders, probably a homeless person or two."

Monty circled Ivan and hopped back on the stool behind the counter, the obsessive light in his eyes undiminished. "If you think about it, since I was looking for the entrance to the tunnel, I wasn't really breaking and entering." He raised a forefinger towards the ceiling. "More like, cutting through. That's hardly a criminal offense."

Monty propped his feet up on the counter, crossing one

on top of the other. "I searched the entire ground floor here for a hidden door—for any possible way to get into a tunnel." He sighed heavily. "But there was nothing."

He pointed his finger at me. "You could have knocked me right over when I walked in the other day and saw that hatch wide open." Monty crossed his arms in front of his chest. His pointy elbows jutted out on either side of his narrow frame.

My gaze pored into the floor, thinking of the dusty room beneath and wondering if this was the reason Oscar had hidden its existence.

"I went up and down the stairs at the back there," Monty said, frustration in his voice. "Then, I headed up to the kitchen." He shrugged his shoulders. "I thought— maybe you had to get to it from the second floor or something."

Monty skewed his face up as if sucking on a lemon. "That place was a mess! Dirty dishes in the sink. And that refrigerator—I saw something move in there."

Isabella chirped helpfully from her perch on top of the bookcase, her voice making a series of sharp clicks and trills.

"My mouse catcher is on the case," I said, interpreting for the rest of the room.

"A mouse would be afraid of what's living in there," Monty shuddered. "I closed the door to the refrigerator, *firmly*." He stretched out his right arm and waved it from right to left. "That's when I saw the sketches on the table. I was studying them when Harold collared me from behind. That grungy little man is a lot stronger than he looks."

This explained the bitter exchange I had overheard between Monty and Harold, I thought.

"I wonder what Harold was doing here?" Ivan asked, almost as if to himself.

"Beats me—he was supposed to have been at the dominoes game!" Monty shook his head ruefully. "The next thing I knew I was taking a ride in the backseat of a police car with one of their slobbering dogs. I ended up in a holding cell in the courthouse until Oscar came to get me out the next morning. He didn't press charges, so they had to let me go."

Monty twisted his right leg around to look at his foot. "I've still got some sort of goop stuck on the side of my shoe."

"Why didn't you tell me all of this before?" I asked, exasperated.

His face reddened again. "Well, it seemed a bit much for our first meeting. And then I just got carried away with the remodel project. When we started talking about potential ideas, it only seemed natural that you should consider Oscar's."

Ivan and I exchanged looks. Monty hopped off the stool and leaned over the counter towards me.

"Don't you think it's kind of karmic that you picked the same design that he was considering? It's almost like Oscar was communicating with you from beyond the grave."

I bit my lip, holding back my retort.

"I had no idea that Ivan had done them," Monty said defensively as he spun himself around the counter. "Of course, I knew *Harold* couldn't have sketched them."

He leaned towards Ivan in a loud aside. "That man's got no talent—*none*."

I picked up the page of sketches from the counter where Ivan had left them. The drawings were just like the ones Monty had sketched for me earlier in the week. The wide glass windows on the front of the store had been replaced with a matrix of one-foot squares. Inlays of a shaded vase repeated intermittently in the glass sections.

Still staring at the sketches, I asked, "Did you talk to Oscar about the tunnel?"

Monty shook his head. "Oscar wasn't exactly chatty when he picked me up from the courthouse. I was afraid he might turn me back in to the police if I told him about the broom closet. . . ."

The afternoon sun hit the gold foil detailing on the antique cash register, and I blinked to avoid the blinding flash of light. When my eyes refocused on the paper, I noticed a penciled squiggle in the bottom right hand corner. "What's this?" I asked, pointing.

Ivan took the paper from me and pulled it up close to his face. Then, he shrugged and handed it back to me. "Beats me. Oscar must have done that."

I held the paper up to the window. Doodled in the bottom right hand corner was a three-petaled tulip—the same design as the handle to the key.

And suddenly it clicked.

Chapter 10

"WILLIAM LEIDESDORFF," I murmured, staring at the tulip scrawled on the bottom of the paper.

"Leidesdorff? Is that what you said?" Monty repeated the name slowly, tasting it on his tongue. "That name sounds familiar."

"Several months ago, Oscar told me a story about a William Leidesdorff," I replied as I looked up from the page of sketches. "There's a street a couple of blocks over named after him—in the financial area. It's more of an alley, really. You've probably walked past it hundreds of times, but you wouldn't realize it has a name unless you were looking for the street sign."

I paused for a moment, remembering that Saturday night's story telling session. Oscar and I had been sitting at the kitchen table above the Green Vase showroom. The remnants of that evening's meal still littered its surface.

"Since the beginning," Oscar had begun that night, "people have been coming here to start over—build a new life for themselves. San Francisco's always been a beacon for second-, third-, and fourth-chancers. That's who planted the seeds of this city—made her who she is today." A far away look swept across his face. "That kind will always feel at home here."

Oscar reached into his shirt pocket, pulled out a pair of rod-shaped gold pieces, and set them on the table. "William Leidesdorff," he said, signaling the start of that evening's Gold Rush story.

One hand dropped near the floor and discreetly passed Rupert a last morsel of chicken. There was a gulping sound from underneath the table as Oscar launched into the tale.

"Leidesdorff left his home in the Virgin Islands when he was just a boy. He landed a job as a deckhand on a ship running the trade route between New York and New Orleans. That was in the early 1800s, before the railroads became king. Back then, everything moved on the water."

Oscar pushed his chair back from the table, wiping the last crumbs of dinner from his mouth. I picked up his plate and carried it over to the sink to rinse it off.

"Leidesdorff slowly worked his way up in the shipping business, gradually acquiring boats, property. He set up his base in New Orleans, but his ships ran all the way up and down the East Coast."

I returned to the table with a jug of water, refilled Oscar's glass, and slid into my seat.

"He bought himself one of those big, antebellum mansions with the white columns across the front. It was the scene of some of the finest parties in New Orleans." Oscar winked slyly at me. "Leidesdorff romanced the cream of the city's crop of debutantes—wooing them with his guitar. He'd built up quite a playboy lifestyle for someone who started out penniless at sixteen."

Oscar wrapped his hand around the glass of water, rotating it back and forth on the scratched surface of the table.

"Then, around 1840, at the height of his business success, Leidesdorff up and sold everything, packed it all in, and moved to California."

"Chasing the gold?" I guessed.

"Nope," Oscar said, leaning across the table towards me. "He came here long before they found those first nuggets up in the Sierras." The bushy eyebrows scrunched together. "No, he came out here to start over." Oscar leaned back in his chair and took a sip of water. "In a place where nobody back in New Orleans would know to find him."

Oscar set the glass back down on the table. "You see, he came out to the West Coast before San Francisco had even been born. At that time, this was just a small Mexican outpost called Yerba Buena. Few people even knew it existed—it wasn't on many maps. It was just a scattering of homesteads and a Spanish Mission, cut off from the rest of the world, clinging to the edge of the continent."

"Why did he leave New Orleans?" I asked.

Oscar stroked his chin, his worn fingers brushing against the wiry stubble of his face. "The story at the time was that he'd been engaged to marry one of those high falutin' debutantes—a young lady from an aristocratic French family. I believe her name was Hortense. But her parents found out about Leidesdorff's family tree and called off the wedding."

Oscar rested his arms on the plump pillow of his distended stomach.

"Leidesdorff had kind of a swarthy, tanned look about him. You'd expect that from someone who'd been exposed to the elements all of his life—like he had been on those ships. But it turned out his mother was a native of the islands—dark skinned, you see."

"Oh," I mouthed. Such information would not have been well received in the social echelons of a pre-Civil War southern city.

"According to local lore, Leidesdorff left New Orleans to soothe his broken heart." Oscar gave me a sideways smile. "There's a lot of people over the years that have been skeptical of that version of events." The bushy eyebrows arched over Oscar's face like foam on the crest of a wave.

"In any event, all of a sudden Leidesdorff decided to move to a remote, lightly manned outpost in the far reaches of a Mexican territory. Over the years, he built up a nice trade business out here in the bush. He was on the town council, the school board, that sort of thing. The little town slowly grew—and at some point the United States annexed the California territory and changed the name from Yerba Buena to San Francisco."

Oscar grabbed a toothpick from a container in the center of the table and stuck it in his mouth. A piece of food had apparently wedged into the space between his dentures and gums.

"There's a plaque about him on an alley a couple of streets over—it's got his picture on it. He had these enormous lamb chop sideburns. They were quite stylish in those days."

Oscar pulled the toothpick out but looked dissatisfied with the result.

"By the time the first bits of gold were discovered, Leidesdorff had acquired several pieces of property here in Northern California."

Oscar gummed his dentures out then slid them back in.

"There was a hotel and a warehouse. And he owned one of the nicest homes in the area—the only one with a flower garden. Whenever anybody important came to town, Leidesdorff would throw a dinner party for them—still suave and debonair even in his outback surroundings."

Oscar tossed the toothpick through the air to the open mouth of the kitchen trash can.

"But the most important piece of property is what he got from the Mexican government. It came out of a land grant deal that closed just before California was transferred over to the United States. The land was up in the Sierra foothills, near where the Sacramento and American rivers meet." Oscar paused, rubbing the side of his nose. "Leidesdorff's property ran alongside John Sutter's ranch—right next to his sawmill. You remember—it was one of Sutter's ranch hands that plucked a nugget up off

of the riverbed and ran into San Francisco with it, babbling about his find to anyone who would listen. That's
what set the whole thing off."

I had been standing in front of the cash register retelling my memory to Monty and Ivan. Monty burst in as I
reached this part of the story. "I remember this Leidesdorff fellow now! He died right before the Gold Rush hit,
didn't he?"

"Yes," I nodded. "Leidesdorff died in the spring of
1848—of encephalitis."

Ivan looked puzzled.

"His brain swelled up," I explained. "Probably from an
infection. It came on suddenly. He was fine one day and
on his deathbed the next." I paused for a moment and
lowered my voice. "Oscar thought there was something
strange about his death."

"Strange? What kind of strange?" Monty asked, his
voice edged with excitement.

I shrugged noncommittally. "Most of the people who
moved to Northern California in those early days were
coming here to get a fresh start." I leaned over the cash
register towards my listeners to make the point. "Almost
all of them had at least one skeleton in their closet."

Ivan shifted uncomfortably as I continued.

"Here's another odd tidbit. Even though he'd just sold
off several pieces of land—the house with the flower garden and the warehouse—Leidesdorff was financially
bankrupt when he died. The proceeds from those transac-
tions were never accounted for. His remaining holding
was the ranch up in the Sierras, land that would be at the
focus of the Gold Rush just days after he died. The property mushroomed in value, almost overnight."

Monty stroked the side of the cash register contempla-
tively as I walked around the counter. "Oscar said that at
least as early as January of that year, Leidesdorff had
commissioned surveys of his land—assessing its potential
mineral content. He and Sutter had probably known about
the gold for quite some time."

Ivan sighed. "What's the connection with the tulip? Why would Oscar have drawn it on the remodel sketches?"

"He must have been thinking about the Leidesdorff story," I replied as my mind drifted back to the memory in Oscar's kitchen.

Oscar reached across the table and picked up the two gold pieces. "I came across these items recently," Oscar said, his eyes gleaming with an antiques dealer's thrill of discovery. "I'm pretty sure they belonged to Leidesdorff— matches some I saw him wearing in an old daguerreotype. That man loved his flower garden, especially the *tulips*."

Oscar held out his hand so I could see. Poking out of his cracked, stubby fingers were two gold cufflinks cut in the form of three-petaled tulips.

It was the same tulip shape as the doodle on the corner of Ivan's sketches. The same shape as the handle of the key from the white envelope.

Ivan spoke before I could reach into my pocket to pull the key out. "About those renovation discussions I had with Oscar," he said, smiling apologetically. "I was going to tell you after we looked at the sketches. I didn't want it to discourage your ideas, if they'd been different."

He sucked in his breath, as if anticipating his next words might ignite a blast. "Oscar had ordered a replacement for the front door of the Green Vase. I delivered it here last Sunday morning—the day he died."

Chapter 11

"YOU WERE HIS Sunday morning appointment?" I asked, confused. I had assumed Oscar had been leaving to go to a construction site when he had the stroke.

Ivan hesitated, a pained expression on his face as he glanced down at the reddish-brown shadow on the floor near our feet. "He seemed fine when I left," he said softly. "I had no idea—I wish I'd been here when it happened. I could have called a doctor."

The scar lining Ivan's jaw pulsed. "Oscar had me carry the new door down to the basement," he said gently. "Can I show you where we stored it? I think you'll be interested to see what Oscar ordered."

"I know I'd like to see it," Monty piped in, popping his right hand up enthusiastically, eager for a chance to prowl around the basement.

"All right," I said, giving Monty a surly stare as I walked across the room towards the hidden hatch. I leaned over, stuck my finger in the hole in the floorboard and removed the cover.

"I can't believe I missed this," Monty muttered to himself.

I pulled up on the handle, and the door swung open, creaking loudly as the steps cranked down below. I grabbed the flashlight and led the way down, my flat footsteps echoing dully on the wobbling staircase before being drowned out by Ivan's tromping construction boots and Monty's flapping dress shoes.

The basement was just as dark and dismal the second time around. The mustiness of the room clamped down on my chest as I moved forward. I played the light against the brick walls and stacks of shipping crates.

"Over there." Ivan motioned towards the back wall.

I pressed forward, stepping around numerous wooden shipping crates, deteriorating furniture, and odd-shaped objects covered in drop cloths. Ivan stayed close behind me, navigating off the light from my flashlight.

Monty, on the other hand, kept stopping to peek behind crates and snoop under drop cloths. He let out a whimpering screech of pain as he tripped headlong over a short wooden stool.

I swung the flashlight back towards Monty, training the beam on the spastic figure trying to free himself from the clutches of the cobweb-filled wardrobe he'd fallen into. Ivan grabbed his shoulders and pulled him back to his feet.

"I'm all right! I'm all right!" Monty called out as he righted himself.

Ivan fished a small flashlight out of his tool belt and led the rest of the way to where a hulking, tarp-covered object leaned against the back wall of the basement. Monty and I caught up to him as he pulled back the covering.

Familiar iron scrollwork framed the edges, supporting beautifully cut—unbroken—pieces of glass. It was an exact replica of the broken door swinging from the front entrance above, except that this one was in pristine condition.

Gold script flickered on the top pane of glass.

The Green Vase

Another line of text was placed further below, near the middle of the door. This gold lettering announced the proprietor of the Green Vase.

I caught my breath, speechless.

"Take a look at that!" Monty exclaimed. Ivan grinned. The name listed was not Oscar's, but mine.

I slid the light down to the doorknob. Here, the design diverged from the original. A circle of twisting tulips wound around the facing, the pointed tip of each petal turning in towards the knob. Forged into the knob's surface was—a three-petaled tulip.

I ran my fingers over the sculpted ridges with my free hand.

It was the same design as the key. The same design as the drawing on the sketch I'd left on the counter upstairs.

I handed the flashlight to Monty and reached into my pocket. Monty's eyes shone as I pulled out Oscar's white envelope.

The flower-tipped key felt heavy in my hands as I brought it up to the opening of the lock.

I was too distracted by the door to notice my companions' reactions—too distracted to notice their greedy-eyed gleam when the key slid into the lock and engaged.

BEEP.

It was Monday morning, and I was returning to work after the previous week's absence. I had just reached the foyer to the accounting firm's office tower. Gaudy stone gargoyles glared down at me from the upper rim of the entrance's atrium.

Half asleep, I didn't hear the tiny error sound as I

swiped my security access card, and I walked straight into the frozen entry bar. Rubbing my bruised abdomen, I smiled apologetically at the suited man in line behind me and waved the card again in front of the scanner.

Beep.

This time I heard the beep and didn't try to charge through the gate. I turned around to fend off the impatient man who was now slapping his plastic card against the metal railing.

"My card doesn't seem to be working." I shrugged. "I'll just try it one more time."

I held my breath as I took one more swipe.

Beep.

A loud, irritated sigh erupted from behind my left shoulder. Gritting my teeth, I turned and said stiffly, "Be my guest."

The man moved aggressively past me, flicking his card in the general direction of the scanner. A slight clicking sound echoed in the stone foyer indicating his card had been accepted. The bar swung easily away from him as he moved through the entrance and turned the corner to the bank of elevators.

I moved off to the side of the foyer, underneath the gaping mouth of one of the elevated gargoyles, and studied my card. It didn't seem bent or disfigured in any way. I was holding it up to the pale, anemic light from the ceiling fixture when a security guard touched my elbow.

I handed him my card and said helplessly, "It doesn't seem to be working."

He read the name on my badge and said in a hushed tone, "Follow me, please."

He was a solid, bulging man with a gut that looked as if it had stored up reserves for a long hibernation. His thick, trunk-like legs seemed to have taken root during his endless hours of standing surveillance. Each plodding step required enormous effort.

The dark, pitted bark of his skin was expressionless as he unchained a side gate and led me down the hall to the elevators. We disembarked at the fifth floor lobby and waited, both of our roots descending into the polished marble tile.

The security guard didn't volunteer any information, but a worrying knot was forming in my stomach. About half an hour later the human resources manager emerged from a hallway and bustled over to us.

"Oh, there you are," she said, as if she'd been waiting on us and not the other way around.

Unlike the security guard, she swished sharply from place to place, never lingering for long in any one position. The words of my firing flew out of her mouth the second her plump posterior dropped into the seat behind her desk.

"But—why?" I asked, although I had already guessed the reason. I had worked at the firm for five years; only a short list of provocations were handled in this manner.

"We understand," she said, her face gelling into a solemn mold that I was sure had been used countless times before, "that you will be branching out on your own, as a solo practitioner."

She paused, the traces of a smirk creasing her lips. "As you know, you are prohibited from soliciting any of the firm's existing clients while you are employed here. We wouldn't want you to be unduly tempted, so we think this arrangement will be best for both parties."

Monty, I steamed internally, had broadcast his harebrained accounting-antiques store idea to all of the Jackson Square board members. Someone from the board must have passed the information on to the accounting firm. The business circles in San Francisco, I knew, ran a tight circumference.

I nodded, red faced, aware that there was no use arguing or trying to explain. Once this kind of decision had been reached, the firm never budged. The security guard led me to my cubicle and supervised as I packed up my personal belongings.

Silently, I unpinned the smattering of photos from the

cloth-covered walls of my cubicle and cushioned my coffee cup in a corner of the single cardboard box I'd been allotted. Deafening stares bored into my back as I exited the electronic beehive of computers, headsets, and photocopier machines.

On the street outside the fortress of the firm's office building, I blinked for several seconds, dazed in the unaccustomed freedom of a mid-morning Monday unleashed in downtown San Francisco.

"Well, Oscar," I said, still in shock as I stared up past the office buildings at the powder blue sky. "I hope you're happy."

I carried my box the couple of blocks over to Jackson Square. I was standing beside the cashier counter just inside the Green Vase, one hand on my forehead, the other on my hip, when a short, rapping sound echoed against the glass behind me.

"Hello there, neighbor," Monty called out from the sidewalk.

I waved weakly at him, hoping he might go away if I didn't move to open the door. Ivan had installed Oscar's replacement before he left the night before.

"Shouldn't you be at work?" he shouted persistently through the glass.

I sighed depletedly and unlocked the door to let him in.

"I was canned," I said flatly. "This morning."

"Oh—well." Monty's face contorted. He seemed to be looking for the right thing to say. "That's fabulous!"

I packaged my most withering look and sent it to him express.

"No, I mean, obviously, the actual event must have been unpleasant." Monty patted me on the shoulder awkwardly. "But, won't it be easier to get started on your new business without having to keep up your other job?"

"I suppose," I murmured, an underlying sharpness in my voice. I had intended to think over my decision on the Green Vase for a couple of weeks before giving up my regular paycheck.

A light flashed in Monty's eyes. "I know just the thing that will cheer you up," he said. "I was going to bring it over later anyway. You wait here." He leapt giddily out the door and sprinted across the street to his art studio.

I sat down wearily on the stool behind the cashier counter and considered my situation. Thankfully, the funds from Oscar's estate would be available once probate was completed. I had some savings of my own that would keep me afloat until then, and I could save on rent by moving out of my apartment and into Oscar's old flat upstairs. My eyes rolled up to the ceiling, thinking about the enormous cleaning job awaiting me.

Monty reappeared, holding a vase filled with fresh, violet-colored tulips. The vase was the epitome of the icon we were planning to use for the inlay to the glass windows. The translucent, green surface of the vase glowed as the light shone through it.

"You're right," I said, somewhat sarcastically. "This is just what I needed."

Monty either misread or ignored my tone. "Picked it up at a flower stall down the street," he said, preening in the pride of his purchase. "The vase caught my eye as I was walking by. It was sitting on a counter at the front." Monty rotated the vase in his hands. "It sucks you in, doesn't it? The owner helped me pick out the tulips. Freshly cut this morning."

I took the vase from Monty and placed it on the cashier counter, sliding it back and forth to find the best light. It was a nice vase, I had to admit.

A movement across the street caught my eye. "Monty, there's someone at the door to your studio."

He whirled around. "Right, that'll be Dilla." He sprung out the door, then pirouetted back and stuck his head inside. "I'll come by later this afternoon, so we can work on the board presentation."

He was gone again before I could spit out my response. I watched as he rushed across the street to greet an elderly woman standing at the door to his studio. She was colorfully dressed in a bright orange suit, trimmed along all of its edges with a detailing of reddish-orange fur. They greeted each other with kisses on each cheek; then he bent to a deep bow as he held the door open for her to enter the studio.

With an appreciative nod to my newly acquired green vase, I locked the door and headed home for lunch.

Chapter 12

FOUR HOURS LATER, I was back at the Green Vase, sitting in the kitchen listening to Monty expostulate on the finer details of historical renovation for our upcoming board proposal. Ivan had managed to escape this torture session due to an alleged prior engagement.

I laid my throbbing head on the kitchen table as Monty gabbled on about brick textures and glass thicknesses. My forehead found a particularly soothing groove in the pine plank surface, and I closed my eyes trying to shut out the whining drone emanating from the other side of the table.

The floor around us was still sopping wet from my first unfortunate episode with Oscar's dyspeptic dishwasher. Trapped in the kitchen with a monologueing Monty, I'd begun tidying up the area. I had scraped several layers of chicken grease off of the stove and—with Isabella's diligent supervision—had removed all sorts of unidentifiable organic matter, in various states of decay, from the refrigerator. But my cleaning frenzy had terminated when I'd gathered up a load of dishes and unwisely flipped the start switch to the dishwasher.

At least the subsequent flood had earned me a temporary break from Monty's endless renovation lecture. He'd stopped long enough to help me mop up most of the water. Unfortunately, he was now back at it, tilted back in his chair, wingtips propped up on the edge of a nearby stool.

Monty's current topic revolved around what shade of green to paint the crenulated iron columns that framed the bricks and windows along the front of the Green Vase. He picked through a reel of paint chips, searching for suitable options.

Holding up one of the small pieces of paper between his fingers, Monty commented, "Dollar bill green—the color of money. Appropriate for an accountant, I should think."

"I thought we agreed not to make any more public statements about the accounting idea," I said warily.

"Right," he responded in a voice I suspected meant the opposite. "Of course."

From my semi-prone position on the table, I had begun to wonder what means Oscar had used to so successfully eradicate Monty from the Green Vase. A hefty frying pan hung from the ceiling near the stove—it looked like just the right size for swinging at his curly, pin-shaped head. I was about to walk over to take a closer look at it when Monty finally started winding down for the night.

"That's probably more than we'll need for the board meeting," he said, carefully filing his sketches in his leather portfolio. He dropped his pencils into their plastic case and straightened up his bow tie. "They probably won't want more than a two-minute summary anyway."

I eased myself up off the table and looked around for the cats; I'd brought them back with me after lunch. I found them curled up together in a dry corner of the kitchen and nodded to Isabella. She responded with a sharp "Mrao" and headed down to the first floor where I'd left the cat carriers. I plucked a sleepy Rupert up off the floor and followed Monty out of the kitchen.

He tiptoed around the last pools of water and started down the steps, the soles of his wingtips clapping on the wooden boards of the staircase.

"These old buildings always make me nervous," Monty said, ducking his curly head under the low-hanging beam in the stairwell. "You never know what might be hiding in all the cracks and recesses. I had a close call not too long ago—over at Frank's. Some sort of exotic spider had crawled up into his rafters. It dropped down and bit me on the ear. The whole lobe swelled up—it looked like I had a grapefruit stuck on the side of my head!"

Monty reached up to his head and tugged on his ears, as if trying to ensure that they were free of any lobe-enlarging arachnids.

"You'd think the spider would have gone after Frank, what with that mustache he's got," Monty said as we reached the bottom of the stairs. "You know, for nesting materials." He gently slapped the sides of his face. "I like to keep a clean shave—for just that reason."

"Mmmm," I mumbled behind him, relieved to be exiting the building at last.

"Frank's mustache reaches way out over the top of his lip," Monty nattered on in front of me. "He must spend hours combing it—there's never a hair out of place. The mustache is so enormous, you hardly notice his nose."

This did not match the description of Napis as I remembered him, but, with my car in sight at the curb outside, I wasn't about to start asking questions. Monty helped me carry the cat carriers out to the sidewalk, and I pulled the iron-framed door shut behind us.

"I'd never be able to grow one," Monty said thoughtfully. "They're too itchy—and I don't know how Frank manages to eat with his." Monty drew a quarter-sized circle on the tip of his chin. "But I've been thinking about growing a micro-beard right about here."

I opened one of the backseat doors to the Corolla and shoveled the two cat carriers inside. Monty was still carrying on about facial hair as I climbed into the driver's seat.

"I saw that Leidesdorff plaque you told us about—the one over in the financial district with his picture on it. It's got me thinking about extending my own sideburns a bit. Not full on lamb chops, mind you, more of a thin line here around the jaw area." He stood admiring his face in the dusty reflection of the Green Vase's windowpanes.

"Good night, Monty," I said, closing the driver's side door and turning the key in the ignition.

"THIS IS QUITE the setup you've put together here," I said, surveying the scene on the sidewalk outside the Green Vase the following afternoon. Ivan was scheduled to come by to review our proposal before the board meeting later that evening. Monty had prepared a tea service for the occasion.

A white china tea set had been laid out on a round plastic table. Delicate pink roses detailed the rim of each cup as well as the handle of the hot water pot.

I pulled out a seat as Ivan walked up.

"My lady," Ivan said, pushing my chair in with an amused look on his face.

"Thank you kind sir," I replied as Monty leaned over to pour steaming water into my cup.

Monty presided over the tea service, directing the small symphony of cups and saucers. Our conversation had turned to that night's board meeting when an elderly Asian man tottered up to the table and greeted us.

"Good afternoon," he said with a slight dip of his head.

The man was frail, his body rail thin. A baseball cap, one size too large, perched on his large protruding ears, while a pair of dark trousers swallowed up his entire lower half. He leaned towards me, his thin lips parting to reveal tobacco-stained teeth. "I'm looking for Oscar's niece?"

"That's me," I volunteered, standing up to introduce myself.

"Hello, Mr. Wayne," Monty called out, waving from his chair on the opposite side of the tea table.

The paper-thin skin on the man's pallid face stretched tensely, but he smiled again and bowed slightly in Monty's direction. "My name is John Wang," he said to me, emphasizing the pronounciation of his last name. "Mr. Carmichael," he paused, nodding in Monty's direction, "stopped by my flower shop the other day."

"Oh!" I exclaimed, making the connection. "Where he got the vase. It's a perfect fit for my store." I motioned to the gold writing on the front of the new door.

"Yes, this is nice," Mr. Wang said as he looked over at the entrance, studying it carefully with alert eyes that seemed to take in every detail. He turned back to the tea table. "I am very sorry for your loss," he said kindly, his reedy voice scratching. "Your uncle was my friend."

"Thank you," I replied gratefully. There was an oddly comforting, grandfatherly way about him, despite the sweaty tobacco aroma exuding from his clothes. A well-used pipe poked out of his shirt pocket.

"Your uncle wanted you to have this," he said, pulling a flat, rectangular package out of his back pocket and handing it to me.

I turned the package over in my hands. It was less than an inch thick and covered with a brown paper wrapping. My name was written on one side in a cramped scrawl I recognized immediately as Oscar's.

"Oscar gave it to me a couple of weeks ago," Mr. Wang said. "Not long before he died."

I turned the package over in my hands, my eyes instinctively looking for yet another three-petaled tulip.

"He asked me to deliver it to you." Mr. Wang looked at me with deep, solemn eyes. "In case something happened to him."

"Happened to him?" I repeated the words, hearing the ominous phrase for the second time in as many days.

Chapter 13

MR. WANG'S FRAIL figure teetered off down the street as I excused myself from Monty's tea service. I climbed the stairs to the kitchen, laid the package on the table, and collapsed into one of the worn seats.

The resilience I'd built up in the days since the funeral melted away. The package sat on the table like a bomb, waiting to explode. I hunched in my chair, biting my lower lip, my eyes trying to penetrate the layers of brown packing paper.

Sighing resignedly, I slipped the edge of a pair of scissors underneath a fold and began to cut through the layers of tape. In typical Oscar fashion, the package was virtually waterproof from his wrapping. Not an inch of the paper remained uncovered by strapping tape.

At long last, I'd cut through enough of the outer shell to access the inside. I reached in and pulled out a weathered parchment that was folded up like a street map. The worn and beaten document cracked as I opened its accordion-like pages. Unfolded, it spanned about two feet by three feet. The printed side contained streets and a shore-

line from an earlier time that I recognized immediately—
it was San Francisco during the first blazing days of the
Gold Rush.

I'd come across several old city maps in the Green Vase
showroom, but this was one of the earliest versions I'd
seen. In this depiction, the shoreline had not quite reached
our block in Jackson Square. The land that the Green Vase
would soon occupy was still under water. The kitchen table
where I was sitting looked to be about forty to fifty feet into
the bay, near the mouth of a small inlet cove. A short bridge
had been built over the narrow opening of the cove to allow
foot traffic to the other side.

I sat back in the chair and rubbed my eyes. Why would
Oscar have asked Mr. Wang to deliver this to me? What
calamitous event had he been preparing for? Had Oscar
sensed his imminent stroke or was there a more sinister
explanation?

I heard a noise outside and walked through the living
room to the window overlooking the street. Monty and
Ivan were carrying the table and chairs back to Monty's
studio. I carefully refolded the map, slid it between two
cookbooks on a shelf in the kitchen, and headed back
downstairs.

Monty and Ivan walked through the front door as I
reached the showroom. From Monty's expression, I could
tell he was about to bombard me with questions about the
package.

"Ouch!" I cried out as I stubbed my toe on the still unopened crate that had covered the trap door to the basement.

"Hey, can one of you help me open this crate?" I called
out. Given Monty's pathological penchant for disseminat-
ing information, I wasn't ready to share this latest development with him. I needed a quick change of subject.

"I've got it," Monty said as he trotted towards the back
of the room where I stood next to the crate. He leaned
over the box and tried to read the water-stained shipping
label.

"Australia?" he called out curiously. "What would Oscar have ordered from Australia?"

I shrugged my shoulders—puzzled, but relieved. His interest piqued, Monty dove into the task, momentarily forgetting about my package from Mr. Wang.

"We're going to need a crowbar on this," he advised, looking at me with an air of crate-opening expertise.

I fetched one from Oscar's toolbox in a closet off the kitchen. "Here you go."

"Right, then," he said, grabbing the handle. He approached the box awkwardly, holding the crowbar in his hands like a pickax. He laid the box down on one of its oblong sides and slid the slanted end of the crowbar into a grooved crack between two of the planked panels.

I squinted at the box. Bracketed hinges appeared to line the edge of the panel Monty had chosen to attack with the crowbar.

"I think you've inserted it into the hinged side of the lid," I offered.

"Yes." He stood up, his voice tetchy. "Yes, it appears that I have."

Monty crouched down and tried to remove the crowbar, but it was now tightly wedged. He threw a leg over the crate, trying to improve his leverage. As I watched him straddling the crate, wrestling with the crowbar, I realized Ivan would have been a much better candidate for this task. So skillful with a sketch pad, Monty was a disaster with any device that might be stored in a toolbox.

"Haven't you done this before?" I asked. "Don't the frames for your art studio come in this type of container?"

"No, not really," he sniped, throwing his weight against the crowbar. "Most of my pieces are done locally. I just go pick them up in the van." He studied the thick shipping bands wrapped around the obstinate crate. "Even when they do come through the mail, they've never been cinched up quite like this."

Ivan heard the commotion and wandered towards the back of the showroom. Monty had rotated the box and was lying parallel to it on the floor, still trying to release the crowbar. Ivan's face twisted as he tried not to laugh.

"Need some help?" Ivan asked in response to my pleading look.

Monty muttered up from the ground near the crate. "No need—I've got it covered." His voice pitched higher as he strained against the crate.

The hinges finally gave under the pressure from the crowbar. A loud crack of splitting wood ricocheted through the room as Monty's head slammed backwards onto the floor with a thud. A snowstorm of tiny cedar shavings from the inside of the box showered the area.

Wincing, Monty righted himself, pulled off the loosened metal bands, and raised the lid open the rest of the way. Despite the dusting of cedar shavings all over the floor, the inside of the crate was still flush with packing materials.

"Shall we see what you've got then?" Monty asked, his hair and eyebrows covered with a dandruff of shavings. He waved his right hand in the air, wiggled his fingers, and plunged them down into the crate. A strange and somewhat horrified look came over his face as he grabbed hold of the item hidden under the cedar shavings.

"What in the name of Helen of Troy is this?" Monty cried as he pulled an enormous furry object out of the box.

Monty wrestled the beast to its feet and stepped back. We all stood there silently staring at it, rotating our heads one way, then another. Isabella hissed; her back arched. Rupert leaned forward, sniffing loudly.

We were looking at a stuffed kangaroo that appeared to have been the project of an amateur taxidermist. The animal was standing upright on its two back legs, with one arm crooked out resting on its hip. The body was slightly misshapen, and the head had been contorted so that the animal looked like it was smiling. It was a pose I couldn't imagine a kangaroo striking naturally.

I was beginning to realize that there was a lot I didn't know about my Uncle Oscar.

* * *

THE BOARD MEETING was held around the corner from the Green Vase in an empty room in a renovated, red brick building.

I followed Monty into the building and up a narrow flight of stairs. Monty clutched his ears instinctively as we rounded each turn of the staircase.

At the top, we stepped out into a bright, window-lined hallway. Double doors opened into a rectangular room, whose high ceiling was covered in a decoratively stamped, copper-colored tin.

I took a seat on the second row of chairs next to Ivan while Monty circled the room, mixing with the crowd.

Five chairs lined the far side of a table that ran horizontally across the front of the room. Ivan confirmed that they would be occupied by each of the board members.

Ivan began pointing out various people in the growing crowd. It seemed that he and Harold had done work for most of them. He nodded towards a lively looking woman with bouncing, brown hair and bright, peppery eyes.

"That lady over there is Etty Gabella. She runs a Spanish-themed antiques store on the corner. She hired us to rewire the place last year. You wouldn't have believed the condition of some of the circuits we stripped out of her walls. It's a wonder the place hadn't caught fire."

Next, Ivan indicated to a tall, well-dressed man with high cheekbones and smooth, espresso-brown skin.

"And there's Essian Diarra. I rebuilt the chimney in his place. Found a diary from the 1850s hidden behind a couple of layers of brick."

On the other side of the room, Monty was engaged in an animated conversation with Etty Gabella. Given the flailing arms gesticulating wildly around his head, I guessed that Monty was telling her his ear-biting spider story.

I shook my head. "What is *wrong* with that man?"

"Oh—he's not so bad," Ivan replied, chuckling. "He means well."

I rolled my eyes in response.

Monty crossed the room, still stroking his ears, and leaned over our chairs. "I talked to the board secretary. We're first on the agenda. He thinks we'll go through without any problems."

I looked over Monty's shoulder, and a sinking feeling plunged through my stomach. A short-statured man had just entered the boardroom. He had the same hawkish eyes and balding head I'd seen a couple of months earlier as I stood on the sidewalk outside the Green Vase struggling to unlock Oscar's front door. No mustache, I confirmed, wondering what Monty could have been going on about.

"I thought Frank Napis wasn't going to be here?" I asked, perplexed.

Monty jumped like a frightened rabbit and whipped his head around in a full-circle contortion, his panicked eyes searching the room.

"What?" he splurted. "What do you mean? Frank's here? Where?"

"Right there," I indicated with my head, not wanting to point. The short, balding man strode through the room, his square middle advancing in front of him. He began greeting various attendees with a grand, effusive hand pump.

Monty noodled his head up and down like a serpent, his eyes frantically pacing the room. "I don't see him. Are you sure?"

"He's heading towards the back window," I said in a hushed voice, trying not to draw attention to us. Monty's anguished antics were spectacle enough.

"That's not Napis," Ivan intoned quietly. "That's Gordon Bosco, the chairman of the board."

Monty collapsed into the seat next to me, his hand on his chest. "Good grief woman, you nearly gave me a heart attack."

AFTER THE MANY hours of preparation with Monty and all of my nervousness leading up to it, I don't remember much about the actual board meeting. It was as if time moved on without me, leaving me frozen in my seat.

Afterwards, Ivan assured me that Monty had made the most thorough, in depth presentation in the history of the Jackson Square Historical Board. When Monty finally finished his presentation, our renovation project was approved unanimously—without comment or debate.

But it had been impossible for me to focus on Monty's speech. Throughout the entire meeting, my eyes never left Gordon Bosco, sitting in the center chair at the front table.

I couldn't help it. I couldn't tear myself away from the gold, tulip-shaped cufflinks flickering on the sleeves of his starched, white shirt.

They were identical to the ones Oscar had shown me at his kitchen table during the Leidesdorff story—the same cufflinks that I had picked out for him to wear during his funeral—the cufflinks that had disappeared along with my uncle as his casket lowered into the earth.

Chapter 14

I LAY IN Oscar's old bed the next morning, groggily contemplating the events of the previous day. The cats slept at my feet, stretched out in the extra folds of the blankets I'd brought over from my apartment.

The air was wet with the thick chill of fog, sending me deeper into the warmth of the bed. One of Rupert's tightly shut eyes cracked open a sliver, warning me that it was far too early to disturb his beauty sleep.

My head burrowed down into the pillow in agreement. Almost instantly, I fell back into a deep, pre-dawn slumber. Bundled in the cushioning cocoon of blankets, every joint thoroughly un-tensed, my head sunk down through the pillows and picked up the thread of an earlier, unfinished dream.

I walked towards a faint, glowing light as the uneven tile floor of the kitchen appeared beneath my feet. The peeling wallpaper rose before my eyes, along with a happily gurgling dishwasher. Happy, I saw, because its owner's hunched back stood near the stove, cooking up a skillet of fried chicken. Oscar turned as I reached out to touch him on the shoulder, and the gruff exterior of his face broke into a broad, warm smile.

Oscar was holding something in his hand. He stretched out his arm to offer it to me. The object glowed a gold metallic in his rough, worn fingers—the image of a tulip flickered in the warm light of the kitchen.

I reached out to take it from him, my fingers curling around the hard metal surface. The object rolled in the palm of my hand. I looked down and saw that my fingers were wrapped around the tulip-shaped handle of the gold key.

My gaze bounced back up to Oscar, but his face was slowly changing. I watched, horrified, as his round, grizzled cheeks flattened into loose, flopping jowls. His gray hair darkened into oily, black strands. His cheery, blue eyes sunk into his skull, shrinking to dark, beady pupils.

Harold Wombler's snarling voice echoed in my head as I stared at the worn, shredded overalls that had suddenly replaced Oscar's stained, navy blue shirt.

"What are you up to Monkey-mery?"

I tried to speak but my voice remained silent, my vocal cords paralyzed, as the face in front of me morphed again. The cartilage of the nose grew into a sharp protrusion, beaking out over thin, nearly invisible lips, and I found myself face to face with Gordon Bosco.

I stepped backwards, trying to distance myself from his portly figure and finely tailored, double-breasted suit. He tugged on his starched white cuffs, revealing tulip-shaped cufflinks that twinkled in the light. . . .

"Whugh!" The sound squeezed out of my throat as Rupert jumped on my stomach and crawled up to my face. Apparently, it was time for breakfast.

I FILLED UP the cats' food bowls and headed down the stairs to the showroom, grabbing the parchment map and a couple of San Francisco guidebooks along the way.

I passed the stuffed kangaroo on my way out the front

door. In this misty light, it looked like a character from a B-grade horror movie.

"I've got to get rid of that thing," I thought, shaking my head as I walked outside.

The fog covered everything like a trench coat. Figures as close as the opposite side of the street retained their anonymity, making it difficult to shake the eeriness of my dream.

A couple of blocks later, I entered the financial district. The streets filled up with crowds of lawyers, stockbrokers, secretaries, and salesmen, littering the sidewalks with the one-sided cackle of their cell phone conversations. The pumping gears of delivery trucks and the screeching brakes of Muni buses filled in a deafening white noise as an army of suited, stone-faced warriors flashed by me, white iPod tails dangling from their ears.

It was 8:55 a.m. on Montgomery Street, crunch time for the army of ants scurrying to their offices. I stood with my ex-brethren on a corner, waiting for the light to change, feeling the heated radiation of their stress and anxiety. The force of my old routine tugged at me, threatening to suck me back in. If I closed my eyes, I felt certain my feet would turn off towards the accounting firm—left at this corner, then two blocks down. I imagined my closet-sized cubicle, forlornly waiting for my return.

The signal turned to green, and everything started to move again. I continued straight across the intersection, bypassing the left turn, wrenching myself free from the siren call of my cubicle. By the time I reached the opposite side of the street, my head was up, my vision sharp and clear. A fresh breeze whistled through the fog-laden streets, chasing the murky spirit back to its ocean lair.

It's funny the things you notice when your perspective changes. I must have passed that corner hundreds of times before, but—for the first time—I noticed a gold-colored plaque set into the brick wall of a bank building. To the consternation of the crowds rushing past me, I stopped to read it.

The marker commemorated the spot where, on July 9, 1846, Captain John B. Montgomery sailed the *USS Portsmouth* into the small settlement of Yerba Buena and disembarked. I leaned forward, squinting to read the raised text mounted on the block as the last office stragglers screeched around me, racing to make their elevators before the clock ticked nine.

From here, I read, the captain had marched his men up the hill a couple of blocks to the center of town and claimed the territory of California for the United States. The few Mexican soldiers on patrol had left a couple of days before his arrival. In that pre-Gold Rush atmosphere, neither the United States nor the Mexican government had much interest in the isolated backwater that would become San Francisco.

The streets emptied as the hour hand broke nine. I crossed the street in decadent luxury, skipping lightly over the cable car tracks, and walked a couple of blocks down to my destination—a nondescript alley fronted by a pair of stately stone office buildings. A narrow canyon of asphalt sliced between the two structures, providing outdoor seating for a coffee shop that occupied a commercial space on the street level of one of the buildings.

A small street sign hung off a lamppost, barely noticeable against the fog-enhanced backdrop. The sign labeled the shaded alley: LEIDESDORFF.

I took a seat at a small table in the alley outside the coffee shop. Sharp rays of sun began to slice through the fog as I pulled the parchment and the guidebooks out of my backpack and spread them out on the table. From the text of one of the reference books, I realized that Leidesdorff's warehouse had been located just across the way, on the other side of California Street.

According to the book, the warehouse had been situated on the water's edge so that at high tide, small runner boats could pull up to it and unload their cargo. The warehouse had been a transit point for raw materials from Northern California ranches, sugar cane from Hawaii, and manufactured goods from the East Coast.

In the present day geography, the city's shoreline was several blocks to the east. Even without the fog's impediment, the water was no longer visible from this location.

I tried to imagine away the towering masonry encircling my table, envisioning a damp bank of sand trafficked by burly frontiersmen hefting bundles of fur and skins. Their heavy boots thunked up the wide, wooden steps of the warehouse into a receiving area where a tall, swarthy, lamb-chopped Leidesdorff entered their goods into his ledger book.

My mental image evaporated with the jarring clang of a trolley car clattering along California Street. I returned to the book.

An American solider named Joseph Folsom had purchased the warehouse property from Leidesdorff right before he died. Folsom built a hotel on the site, expanding it into the landfill lot next-door.

In its day, the Tehama Hotel had been a landmark for the city's social elite. Famous financier William Ralston and his wife lived there for several months after their marriage while they waited for their prestigious Nob Hill residence to be built. Ralston had been so taken with the hotel's location that he later purchased the land for the site of his bank.

The bank's first building had burned down after the 1906 earthquake, but its replacement was equally grand. I walked around the corner of the coffee shop to study it in person. Elaborate, stone pillars supported a Parthenon-like structure; Italianate detailing trimmed every edge. Despite the elaborate décor, the bank presented a solid, dignified front.

A delivery bike screeched up in front, and a slim, heavily tattooed man with bulging calves dismounted and clacked up the steps in his plastic biking shoes. I was still staring at the building when he returned moments later, whipped up his bike and pedaled off, iron leg muscles gaining momentum to pound him up the next hill.

I held up the parchment, searching the map for the location of Leidesdorff's warehouse. Another red trolley car rolled by, its wheels banging loudly against the rails, the fog-piercing sunshine glinting against its brass finishings. As the ringing of its bell disappeared up the hill, I saw it.

On the bottom right-hand corner, an imprint had been pressed into the paper. I brought the map up close to my glasses, squinting at the mark.

It was a three-petaled tulip. The same design as the handle to the gold key. The same design as the sketch on Oscar's renovation drawings. The same design as the gold cufflinks Oscar had traced back to Leidesdorff.

I wondered again about the gold, tulip-shaped cufflinks Gordon Bosco had worn at the board meeting the previous evening. The image of Oscar's casket sinking into the deep, black earth flashed before me as the ubiquitous phrase echoed in my head—*in case something happened to him*.

I pulled out my cell phone and called the police station. A switchboard operator picked up. "Hello? Can I help you?"

"Yes, hello," I replied, hesitating for a moment, intimidated by the spontaneity of my action. "I'm calling about an autopsy that was done on my uncle about a week ago."

"I'll transfer you."

I waited as the line rang. The sound of plastic knocking on plastic banged in my ear as someone scooped up a receiver.

"Yes," came the answer. It was a man's voice, flat and pickled, as if it had been soaked in formaldehyde.

"Yes, hello, I had some questions about an autopsy that was done recently on my uncle," I said and gave him Oscar's details.

Computer keys clicked in an otherwise silent void.

"I don't see any records of that here." The voice was cold, sterile. "I'm sorry, you must be mistaken."

"But—someone called and told me that there'd been a preliminary autopsy. That my uncle had died from a stroke," I insisted, growing frustrated.

"I don't know what to tell you, Ma'am. We have no records of any autopsy being done." He coughed uncomfortably. "As far as I know, we don't *do* preliminary autopsies."

Chapter 15

I WALKED PENSIVELY back to the Green Vase, my brain more fuddled than when I left, unsure of how to process the information from the police department. *Someone* had called to assure me that Oscar had died of a stroke. That diagnosis now seemed less and less likely. My head swam with grim possibilities as I turned the tulip key in the door and walked inside.

Rupert was fast asleep on the cashier counter, soaking up the sun streaming in the window. A couple of stray pieces of litter had shaken out of his coat onto the counter. One paw hung lazily off the edge, swinging back and forth like the pendulum on a grandfather clock.

"Glad you're keeping an eye on the place," I said sarcastically.

A light snuffle was his only response.

Isabella chirruped a warning from her perch on top of the bookcase. A half-second later, the floor creaked behind me. I turned to find that my curly-haired, omnipresent neighbor had followed me through the front door.

"Afternoon, everyone," Monty greeted us.

The feathery tip of Rupert's tail twitched slightly in response.

"Hi, Monty," I said, appreciating more and more the value of an underground tunnel that might allow me to come and go unnoticed by my nosy neighbor. "How's it going?"

"I've come to see you about an opportunity." He smiled winningly. "Actually, I've already put you up for it, so you have to accept."

I cringed. "Um, you know, things are really busy right now," I responded evasively. "I've got a lot of work to do here. . . ."

"Oh, this will be great for your business! I'm sure you can fit it in." He began to pace back and forth. His hands stretched above his head as his long fingers gripped at the air, gathering his thoughts.

I could see that I was about to be treated to an in-depth presentation, so I began to look for a place to sit down. I glanced at the dental chair, but, remembering the episode with the recline lever, decided to aim for the stool behind the cashier counter instead.

Monty was just getting warmed up. "I've got this client who runs an auction house—her name's Dilla. She's a dear, you'll love her. She dropped off a painting the other day that I think you'll be interested in." He waved his hand as if setting this thought aside on a mental shelf. "I'll show it to you later."

Rupert yawned and joined Isabella on the floor in front of the pacing Monty. Monty nodded to him, acknowledging the added audience.

"Dilla grew up in this big Victorian up on Nob Hill. It's a bit run down now, but it must have been a beautiful house in its day."

I could see the corner of the metal stool behind the cashier counter. I began circling Monty, trying to get close enough to slide onto it.

"Dilla's a peach." Monty gave me a knowing look. "She's old San Francisco society."

I eased over towards the stool. A few more feet, I

thought, and I could fake a fall and make up the rest of the distance.

"So, Dilla's liquidating this estate for a client, someone's aunt or other who passed away. They were going through the goods and came across a box of costume jewelry. It's made up to look like diamonds, emeralds, sapphires—very convincing imitations. The client has decided to donate the costume jewelry to charity to help defray some of the inheritance taxes."

Monty paused and looked pointedly at Rupert. "They're donating the whole kit and *kangaroo* to a cat rescue operation down on the peninsula."

Rupert began hopping up and down in a circle around the stuffed kangaroo. Monty watched, a jubilant expression on his face.

"What have you done to my cat?" I demanded.

"Just a little kangaroo joke between me and Rupert," Monty said smugly. He paused, proudly watching Rupert's antics.

Muttering under my breath, I stalked around the counter and took a seat on the stool as Monty jumped back into his spiel.

"Dilla's going to hold the charity event in the ballroom at the Palace Hotel a week from Friday. They're selling tickets, the whole nine yards. And, she's going to get the Mayor to come. That will ensure a big turnout."

Our Mayor was young, dashing—and recently divorced. Any event that could advertise his participation was sure to be inundated with swooning females hoping to catch his eye.

"That sounds exciting and all, but I don't think . . . "

Isabella pounced on the bouncing Rupert, and the two of them began wrestling and rolling across the floor in a furry, white blur.

"I haven't got to the best part yet," he interrupted. "The original owner of this jewelry must have been crazy about cats. This costume jewelry—it's done up for cats! It's cat jewelry!"

Isabella looked up at Monty's latest revelation, and Rupert decided to take advantage of her momentary distraction. He coiled up for a full body leap and launched himself through the air. Isabella stepped aside at the last second, and a sprawling Rupert went spinning across the hardwood floor. Isabella, smiling triumphantly, turned her focus back to Monty.

"Dilla was going to use stuffed animals to display the cat gear, but I said, 'Hang on there, I know just the cats for this job!' Rupert and Isabella would be great for it. They're comfortable around people, and they wouldn't cause any fuss. I've never met such social cats. Their white coats are the perfect color for showing off baubles. It'll be brilliant!"

Rupert looked up at him adoringly; even Isabella started to preen. I could see that I was going to have a tough time vetoing this idea.

"We'll think about it," I said, ushering Monty out the door.

"Excellent. Dilla will be by this afternoon to meet Rupert and Isabella."

"Well, I might have to step out. . . ."

He chose not to hear me. "Right then, I'll see you later. This is going to be a great gig."

I sighed as Monty finally left us. Two furry heads stared up at me inquiringly.

"This is a ridiculous idea," I said, my hands on my hips. "Even by Monty's standards."

I looked at Rupert. His eyes had glossed over, filled with visions of a glamorous photo shoot with himself playing the role of a fat, rock-star cat spread out in the middle of a gluttonous array of gourmet cat food.

"We'll talk about it later," I said resignedly.

I moved upstairs so that I could pretend not to be at the Green Vase when Monty's cat-jewelry person arrived. I turned the tulip key in the lock in the front door, grabbed my backpack holding the parchment and guidebooks, and headed up the stairs.

An hour later I was seated at the kitchen table, studying the history section of one of the guidebooks. Isabella sat on a chair watching me work while Rupert slept soundly, beached like a whale on the floor nearby. Isabella's ears jumped at a sound downstairs.

"What was that?" I asked as Isabella headed for the stairs, quick and quiet, stalking the sound. Rupert wheezed out a snore as I jumped over him.

I nearly squashed Isabella as I rounded the bottom of the steps. She was in hunting mode, flattened against the ground. Her sharp, blue eyes were locked on what looked like a giant peacock in the middle of the showroom, bent over a display of assorted gold trinkets.

Isabella licked her lips and prepared to leap as I called out, "Can I help you?"

The creature turned around revealing an elderly woman wearing an outfit comprising every possible form of feather-related accoutrement. Her light blue suit was trimmed with feathers around the hems of the skirt and jacket. A feather boa circled the loose folds of her neck and dangled down to her bulging midsection. Still more feathers poked out of her hat, front suit pocket, and purse.

Isabella backed off of her hunting posture, but her eyes retained a wistful, hungry expression.

"Ah, there you are. Such a cute little shop! I've always thought so. Of course, I haven't been in here in quite some time. I was so sorry to hear about your uncle. The place seems altogether different without him in it." Her eyes wandered around the room. I had the strange sensation that she was looking for something.

"Monty sent me," she continued. "He said I should just knock and come in—that you were probably upstairs. I'm Dilla Eckles. I'm running the auction for the cat jewelry."

I fought off a strong urge to sneeze as the plumed woman walked towards me.

"A pleasure to meet you," I said, introducing myself as I shook the hand that shot out at me from the feathers. I glanced at the front door, now wide open. The tulip key rested on the cashier counter.

"That's a lovely door, dear. That's new, isn't it?" Her voice twittered like the bird her clothes were impersonating.

How had this woman managed to get inside the store, I wondered, perplexed.

"Yes, the old one was broken. . . ." I scratched my head, still staring at the open door.

Isabella stepped out from behind me and sat down in front of our strangely dressed visitor.

"Oh, what a beauty!" Dilla trilled. "Monty said they would be perfect for the job. He's got wonderful taste that man."

Rupert staggered into the room, still half asleep. Our voices had woken him. Afraid he might miss something, he had hurled himself down the stairs. He wasn't prepared for the whirlwind of feathers that suddenly swooped him up. I heard him gulp as Dilla grabbed him around the belly.

"Oh, and here's the other one. Soooo cute! The color is just right—wait 'til you see them in the costumes!"

Rupert tried to manage a pleasant look. He was having a hard time breathing with the way she was holding him around the middle.

"So," I said, trying to figure out a way to rescue Rupert. "Monty mentioned you might need some cat models." Rupert was starting to look a bit faint.

"Yes, yes, dear. Monty said that they would be perfect for this, and I can see that he was right. They're just the right color. The white fur will really highlight the stones."

Rupert's panicked eyes pleaded SOS.

"And that nice, young Mayor is going to come. Well, I'm sure he will once I catch hold of him." She gave me a wink. "If I was just a few years younger. . . ."

Isabella and I looked at each other. Maybe a bit more than a *few* years younger.

Rupert gave a feeble cough.

"Oh, I think he's got a hair ball. Here dear, maybe you should help him." She handed a nearly expired Rupert over to me. Relieved, he took a big, unobstructed gulp of air.

"Now, we'll need to do a fitting," she said, wiping her hands across the front of her suit, trying to brush off the dirt and Rupert hair that had stuck to it. "How about tomorrow afternoon? I'll serve lunch. I'm sure Monty can close up the gallery and join us."

Even Rupert looked like he was starting to have second thoughts. I was about to politely decline Dilla's offer when Isabella started purring loudly and rubbing up against the peacock's legs. Rupert looked down at her as if she'd lost her mind, but I had just caught on to what Isabella's sharp eyes had seen, hidden beneath the flurry of feathers.

The ploy worked and up sailed Isabella. She was more nimble than Rupert in positioning herself in Dilla's arms and, thankfully, breathing freely. Ever so subtly, Isabella flicked aside the feather boa with her paw, revealing a silver and gold necklace.

"Oh, what a lovely necklace," I said, dumping Rupert to the floor. He scooted a good five feet behind me to ensure he was safely beyond the feathery creature's wingspan.

Dilla smiled and set Isabella on the counter. "Thank you, dear." She brushed back the plumage to show off more of her neck.

It was, in fact, a lovely necklace, but my interest went beyond typical female whimsy. The necklace was made of gold and silver pieces interlocked to form the now familiar motif of three-petaled tulips.

"It's one of my favorite pieces of jewelry." Dilla wagged a pudgy finger towards Isabella, who was studying the necklace closely from her vantage point on the counter. "It's for humans, not kitty cats." She sighed pleasantly and pointed at the key on the counter. "Strange how similar the tulip shapes are to the one on that key you've got."

Not for one second did I believe that this latest tulip sighting was a coincidence. "So, for the fitting session, then," I said. "What time would work best for you?"

"How about two, darling? It'll be a late lunch. Monty has the address." She looked at Rupert's wide belly. "We can try on the costumes and make any adjustments we need to get them to fit."

I followed her swishing feathers to the door. She placed her hand on the handle and rubbed her thumb across the raised tulip embossed on its surface. Then, she turned back towards me, her voice dropping to a whisper as she nodded towards the middle of the room where Rupert sat on the floor looking warily up at us. "You might want to give him a *bath* before the big event."

I smiled in response, hoping that Rupert hadn't heard her last comment. "Two it is. We'll see you then."

She walked through the doorway and called out from the sidewalk. "Can you tell Monty? I've got an appointment downtown and don't have time to stop at his place. He likes to talk, that man."

I nodded. "Maybe I'll leave him a note."

I shut the door behind her and turned the tulip key in the lock. I stared at the tulip shape on the handle for a moment before climbing the stairs to the kitchen to fetch the padlock.

Chapter 16

MONTY SHOWED UP early the next afternoon, bursting with ideas about the auction. He peppered me with a constant stream of them as I pulled out the cat carriers for our trip to Dilla's.

"Little cupcakes in the shape of a cat's head. White, creamy frosting with tiny, sparkling candy around the neck." Monty stood in the middle of the kitchen, lecturing to the microwave as I stuck some older towels in the bottom of the carriers.

"No," he turned now to the refrigerator. "No, no. Cookies. Then you can get the whole cat in."

Isabella sauntered into her crate. Rupert sat on the floor, giving Monty a disturbed look.

"The whole cat *shape*, mate. No one's going to cook any cats for this event, I assure you."

I bent down towards the floor trying to convince Rupert to climb into his crate as Monty resumed his list. "We'll need champagne and strawberries . . ."

Rupert was still sore around the ribs from yesterday's encounter with Dilla, and he was not eager to repeat the experience. He finally backed into the cage, giving me a look that indicated he might not exit until the crate returned to the Green Vase.

". . . candles, in the shape of cats," Monty prattled on.

I stood up, grabbed a water bottle, and stuffed it into my shoulder bag. "Let's go."

We headed out the door, each of us hefting a cat carrier. It had been Monty's idea to take a cable car up to Dilla's, since parking was difficult to find in her neighborhood. I had argued for a more practical taxi ride, but Monty insisted he—and his buddy Rupert—needed the fresh air of the cable car.

As we walked the couple of blocks to the nearest trolley stop, we approached a colorful display that I suspected was Mr. Wang's flower stall. It was a low-slung structure of exposed plywood and two-by-fours that looked as if the next strong gust of wind might do it in. Rolling racks of blooming vegetation had been pushed out onto the sidewalk to alleviate the cramped space within the stall.

Mr. Wang greeted us as we approached. "You've come to buy more flowers?" he asked, his voice as thin and reedy as the previous day.

"Sorry, not this time," I replied. "We're on our way to visit someone up in the city."

"All of you, it seems," he said, pointing to the cats. Rupert and Isabella peered up at him through the grilled openings in the tops of their crates.

Monty set Rupert's crate on the pavement and wandered into the maze of racks, perusing the brightly packed rows. "Maybe we should bring Dilla some flowers."

"Tulips are a very good choice," Mr. Wang offered.

I looked over at him sharply; I was now extraordinarily sensitized to tulip references.

"Oh, I don't know." Monty paused behind a rack of calla lilies, his forehead furrowing as he considered. "I'm kind of partial to roses."

"Tulips," Mr. Wang pressed, winking at me as Monty

ambled into the covered portion of the stall. "Today, I can give you a discount on tulips."

The temptation of a bargain was too much for Monty. He turned around, a broad smile on his face. "Tulips it is," he pronounced.

I opened my mouth, but I was too flustered to comment. Monty fished in his wallet for the total, seemingly oblivious to the conspicuous tulip references. I tried to convince myself that I was reading too much into Mr. Wang's comments as he wrapped up the flowers and handed them to Monty. "I hope you have a good visit."

We reached the corner of California Street and waited with a crowd of tourists for the cable car to arrive. Another morning's cool, damp fog was succumbing to a blazing barrage of sunlight. I shielded my eyes from the glare as the clang of the trolley's bell approached us.

We climbed into the carriage, squeezing our cargo into the limited space at our feet. I pulled my knees up to my chest, propping my heels on the roof of Isabella's crate. My mind raced as we rose up through the last wisps of fog, rocking back and forth each time the driver hooked the cable running beneath us. Beside me, Monty chatted merrily along with Rupert, showing no indication that he had registered any significance to Mr. Wang's persistent pushing of the tulip sale.

"I've got tulips on the brain," I thought to myself, letting it go.

We got off at the top of the hill, walked half a block down a side street, and stopped in front of what must have once been a magnificent Victorian house. Time and lack of maintenance had not been kind. The battered structure teetered at least four stories up from the street; rotting gables clutched at its crumbling edifice; sad, broken steps clung feebly to the steep side slope.

Dilla stood in the doorway waiting to greet us as we climbed up the weather-beaten stairs, her vibrant smile a sharp contrast to the tired, defeated expression of her house.

She wore a vivid ensemble of Hawaiian-inspired colors. Her mango-orange jacket and slacks were decorated with a scarf streaked with azure blues and guava pinks. She had further adorned herself with a pineapple-shaped broach and matching earrings. Underneath the brilliant colors of the scarf, her tulip necklace seemed somewhat out of place.

"Welcome, welcome. So good to see you!" she said, ushering us inside to the living room. A plate of triangle cut sandwiches had been placed on a long, rectangular coffee table. White, porcelain bowls waited for the cats on the floor. I set Isabella's cage down on the faded rug and massaged my cramped hand as Monty handed Dilla the tulips.

"Oh, these are lovely!" she gushed to Monty. "Thank you so much!" She dove her nose into the flowers. "Tulips—how appropriate."

Monty somehow missed Dilla's exaggerated wink at my startled expression.

"Please, have a seat," she said graciously, directing us to a threadbare couch in front of the coffee table.

Rupert spied the bowls and looked up at me with anticipation.

"You can go ahead and let them out of their crates, dear, if you like," Dilla said brightly. She opened a container of Tupperware and dished out a brown, mushy mixture into the cat bowls. "I hope they like it," she said proudly. "I made it myself."

I reached over to open Rupert's cage. "Mind your manners," I hissed at him under my breath.

Quickly forgetting his intention to stay inside his crate, Rupert bounced out onto the rug and sat down in front of the bowls, waiting for the go-ahead sign to dig in. Isabella followed him, suspiciously eying the brown sludge in her dish.

Monty and I sat down on the couch as Dilla left with the tulips to find a vase. Rupert looked up at me questioningly.

"Just wait a minute until she gets back," I whispered to him.

Monty leaned back in the couch, casually throwing his arms across its back. "So," he said, pumping his eyebrows at me, "that was kind of odd the other day—Oscar sending you a package through that flower shop guy."

I shifted uncomfortably on the lumpy cushions of the couch. Dilla returned to the living room before I could come up with a response.

She opened a bottle of water, poured it into the three glasses on the table, and then leaned over to the floor to pour some for the cats.

Rupert stared intently at the food in front of him.

"Well, go on then, sweetie. It's all right," she urged him.

That was all the signal Rupert needed. He dove in, his lips smacking as he slurped up the sticky muck. Isabella hung back, tentatively sniffing her bowl.

"This is a wonderful house, Dilla," I said, cautiously taking a sandwich from the tray. The crusts had been cut off, leaving neat, sharp edges. The filling looked suspiciously similar to the lumpy, brown mixture in the cat bowls. "How long have you lived here?"

"All my life, dear, all my life. I couldn't imagine being anywhere else." She stopped and looked around the room, a misty look of remembrance on her face.

The walls and shelves were cluttered with knickknacks and family pictures. I recognized a much younger Dilla in many of them. Even in the black-and-white photos, her flair for bold fashion came through.

To the right of the couch, the room boasted a large picture window that spanned across a wide swatch of the bay. It was one of those million-dollar views the city was famous for. Coit Tower was visible on the right side and, with the fog lifting, Alcatraz spread out on the left. It was mesmerizing.

Monty broke the silence. "Shall we break out the goods? I can't wait to see the cats decked out in the fake jewels."

A delicious smile spread across Dilla's face as she brought a long, flat, wooden box over to the coffee table. She raised the lid to reveal a red, plush, velvet interior.

Isabella's eyes peeked over the edge of the table, curiously studying the box, while Rupert, having licked his bowl clean, began wolfing down Isabella's nearly untouched portion.

Dilla moved aside a sheet of cloth to reveal the first piece, a collar inlaid with a row of green, emerald-like stones.

My head reminded me that it was costume jewelry, but my eyes thought it was the real thing. The stones hued dark against the red background, but when Dilla held them up to Rupert's white coat, the dozens of small, faceted edges caught the light, twinkling.

Rupert stopped eating and sat perfectly still while Dilla fastened the clasp—I think he was afraid she might try to pick him up if he squirmed.

She fastened the hook and stepped back, clapping her hands together in delight. "Oh, he looks so handsome!"

Dilla reached back into the box and pulled out a silver and gold chain, interlaced with several mock diamonds and a rainbow full of other stones. Red, blue, purple, and green sparkled in her hands. "This one's for the lady. Come here dear, I'll help you into it."

Isabella stepped forward and daintily put her front paws through the hole in the chains that Dilla framed with her hands. Slowly, Dilla moved the links into place until Isabella was covered in what looked like a suit of cat chain mail. The netting of bejeweled chains wound around her legs, back, and stomach, then over her head so that one of the blue, sapphire-like stones rested on her forehead between her ears. I wondered if it might feel heavy, but Isabella, admiring herself in a mirror hanging on the wall opposite to the sofa, didn't seem to mind.

Next, we fitted Rupert with a jewelry chain jacket similar to Isabella's costume. It barely closed around his bulging midsection. Cat-sized, elastic cuffs fit around his ankles to complete the outfit.

"You look like Elvis," I told him as he strutted in front of the mirror. Rupert grinned back at me.

"So, Dilla," Monty said, eager to dive into his ideas for the auction. "I was thinking about the layout of the ballroom. Right down the middle, we could construct a raised walkway for the cats to walk up and down wearing the costumes. It'll be like a fashion show—with a real *catwalk*."

I had already heard more than enough about the catwalk proposal and was still pondering the significance of Dilla's tulip-related wink. I interrupted Monty's spiel. "Dilla, I was intrigued by your necklace the other day. Could I take another look at it?"

"Certainly dear," she said, reaching up to her neck. I thought I saw her eyes gleam as she handed the necklace to me and turned back towards Monty. "Oooh, I like that idea. And weren't you talking to me about cupcakes on the phone earlier?"

Monty and Dilla became deeply engrossed in the auction discussion and didn't appear to be paying any attention to me. I turned the necklace over in my hands, gently twisting the alternating silver and gold links. I held the necklace up to the light and found what I was looking for. A miniscule hinge ran along the side of one of the tulip-shaped links. I slid my fingernail into the seam and sprung it open.

A faded photo of a dark-haired man with a swarthy complexion looked out at me. His facial hair had been neatly trimmed—into a thick mustache and lamb chop sideburns. I recognized the image immediately.

It was William Leidesdorff.

Chapter 17

I SQUEEZED MY hand, closing the leaves of the locket, the metal of the necklace cold against my pulsing palm.

"Dilla," I said shakily, breaking into Monty's rambling dissertation on the feasibilities of feline resemblance in cupcakes versus cookies. "May I use your restroom?"

"Down the hall on the right, dear," she said, pointing vaguely, her head turned towards Monty, thoroughly engrossed in the discussion. "I think there's something about the texture of the cupcake that evokes the fluffy airiness of cat fur, don't you?"

I laid the necklace on the table and walked down the hallway, trying to collect my thoughts as my eyes adjusted to the dim light in the windowless corridor. The restroom was small and box shaped, barely large enough to turn around in. A cracked, pedestal sink leaned against the wainscoted wall, its exposed, rusting pipes hanging down from the ceiling like the gutted innards of a carcass.

I stepped inside, pondering as I leaned against the closed door. How did Dilla fit into the Leidesdorff story, and why was she wearing a tulip necklace with his picture in it?

I dug my hand into my pocket and pulled out one of Dilla's sandwiches. I'd discreetly wrapped mine up in a paper napkin. Desperately hoping that her mysterious filling wouldn't plug up the ancient plumbing, I chunked it into the toilet and pushed down on the lever. There was a satisfying swish as water rushed through the rusting pipes, rattling them against the peeling surface of the wall.

Mission accomplished, I left the lavatory and retraced my steps back towards the living room. As I walked along the hallway, I scanned the lineup of family photos, my eyes now adjusted to the dim lighting, rejecting one after another as having any resemblance to the picture of Leidesdorff in the locket. I was so focused on my search for Leidesdorff facial features, I nearly missed the familiar face staring out of one of the larger frames.

Longer locks of auburn hair bounced youthfully around her shoulders, but the curls did nothing to soften the hard edges of her mascara. My stomach quaked as I recognized the portrait of a younger Miranda Richards.

"That Mayor of ours has been playing a little hard to get." Dilla's voice carried down the hall from the living room. "I haven't been able to swing an appointment with him yet." Her voice dropped slyly. "Not to worry. I've decided to try a more creative approach. . . ."

I missed Dilla's latest scheme to induce the Mayor to attend her cat costume jewelry event. Her voice broke off as the house began to shake—gently at first, like the vibration of a distant train still several miles down the tracks. The rumbling steadily increased, growing into a more persistent, violent shaking.

It was an eerily familiar sensation in the city. Most of the earthquakes were a low magnitude and lasted only five to ten seconds. Depending on where you were when one hit, you might not even feel it at all.

This one was stronger than most. For the eternity that spanned those ten wobbly seconds, all of San Francisco mentally united in a single, collective hope that this wouldn't be the next 'Big One.'

I reached out my hand to steady myself against the nearby wall. The building creaked; its wood frame groaned. Nails twisted and torqued in their holes. I became uncomfortably aware that I was standing on the first floor of an extremely old building. Throughout the house, glass fronting rattled in picture frames. A china cabinet chattered nervously as a thousand tiny pieces of ceramic knocked against each other.

It ended as quickly and as subtly as it had begun, and a gushing sigh of relief rushed through the city. I stumbled forward into the living room, rejoining the others.

Uncle Oscar had once told me that you could tell a lot about a person by how they responded to an earthquake. The scene in the living room showcased a wide range of reactions. Rupert and Monty were crowded together under the coffee table, Monty with his arms covering his head, both of them with their eyes tightly shut. Isabella hissed wildly at the room, her back arched, her hair spiking out through the chain-mail costume. Dilla stood serenely in the middle of it all, seemingly oblivious to the chaos around her.

"That was a good, strong shake, don't you think?" she said, sounding strangely pleased.

Monty opened his eyes to give her an exasperated look as I crouched under the table and retrieved a still quivering Rupert. A phone began ringing in the back of the house, and Dilla rushed off to the kitchen to answer it, cutting off the earthquake survival lecture Monty was about to launch into.

I freed both cats of their costume jewelry, carefully tucking the kits back into the wooden box. They jumped into their carriers, relieved to be heading home.

An edge of Dilla was barely visible from the living room. Parts of her conversation floated back to us.

"Yes, yes, dear. Everything's fine. Don't worry. You're coming to our little soiree at the Palace Friday night aren't you?"

Monty looked at me, "Her daughter," he guessed in a loud whisper.

"Daughter?" I asked, sensing Miranda's searing stare from the hallway.

Monty nodded knowingly. "Miranda Richards." He smirked. "I believe you've had the pleasure."

Dilla reentered the room. "Well, that was something, wasn't it?"

Monty opened his mouth to respond, but I cut him off before he could start in. "I think I should go ahead and take the cats home. They're a little unsettled from the quake."

I'll take any excuse to get out of this place as quickly as possible, I thought.

Monty yawned, looking at his watch. "And I've got another appointment this evening, I'm afraid," he added, "so, we really must be off."

"Oh, it's going to be a fantastic evening," Dilla said, her eyes gleaming. "I'm so glad Monty suggested using your kitties. That's going to make the whole event."

Monty leaned in to give Dilla a kiss on each cheek. "Thanks for the lunch, Dilla."

Dilla watched us from her porch as we headed back up the street towards the cable car stop.

The sun shone serenely down on the city's citizens. Cars and buses scooted up and down the steep hills, undisturbed by the afternoon's jiggling.

San Francisco had restarted as if nothing had happened. Her pearly, pastel-shouldered streets stretched up to reach the perfect blue sky, a dazzling display that masked the city's precarious perch on the edge of a dark, menacing precipice.

I lumbered along behind a babbling Monty, carrying Isabella's crate, silently pondering the significance of the tulip-embossed handle I'd seen out of the corner of my eye as we walked out of Dilla's front door.

OUR LITTLE GROUP reversed its path back down the hill towards the Green Vase. It was just after 4 p.m. when

I turned the tulip key in the door. Monty left Rupert's crate on the floor inside and rushed off to get ready for his appointment. I let the cats out and went upstairs to the kitchen to make a late lunch.

The cats curled up together in the corner and were fast asleep by the time I sat down at the table. Munching thoughtfully on a salad, I flipped through a book on the history of San Francisco that I'd found in one of the bookcases downstairs.

As I cracked open the chapter on Leidesdorff, I realized that Oscar must have read this section before—the book fell open there naturally. I spread it out on the table and studied the photo on the page, confirming the identification of the man in Dilla's tulip necklace.

The book gave a slightly less nuanced summary of Leidesdorff's life than Oscar's telling of the tale. William Leidesdorff was born on St. Croix, in the Virgin Islands. His father was a Dutch sailor who had settled there and set up a sugar plantation. His mother, Anna Spark, was a native Caribbean woman. Their son had been born with a light, caramel-colored complexion that masked the Caribbean half of his heritage.

Leidesdorff left home in his teens and found work on a steamer vessel bound for New York. From these modest beginnings, he worked his way up in the shipping business, eventually building a prosperous operation transporting goods between New York and New Orleans.

A beautiful young woman named Hortense caught his eye, and they were soon engaged to be married. But on the eve of the nuptials, her aristocratic French family found out about his mixed ancestry, and the wedding was called off. The unfortunate maiden reportedly died of a broken heart the night Leidesdorff sailed out of town.

Isabella yawned, stretched, and walked over to the table. I reached down to scratch her back, still ruminating on the Leidesdorff story. As I picked up my salad bowl to take it to the sink, I accidentally knocked the book onto

the floor. It narrowly missed Isabella, earning me an in-
jured, offended look.

"Sorry, I didn't mean to scare you." I said, leaning
down to pick up the book.

The collision with the floor had knocked loose a piece
of paper that had been tucked into the inside cover. I unfolded it on the kitchen table. It was a printout of an article from the Internet.

The article focused on the efforts of Joseph Folsom,
the army captain who purchased Leidesdorff's warehouse
from him before he died. After Leidesdorff's death, Folsom tried to acquire the remainder of the Leidesdorff
property up in the Sierras.

Since Leidesdorff died a bachelor without any children,
Folsom traveled to the Virgin Islands to try to purchase the
estate from Leidesdorff's mother, presumed to be his closest living relative. He managed to locate Anna Spark and
convinced her to sell him all of Leidesdorff's remaining
California assets for $75,000. It was a significant amount of
money at the time, but nowhere near what the land was
worth after the gold on it had been discovered.

Folsom returned to San Francisco, and litigation
over legal title to Leidesdorff's land began. The dispute
bounced from court to court over the next decade, com-
plicated by conflicts between Mexican, American, and
Caribbean inheritance laws, as well as several factual
discrepancies about Leidesdorff's life before he came to
San Francisco.

During the court proceedings, the leaves of an alternative family tree began to emerge, and questions arose as to
whether Anna Spark really was Leidesdorff's mother.
Doubts were even cast on the tragic details of his New
Orleans love affair.

I stared at the printout for several minutes after I
finished reading the article. The date printed across the
bottom, I noticed as I looked up at Oscar's calendar, was
only a week or so before he died.

Today's date, a Thursday, was marked on the calendar

with a large 'D.' I stared at the wall for a moment before its meaning hit me.

"Oscar's dominoes game," I said, translating the symbol.

Oscar had gone to his dominoes game the Thursday before he died—the same night Monty snuck into the Green Vase looking for the entrance to the theoretical tunnel.

Harold's rusting voice echoed in my head. "Guess we'll need to find another player for this week's game."

I pulled out the phone book from a drawer near the kitchen sink. The book was well worn—and at least five years old. Smiling, I remembered Oscar's cranky commentary on the topic.

"They're always sending me new ones, but I just throw them out. I've got everything in this one marked!"

I flipped through the brittle pages and found a listing under "dominoes" that had been circled.

"Maybe they'll deal me in," I said, grabbing my coat and heading out the door.

Chapter 18

DINNER CROWDS THRONGED the street as I rounded the corner onto Columbus, looking for a cab. The overpowering smell of garlic welcomed me to North Beach, the Italian neighborhood just north of Jackson Square.

At this point in the evening, cabs were easy to come by. They weaved in and out of traffic, dropping off patrons for the endless row of family run, Italian restaurants. In a couple of hours, the ratio would flip, and a starch-stuffed mob would swarm the few unoccupied taxis that stopped on this block.

I waited for a boisterous group to vacate a blue and black painted, DeSoto sedan. As I slid across the backseat, I gave the address of the bar hosting the dominoes game to a heavyset driver with spiked hair dyed a flaming, florescent red. Painful looking metal piercings had been threaded into every available inch of cartilage on her head.

The car fought its way through a couple of stoplights and turned down Broadway, its tired shocks bottoming out as we picked up speed and swooped down the hill towards the Embarcadero. Joggers chugged along the palm tree lined promenade in the flickering orange sunset, the billowing colors enhanced by the swollen clouds glowering on the horizon.

Pier after pier flashed by as we approached the undercarriage of the Bay Bridge. Rows of tiny, white lights formed the looping outline of its suspension lines, illuminating the sooty, gray structure against the darkening sky.

The cab pulled up in front of my destination as the dark storm clouds bullied their way into the bay. Another drenching downpour was on its way.

I tipped the driver and got out, cautiously surveying the tiny shack of a building leaning out over the water. It looked as if it might teeter off and splash in at any moment. A neon sign flashed in the grimy front window, illuminating a couple of beer-laden tables filled with gray haired men zealously guarding their black-and-white tiles.

"You sure you got the right place, doll?" the driver yelled at me through her open window.

I nodded skeptically as she drove off. Dodging traffic, I scurried across to the other side of the street. A moldy, fishy smell assaulted my senses as I pushed through the door marked as the entrance. Several wrinkled faces looked up at me suspiciously.

I smiled weakly and sidled up to the bar, pretending to survey the offerings. From the looks of the greasy, cracked glassware stacked on the back wall, it had been a while since the last visit from the health inspector. Trying to avoid the bartender's attentions, I turned my stool towards the tables of clicking tiles.

A head of dark hair stood out from all of the gray ones. I studied it closely. I had been expecting to find Harold Wombler among the players, but it was definitely not his greasy black mop that caught my attention.

The man had rotated his head to hide his face, but I'd spent far too much time with those frizzy, brown curls in the last couple of days to be mistaken. My lips twisted together as I strode over to him.

"So," I said, thunking the back of his chair, "I see you made it to your appointment."

"Oh, hello," Monty said meekly, turning to look at me. "I didn't see you come in."

A deep voice interrupted my glare. "Would you like a seat at the table, dear?"

I felt my insides seize up as I glanced at the occupant of the chair on Monty's right side. In the dim, hazy light of the bar, the balding head seemed even smaller, the hooked nose even larger.

"I didn't get a chance to meet you after the board meeting," he said, extending a hand towards me. "Gordon Bosco. I'm so sorry about your uncle. Oscar was a good man."

I met his hand, my fingers brushing up against the tulip cufflinks at his wrist.

"So good to meet you," I managed to whisper, my lungs paralyzed by the hard lines of his thin lips.

"He was one of our best players," Gordon said, the black pits of his eyes never leaving my flushing face. "It's a shame he missed his last game."

"He missed it?" I asked. "Oscar wasn't here that night?"

Gordon shook his head sadly. "Something came up at the last minute, and he had to cancel." The tulip cufflinks reached over and wrapped around Monty's slender shoulders. "Carmichael's offered to fill in, but I'm afraid he's still getting the hang of the game."

Monty's face plumed a flamingo pink. "Never been my forte," he mumbled. "What with all of the numbers." He shrugged helplessly.

"Ah, well," Gordon said smoothly, patting Monty on the back. "You can't expect to fill a pro's shoes on the first try." His beady gaze returned to me. "I'm glad you stopped by tonight. There's something here of Oscar's that you should have."

Gordon stood up, not that it gained him much of a vertical advantage. At full height, he barely topped the curls on Monty's seated head. He walked over to the bar and leaned in to speak with the bartender.

I followed him. Without turning to look, I knew Monty was tracking right behind me. I could hear his shoes flapping against the concrete floor of the bar.

The bartender reached beneath the counter and handed a leather, rectangular case to Gordon. My breath caught as the rounded man swiveled towards me and placed it in my hands.

My fingers slid along the worn surface of the case, fumbling to unhitch the latch. The lid creaked open to rows of thumb-sized tiles lined up on their edges. I turned the lid into the light, reading Oscar's familiar, scrawled handwriting that identified him as the owner.

I pulled one of the tiles out of the case. On one side, bold white dots counted out a numerical value against a dark background. I flipped the tile over and studied the image painted on the opposite side.

Monty, who had been leaning over my shoulder to get a better look, gasped loudly and poked me in the side of my stomach with one of his long, painful fingers.

Gordon stroked the flat plate of skin above his nonexistent upper lip. "It's a fairly new set," he said softly. "The tiles, that is. Oscar had the case for years." I felt the probing, aquiline eyes studying my face as Monty tapped my shoulder.

"Thank you for giving these to me," I responded, wincing as Monty poked me in the small of my back. "I had no idea he kept a set here."

"Almost all of the players do," Gordon said. One of the gold cufflinks clinked as he spread his right hand out on the surface of the bar. "It's easier than carrying them back and forth."

"Well, Gordon, thanks so much for inviting me to participate in the game tonight," Monty said, his voice pitching feverishly. "I'll have to study up for the next meeting." He pulled on my arm. "We've got to go."

Gordon smiled serenely, ignoring Monty's antics. "Perhaps we could meet sometime soon," he said to me, the expression on his face blankly placid as his upper lip twitched. "Your uncle and I had some business dealings that I would like to discuss with you."

"Yes, that—would be—nice," I said, struggling against Monty's persistent pull. I fastened the lid, clasped it to my chest, and waved goodbye to Gordon with the tips of my fingers as Monty dragged me outside.

A hulking storm had shrouded the city while I'd been inside the bar. Its gusting wind wrapped whipping arms of air around me as Monty grabbed my shoulders and started to jump frantically up and down. "That's it! That's it!" he shouted. "It's the kangaroo! You've got to check the pouch in the stuffed kangaroo!"

I studied the tile I'd pulled out of the case as lightening shot across the dark sky, piercing the water somewhere out in the Pacific. The personalized image painted on the backside of Oscar's domino was of a kangaroo. In my opinion, the painted kangaroo bore a much greater likeness to the real thing than the stuffed one guarding the Green Vase.

Another flash of light flickered on the tile, illuminating the detail that had presumably sent Monty into his current tizzy. Streaming up out of the kangaroo's pouch was a rainbow of sparkling gold stars.

"ARE YOU SURE there's not some other pouch-like object somewhere, *anywhere*, around here?" Monty asked as he pulled a latex glove over his right hand.

It was rare to have thunder and lightening in the Bay Area, but tonight's storm definitely carried an electrical charge. Low, rumbling reverberations followed occasional flashes of light as we stood in the showroom to the Green Vase, staring at the spooky specter of the stuffed kangaroo.

"I don't see any way around it. You're just going to have to stick your hand in there," I said, amused at Monty's last-minute anxiety.

I wasn't at all convinced that we'd find anything inside

the kangaroo's pouch, but during the entire cab ride back, Monty had been absolutely certain of his intuition.

Rupert sat on the floor, staring up at the kangaroo. He had already exhausted himself hopping circles around it as we examined the outside of the pouch.

Monty looked more and more squeamish as he tugged on the glove. "Maybe I should put a rubber band around my wrist to hold it closed."

I dug around in the drawer under the counter by the cash register and found one to snap around his wrist. Monty held up his gloved hand, studying it like a surgeon about to enter an operating room.

The corners of his mouth turned down as he sucked in his breath. "Right then. Let's get this over with."

Monty stepped in front of the kangaroo, placed his left arm on its shoulder, and looked into the pair of glass eyes. "No offense, mate," he said solemnly. "I just need to reach in there to get whatever it is Oscar's hidden."

Monty moved his gloved hand gingerly to the outside of the furry flap and slowly eased it in.

I looked away. Rupert hid behind Monty's pant leg. Isabella watched closely from on top of the cashier counter.

A bright flash of lightening lit up the room, quickly followed by a fireworks-decibel boom.

We all jumped.

Isabella jumped on the kangaroo. Rupert jumped on Monty's leg. Monty jumped in the air, both arms still entwined with the kangaroo. I jumped out of the way as a tangled mass of Monty, white cat fur, and the seemingly possessed kangaroo fell to the ground.

"Ahhhhh," Monty howled. A high-pitched, tortured sound emitted from the bottom of the wreathing pile. Then I heard him call out from underneath the kangaroo, "Oooh, I think I've got something!"

I crouched down to the floor near his face, which contorted as he struggled to grasp the object with his slippery, gloved fingers.

"I can't—quite—get hold of it." He jerked his hand out of the pouch and thrust it in my direction. "Oh, good grief! Take the glove off my hand."

I pulled the glove off, and he plunged his unprotected hand into the belly of the beast.

"There!" he said triumphantly. "There, I've got it!" Monty pulled out his hand, which was now completely covered with short, fuzzy, brown hairs. I pulled the kangaroo off of him and righted it next to the cashier counter.

Monty stood up, holding a small plastic bag. We both looked at it silently. Isabella crawled back up on the counter to make a closer inspection.

It contained a used, scruffy-looking toothbrush.

"Your Uncle Oscar had a sick sense of humor," Monty muttered as he dropped the bag on the counter and stormed out the door.

I leaned against the counter, staring at the ruffled kangaroo, wondering what to make of the toothbrush.

Even more intriguing, I mused, what hidden object had Monty been so convinced he would find inside the kangaroo's pouch?

Chapter 19

GINGERLY CARRYING THE toothbrush, I climbed the stairs to the kitchen, trying to rationalize the collection of tulip-related messages, maps, and keys I'd stumbled across since Oscar's death.

It had all begun with the tulip key and the note Oscar had left for me in the white envelope: *There are so many doors left for you to open. All you need is the right key.*

The key had fit into the replacement front door that Oscar had directed Ivan to stash in the basement. Was that what Oscar had meant by his note—a last, prodding message to urge me to leave my accounting job? Or was there another, still unopened door for me to find?

I slid into a chair at the kitchen table. Isabella hopped up into the one next to me, eying me curiously as I stroked her soft, shiny fur.

It seemed like people were flashing tulip-inspired jewelry at me all over the place. There was Dilla with her tulip necklace holding a miniature picture of Leidesdorff in its locket . . . and Gordon Bosco with his tulip-shaped cufflinks—cufflinks that looked almost identical to the ones Oscar had pulled out of his shirt pocket when he'd told me the Leidesdorff story—the same cufflinks my deceased uncle had worn on the sleeves of the starched shirt I'd purchased for his burial.

Brow furrowed, I stood up and pulled the parchment with the old map of San Francisco from its storage location between the cookbooks. I spread it out on the table, focusing in on the tulip imprint on the corner. I stared at it for several minutes, and then pulled back for a wider view, my eyes walking along the streets, trying to imagine the scene as Leidesdorff had discovered it upon his arrival.

The crisp, temperate climate would have made a stark contrast to the heavy humidity of New Orleans. Sailing in through the Golden Gate, Leidesdorff would have been welcomed by the shimmering surface of a pristine bay that was surrounded by rolling green hills and lush vegetation. He would have marveled at the natural port that provided one of the few points of access to an expanse of thickly forested interior teeming with wildlife and raw materials.

For Leidesdorff, all of this natural splendor would have been even further enhanced by Northern California's free-flowing society—as yet uncramped by traditions, stifling social structure, or entrenched dynasties. In my mind's eye, I saw Leidesdorff standing on the shore, the wind coming up off the Pacific, whiffling through his thick, lamb chop sideburns, cleansing his shipper's soul of the demons he'd left behind.

That was how Oscar had felt when he'd arrived here, albeit, I hoped, without the lamb chops. He'd landed in San Francisco after he returned home from the war and never left it.

"A man can make anything of himself here," he'd told me. "Or a woman, for that matter," he'd winked teasingly. "There's nothing here to hold you back. You can do—or become—whatever or *whoever* you want."

My head was still tilted towards the map, but I hadn't

actually seen it for several minutes, musings distorting my vision instead. As I refocused on the parchment, sliding my glasses back up my nose from where they'd slipped, I noticed a faint shadow of a line running across the map. I grabbed the flashlight and shone its bright beam on the paper. A barely visible, charcoal-colored mark looped along the shoreline, then cut up along the city streets.

I shifted my glasses, trying to focus through my bifocals. The line looked as if it had been drawn with a pencil.

I pulled out one of the guidebooks from the previous day and opened it up to a modern day map of San Francisco. Rotating the book's map to align with the parchment, the closest modern day landmark that correlated to the pencil line was—Leidesdorff's alley.

The pencil mark curly-cued out on either end of the narrow street. I traced one end as it circled up to the corner of California and Montgomery.

On a hunch, I thumbed through the guidebook, looking for a citation to the location of Leidesdorff's house. I confirmed the correlation and planted a tingling finger on the marked corner. The tulip garden must have been right behind the house.

Isabella, catching my excitement, made a whirring sound at the map. I glanced over at her, then back down at my finger. The modern day location of Leidesdorff's garden was smack on top of Mr. Wang's flower stall.

The printout of the Leidesdorff article from the Internet poked out of the front cover of the guidebook. I stared at it for a moment, pensively biting my bottom lip, listening to the rain pouring down outside. Oscar didn't have a computer here at the flat. He must have used one at the library. It was only 7:30, although it felt like it should be much later. The library would be open for another half hour.

I slid into my raincoat and raced outside to the Corolla.

I RAN THROUGH the doors of the library's massive, fortress-like building, panting as I pulled back the hood to my coat. I'd finally found a parking spot several blocks over and had been thoroughly soaked on the sprint to the entrance.

A voice came over an intercom speaker announcing the building would be closing in ten minutes.

Drying my glasses on the edge of my shirt, I approached the circulation desk where a bookish young woman wearing thick-rimmed glasses and a "Sarah" name tag stared into a computer screen.

"Excuse me," I said, still trying to catch my breath.

She looked up, smiling warmly. "Yes, can I help you?"

My oxygen-deprived brain suddenly seized up. Instead of inquiring about the library's public use computers, a string of awkward, panicked words tumbled out of my mouth. "Yes, um, my uncle died—a couple of weeks ago."

"I'm sorry," she said, understandably perplexed by my pronouncement. There was a long, painful silence while I tried to think of something—*anything*—rational to say.

The librarian looked at me quizzically. "Did he have any library books outstanding?"

I grabbed on to the lifeline. "I'm not sure. Can you check?"

I gave her Oscar's name, and she punched it into her console. She squinted at the screen, and then tilted her head, looking puzzled. "When did you say he died?"

"It'll be two weeks on Sunday," I replied wearily. "Why?"

She looked at me strangely, swallowed, and dropped her gaze back down to the face of the computer monitor. "Because our records show he checked out a book earlier today."

My hands gripped the counter. "Which book?" I whispered hoarsely.

She rotated the screen, so I could read the title. "It's about William Ralston," she said. "He was the founder of the Palace Hotel."

I took in a deep breath. "Do you have another copy?"

* * *

BACK AT THE kitchen table above the Green Vase, stray
strands of rain-soaked hair dripped onto my shoulders as I
stared down at the extra copy of the Ralston book, wondering why someone would have impersonated Oscar to
check it out of the library. I began to read.

Ralston, it seemed, had been a controversial figure.
Depending on your perspective, he was either a keen vi-
sionary or a reckless gambler. He'd come to San Francisco in the 1850s, a self-made financier following the
Gold Rush. Over time, Ralston amassed an immense fortune by repeatedly taking outrageous risks that, against all
odds, paid out for him. The farther he stepped over the
line, the greater his success. Each spectacular gain spurred
him on to more and more extravagant excesses.

Fate finally caught up to him when he bought into a
fraudulent scheme purporting to sell shares in a nonexistent diamond mine deep in the California wilderness.
The perpetrators of the hoax had purchased raw, uncut
diamonds on the open market in Europe; then they
brought them back to California where they pitched them
as newly discovered stones from a diamond field in the
western United States.

So strong was Ralston's belief in his own innate luck,
he hardly questioned the veracity of the claims. His judg-
ment may have been swayed, in part, by the spectacular
size of one of the diamonds in the sample. When the scam
collapsed, the subsequent scandal triggered the beginning
of a decline in fortunes that would end with Ralston's
financial ruin and death a few years later.

The seed diamonds that had been used to lure Ralston
and other investors into the scheme had been held as col-
lateral in a vault at his bank. The diamonds went missing
in the melee following the exposure of the fiasco and were
never recovered. Speculation on the modern day value of
the largest missing gem ranged to the millions of dollars.

Ralston's bank, I remembered as I pulled my head up
out of the book, had been built on the site of the Tehama

Hotel—previously the location of Leidesdorff's warehouse.

I tried to imagine the transformation of that pivotal piece of property. First, there was Leidesdorff's rustic, barn-like warehouse, barrels, and crates of all sizes lining its walls, bundles of animal fur and sugar cane trundling up and down its entrance ramp.

The warehouse then provided the foundations for the dainty, doily-filled Tehama Hotel. Men in top hats and women in waist-slimming corsets had mingled in its parlor amid the scents of fancy cigars and bottles of scotch.

The same flooring later supported Ralston's audaciously glamorous, marble-trimmed bank—and the vault, which had held the missing diamonds.

I reached across the table for the parchment and slid it towards me, focusing the flashlight beam on it again. This time, I followed the curling pencil line the opposite direction, tracing it along the water's edge and out into a small inlet of water. With a start, I realized that the line terminated near where the Green Vase now stood.

My fingers trembling, I pulled the tulip key out of my pocket. Isabella tilted her head and chirped encouragingly.

"I hope you're coming with me," I replied as I started down the stairs to the first floor, "because it's really creepy down there."

If Oscar had discovered an entrance to a secret tunnel in the basement, it was time for me to find it.

Chapter 20

I PULLED UP on the handle to the basement door, and the stairs unfolded into the darkness, clapping loudly as they hit the concrete floor below. Isabella bounded past me as I flicked on the flashlight and started down into the hole. Rupert woke up from his nap and groggily trailed behind us.

I paused for a moment at the base of the steps, searching the damp darkness with the beam of light. The clutter of shipping crates, cardboard boxes, and cloaked furniture felt overwhelming.

"This place is a mess," I sighed, brushing a spiderweb from my forehead.

I wandered through the room, finally arriving at the far end where Oscar had directed Ivan to stash the replacement door. The cold, dark wall stared back at me—unyieldingly blank.

I took the key out of my pocket and twisted it in my fingers, still staring at the wall. Isabella sat down next to my feet, her tail waving back and forth on the dusty floor.

I knelt down to stroke her head, and a small whisper of

air grazed my cheek. I stopped in my half-bent stance and waited.

There, I felt it again.

A rank, moldy smell oozed out from the wall. The bricks were of the same vintage as the ones on the storefront upstairs. Many were cracked or chipped in places; here and there, chunks of mortar had crumbled onto the floor.

I held up my hand about an inch in front of the wall and began moving it back and forth, searching for the source of the air. Finally, at about four and a half feet off the ground, in the exact spot that had been covered up by the door, I felt the faint whisper of a breeze.

The air seemed to be coming out of a two-inch vertical gap between two of the bricks. At first, I thought it was another instance of the mortar cracking and falling out. But as I examined the wall more closely, it looked as if the opening had been tooled. The edges were smooth and rounded; the bricks on either side of the gap were slightly cleaner than those on the rest of the wall.

I took the tulip key out of my pocket and held it near the opening between the two bricks. The vertical length of the hole was about the same width as the key. I slid the key in, but it simply rattled in the space. When I yanked it back, a handful of stringy cobwebs came along with it.

Isabella stared up at the key, her blue eyes seeming to bewitch it. She rotated her head first one way, then another.

"Mreow," she said, waving one paw in the air.

"Well, that's just silly," I replied, but I tried it anyway, shoving the key into the slot tulip-end first. This was a much snugger fit. For a moment I feared that the key was stuck, but it engaged with unseen metal fixtures, and the wall suddenly seemed to give.

I stepped back, worried that the earthquake earlier that day had weakened the structure of the building. Carefully, I crept back up to the wall, put my hands against it, and gave it a nudge. A four-foot-wide section started to swing,

and the outline of a door emerged from the pattern of
bricks. Now, I gave it a proper shove. The whole thing
creaked and swung open into the basement, rotating on a
hidden, interior hinge.

I leveled my flashlight into a pitch-black corridor.

Isabella leaned into the tunnel, ears pricked, nose crinkling. She walked through the opening, and I fell in line
behind her.

Rupert sat on the basement floor, looking apprehensive. He wanted nothing to do with this murky, gaping
hole in the wall.

"It's okay," I assured him. "You can stay here—in the
cold, dark basement—without the flashlight."

Rupert gave me a nasty look and cautiously followed
us through the opening in the bricks.

I tried to shine as much light as possible into the passage as we crept forward. The sides of the tunnel were
made of the same type of bricks as the basement, but the
surface was slick and slimy. There was no light except for
my flashlight and no sound except for our feet sliding
forward. I tried not to look too closely at the walls, certain
they would be crawling with insects.

No matter, the bugs introduced themselves anyway. A
shiny black beetle fell from the ceiling right in front of my
feet. I jumped, stifling a scream. Isabella spun around,
pounced, and swallowed it in one motion. She licked her
lips, savoring the snack, as I turned to check on Rupert.
He had flattened himself to the ground; his eyes were
tightly closed.

I reached down and scooped him up. Somehow, I felt
more invincible holding a terrified ball of fur in my arms.

We continued deeper into the tunnel. The passage
turned several times, and I quickly lost my bearings, but
we seemed to be gradually descending deeper into the
earth.

The brick walls gave way to a slime-coated concrete.
Corroded pipes, the same vintage as those in Dilla's bathroom, ran along the ceiling.

"I'm in an abandoned sewage line," I murmured, re-membering Ivan's comments.

I was starting to think that we should turn back when Isabella stopped short and chirped. I almost dropped Rupert as I goose-stepped around her.

She put her two front paws up against the wall; something above us had caught her attention. Tracing the flashlight beam upwards, I saw a column of metal rods that had been cinched into the concrete—like primitive steps to a ladder.

"Up has got to be better than down," I said deter-minedly, setting Rupert on the floor and hooking the flashlight into a belt loop on my jeans.

I put my foot on the first rung and started climbing. The ladder took me up through an opening in the ceiling of the tunnel. After about ten feet, I hit a trap door similar to the one in the Green Vase. I grasped the handle with my free hand and eased the door up a couple of inches.

The room above was dark. I perched on the top of the ladder, listening, but it was deadly quiet. I lifted the hatch open the rest of the way and stuck my head up into the dark room.

Waving around the flashlight, all I could see were vent-ing ducts and a couple of brooms leaned up against the wall. Otherwise, the space was vacant.

A furry body brushed past, almost knocking me off the ladder; Isabella had climbed up the stairs behind me. A plaintive wail echoed from the tunnel as she leapt from the top rung of the ladder and into the room.

"Hold on," I called down to Rupert, who was not agile enough to climb the iron ladder. "I'm coming back to get you."

I scrambled back to the floor of the tunnel and picked him up. Rupert's claws gripped nervously into my sweater as I lumbered back up the ladder. I unhooked him at the top and pushed him through the opening. Isabella was already busy casing the room.

I clambered through the hatch, joining the cats. The best

I could tell, we were in a broom closet—the upright entrance to which stood directly in front of us. I put an ear up against the door as Isabella sniffed at the crack underneath. I couldn't hear anything, so I gently tried the doorknob.

It was locked.

"Why would someone put a lock on this side of a broom closet?" I thought. There was only one answer I could think of, and its implications made me uneasy. This lock was meant to keep out entrants from the tunnel.

After an uneasy glance at the open hatch, I trained the flashlight on the gold-plated handle of the door. It was framed with iron scrollwork—in what was now an eerily familiar design.

I pulled the tulip key out of my pocket and slid it into the lock, this time nubbed end first. There was a faint clicking sound as the handle turned.

The broom closet was the same cool, damp temperature as the tunnel below, but I felt a bead of sweat roll off my forehead. I brushed it off with the sleeve of my sweater and eased open the door.

The overpowering scent of fresh flowers rushed through my nostrils. I slid the flashlight through the opening and ran the beam over the rack of tulips in front of me.

On the ground near my feet, Isabella nosed through the slit in the doorway and, before I could stop her, pushed her way into the flower stall. With an exasperated sigh, I picked up Rupert and stepped through the door in time to see Isabella trotting past the tulip display and around a corner.

"Isabella," I hissed. "Come back here."

The Rupert shield pressed firmly up against my chest, I tiptoed to the edge of the rack and peered around the corner. There was no sign of Isabella. I crept forward, growing frustrated as I headed towards the front of the store.

"Isabella."

She was nowhere to be seen.

"*Isabella!*"

The faint aroma of a clove cigarette tickled my nose as

I stopped next to a stand of potted begonias. I heard the low rumble of Isabella's purr as I turned the flashlight towards the source of the smoke.

Mr. Wang sat on a metal folding chair beside the entrance to the flower stall, smoking a cigarette while Isabella rubbed up against his knees.

Chapter 21

"JUST LIKE YOUR uncle," the tiny Asian man chuckled from his folding chair.

I wasn't sure if I should be terrified or amused. Light from a streetlamp outside shone a ghastly spotlight on his pale face. The cigarette teetered on the edge of his thin lips as he laughed.

"You found the tunnel," he said. "I knew you would."

"Just like Oscar?" I repeated his greeting as a question.

"Yes," he replied. "Although Oscar came without cats."

I watched, my stomach tightening, as he picked up Isabella and stroked her head with a small, bony hand. I was still holding Rupert clasped tightly to my chest, but he wriggled around so that he could see what was going on.

"The Jackson Square crowd has been looking for the entrance to Leidesdorff's tunnel for years," Mr. Wang continued, beaming me a knowing smile. "But Oscar always suspected the entrance was in his basement."

Isabella curled up comfortably in Mr. Wang's lap, still purring loudly.

I shifted Rupert's weight in my arms as I struggled to

take all of this in. "Leidesdorff's tunnel—you mean William Leidesdorff?"

Mr. Wang nodded solemnly, then amended. "Technically, the brick section that now connects to the basement of the Green Vase is all that remains of the original tunnel. Most of it was torn out in the early 1900s when the city installed the downtown sewage system. Someone arranged to have one of the sewage lines taken out of use and joined to the remaining brick section. I daresay a number of people have made their way through that passage over the years."

My nose crinkled, remembering the slimy walls and rank odor.

Mr. Wang noted my expression. "Water occasionally backs up into it. Leaves kind of a bad smell in places."

I puzzled on his explanation. "But, Leidesdorff—he couldn't have built the tunnel. The Green Vase was still under water when he died. That section of landfill hadn't been filled in yet."

Mr. Wang scratched the back of his neck thoughtfully and tilted his head towards me. "Death—is a relative concept. It depends a lot on your perspective."

I stared at the small, wrinkled man, my brow furrowed.

"Tell me, dear," he said, his gray eyes studying me closely. "What date of death are you using for your calculations?"

"The date," I stopped, stuttering. "The date all of the guidebooks give." I felt like a pupil in a classroom. "1848." I gave the number tentatively, almost as a question. "Just before the Gold Rush hit."

"Consider," Mr. Wang replied, his voice even and unemotional. "An alternative possibility."

I shrugged my shoulders.

Mr. Wang took a puff on his cigarette as he stroked Isabella's smooth white coat. "Mr. Leidesdorff was a very *resourceful* man," he said slowly. "The city was engulfed in unprecedented chaos right after his funeral. Minus those enormous lamb chop sideburns, I don't think it would have taken too elaborate a disguise for him to slip under the radar—and into his new place of employment."

"You mean he faked his death?" I asked incredulously, trying to recall facts from my research on Leidesdorff. "What about the encephalitis? He fell sick with fever. Everyone saw him pass out . . ."

"Yes," Mr. Wang replied, his eyes twinkling. "They all *thought* they saw him die."

"There was a funeral procession through town," I protested. "He was buried in the floor of the Mission Dolores chapel."

Isabella purred loudly as Mr. Wang's bony fingers rubbed the space on her head just behind her orange-tipped ears.

"You've heard of the famous architect, Willis Polk?" he asked. "Back in 1916, he was commissioned to do a restoration of the Mission to try to protect it against future earthquakes. He put steel girders into the walls, supports into the ceiling, and laid tile over the dirt floor." Mr. Wang paused and ran his tongue over his nicotine-stained teeth. "In order to sink the footings for the tile, Polk had to move Leidesdorff's grave—it was located too close to the wall. The workers dug down underneath the marker, looking for the body. They dug and dug, but they never found him."

I sucked on my bottom lip, still skeptical. "What do you mean by new place of employment?" I asked. "*Here*, in San Francisco?"

Mr. Wang nodded. "There have always been rumors and speculations about William Leidesdorff, particularly his suspicious death. According to one story, Leidesdorff picked up a special sleeping drought during his travels . . . one that would mimic the symptoms of a heavy fever, then induce a deep, almost undetectable sleep."

Mr. Wang smiled indulgently. "Your uncle tracked down writing samples from the ledger for Leidesdorff's warehouse and that of the Tehama Hotel. They were an exact match."

At any second, I felt as if I might fall backwards into the begonias. "The hotel that Joseph Folsom built—where Leidesdorff's warehouse used to stand?" I asked.

Mr. Wang nodded appreciatively. "Ah, you've been doing your homework. You see, Captain Folsom wasn't really around much." A whimsical expression flickered across his thin face. "What with all of his trips to the Virgin Islands trying to prove that Anna Spark woman was Leidesdorff's rightful heir."

The text of the Ralston book I'd been reading earlier that evening leapt in front of my face as I murmured, "The Tehama Hotel was later replaced by William Ralston's bank."

Mr. Wang gleamed, his yellow teeth even more dingy in the lamplight. "When Ralston bought the land, he had the entire structure of the hotel carted off to another lot down the street. He told people he couldn't bare to destroy the lovely, old building. That allowed him to have the bank built directly on top of the old foundations."

Mr. Wang stroked his chin, his grin growing wider. "Of course, the tunnel's access to the bank has been closed off for almost a hundred years now."

"And this," I said, scanning the cramped confines of the flower stall. "This is where Leidesdorff's flower garden used to be. Behind his house."

"In the beginning, this was the start of the tunnel. It allowed Leidesdorff to travel between his house and warehouse undetected. Now, it's just one stop along the turnpike." Isabella looked up at Mr. Wang as he chuckled raspily. "The city engineers had a dickens of a time shoring up around that old sewage pipe when they put the BART line in underneath Market Street. They couldn't understand why they weren't allowed to tear it out."

BART, short for Bay Area Rapid Transit, ran a subway line underneath the bay between San Francisco and Oakland. The train traveled underground for several stops in downtown San Francisco, running along Market Street.

"The tunnel runs all the way to the other side of Market," I said, trying to follow in my head the pencil line I'd studied on the parchment. "Where does it go from there?"

Mr. Wang stroked Isabella's head and then looked back up at me, his narrow eyes squinting in the meager light. "I think I mentioned that Mr. Leidesdorff was a resourceful type. You see, while Captain Folsom was scouring the Virgin Islands for Mrs. Spark, Leidesdorff became close to a particularly influential guest at the Tehama. A man who could appreciate the value of an underground tunnel—one that could give him secret access in and out of his bank. One that could be expanded to run to the site he planned for his fancy new five star hotel."

"William Ralston," I said, finally understanding the connection. "The tunnel goes across Market to the Palace Hotel."

I looked back towards the broom closet, disbelievingly. "And Oscar figured all of this out?" I demanded, pursing my lips. "Before he died?"

Mr. Wang's expression grew serious. "I'm afraid, my dear," he said softly. "That may have been the reason *why* he died. I think he may have uncovered something more than the tunnel in his research."

The rain poured down steadily outside. I listened to the drops beating against the window, pondering on Mr. Wang's revelations, each train of thought inevitably traveling to the missing diamonds, which had last been seen in the vault at Ralston's bank.

There was a bump at the door leading to the street. Isabella leapt lightly from Mr. Wang's lap as he dropped the remains of his cigarette on the floor and smashed it with his foot.

"Excuse me for a moment," he said.

He opened the door, and a young woman with long, black, silky-straight hair leaned in. She gave him a reproachful look, whispered something to him, and left.

"My daughter's giving me five more minutes before she turns me in," he said. He patted the cigarette box in his pocket and smiled ruefully. "I'm not supposed to be having these."

"It's a disgusting habit," I said stiffly. I stepped closer towards his chair. "You don't think that Oscar had a stroke that morning, do you?" I bit down on my lip, unable to voice the horrifying implication.

"That," Mr. Wang said, pulling out a small, black wallet from his coat pocket and flashing a police badge at me, "is what I'm trying to find out. I retired from the force several years ago, but I still have some connections there. I've been making some discreet inquiries."

"The autopsy?" I asked, my voice faltering.

"There was no autopsy," he confirmed, shaking his head.

"But, someone called me," I insisted.

Mr. Wang stroked his upper lip thoughtfully, his fingers instinctively searching for the ever-present cigarette. "What do you remember about that conversation?"

I shrugged my shoulders. "There wasn't much to it—it took less than a minute. It was a man's voice. He told me that Oscar had died of a stroke—and that he didn't suffer much."

I gave Mr. Wang a disapproving look as he pulled out a second cigarette and lit it. He puffed silently for a moment, his eyes glazing over as he savored the toxic smoke.

"You know, when Leidesdorff first came to this part of California, it was just a small Mexican outpost that few people knew about. It must have seemed like a perfect place to escape from all his troubles—to start a new life."

Mr. Wang took another pull on the cigarette. The smoke was starting to irritate my eyes, but I couldn't turn away.

"But then the United States annexed the territory of California, and gold was beginning to be discovered up in the Sierras. Leidesdorff knew that everything was about to change—that soon this place would be flooded with people. People who might recognize him and send word back to New Orleans."

Mr. Wang wheezed weakly, his face bluing as his body

seized for oxygen. He held up a pale, veined hand as his incapacitated lungs struggled to compensate. Finally, he continued.

"Leidesdorff sold his warehouse to Folsom, but he was still using the secret room underneath it to store all of the gold he was collecting—from liquidating his assets and from what he'd been able to collect so far on the property in the Sierras." Smoke funneled over his head as Mr. Wang crossed his scarecrow legs at the knees.

"Leidesdorff snuck in and out of the room using the tunnel. At that point, it ran along the shoreline. It opened up at a little inlet cove, away from the main center of town, so that he could come and go unseen. The tunnel was a lot less stable in the beginning. Just a hole in the mud propped up by wooden beams. Ralston financed the up-grade to brick when he built his bank building—and its extension through the landfill to the basement of the Green Vase."

"The line on the map represents the tunnel," I muttered, almost to myself.

"On Oscar's map?" Mr. Wang coughed again, smoke furling out through the narrow slits in his nose. "Yes, he was quite proud of himself for mapping it out. I assume that's what was in the package I gave you."

Mr. Wang looked down at his watch, then glanced nervously at the front door. "There was one other person who knew Leidesdorff's secrets. When he came to California, he brought with him a young woman to work as his maid. She ran his house, took care of him."

Mr. Wang dropped the half-smoked cigarette near the first stump and squashed it as a stern, gray-haired woman walked quickly past the window and pounded on the front door.

"Uh oh," he said, giving me a wink. "That's the boss. My time's up." His knees cracked as he stood up and hobbled to the door. His thin voice was almost a whisper as he concluded, "The last anyone saw of the housekeeper was at Leidesdorff's fake funeral."

Keys clicked in the lock, and the door flew open. The withered old woman strode across the threshold like a sumo wrestler. Mr. Wang gave her a humble, apologetic look as she scolded him sharply in a language I couldn't understand.

I scooped up the cats, struggling to arrange one on each arm, and followed Mr. Wang outside where the rain had slacked off to an intermittent drip.

Mr. Wang waved goodbye. His wife locked the door behind us and steered him down the street as I turned towards the Green Vase.

"Wait," his wheezing voice called out behind me as he shuffled breathlessly back. "Let's," he said painfully between gasps for air, "let's keep this a secret for the time being." He patted the shirt pocket where he'd stuck his badge in behind the carton of cigarettes.

"Those things are going to kill you, you know," I said reproachfully.

"I'm afraid, my dear, they already have." He chuckled ruefully. "Death is a relative concept."

Chapter 22

THE FURRY, ROUND rump of Rupert squeezed under the six-inch crawl space of a credenza in the musty showroom of the Green Vase. Several half-empty boxes stacked haphazardly on its surface swayed back and forth as Rupert wiggled along underneath, tunneling his way through the substructure's undergrowth of spiderwebs, lint, and dust. I could just make out the apricot-orange tips of his ears as his shadowed, blue eyes peeked out the other side, stealthily tracking his target.

She sauntered past his hidden position, feigning interest in the corpse of a long-deceased cricket swinging enticingly from the frayed upholstery of the swivel-mounted dental chair. The pipe of her long, graceful tail arched into a question mark, its orange tip flashing like a lure on the end of a fishing line.

Rupert studied her carefully, hardly believing the luck of his location. The bushy end of his feather duster tail thwumped against the floor underneath the credenza as he plotted his next move. He shifted his weight back and forth, the white wires of his whiskers twitching with anticipation. His back legs coiled up, and he prepared to launch.

Isabella paused and stared, as if mesmerized, into the dead eyes of the bug, her head following it back and forth, back and forth. Rupert quivered like a tightly wound spring; he couldn't bear to wait any longer.

There was a poof of dust as he charged out from under the dusty piece of furniture. Isabella hopped up onto the seat of the dental chair, the pads of her feet touching it for only a second. A sly smile spread across her face as she leapt nimbly from the seat of the recliner to a spindly side table three feet over.

In hot pursuit, Rupert pounded onto the dental chair—already slightly spinning from Isabella's touch and go. His added momentum increased the rotation of the chair, moving him farther away from Isabella, but he was determined to keep up the chase.

Rupert clambered up onto the thick, leather back of the swiveling recliner and hurled his heavy mass towards the delicate table, but his arrival sent it tipping. He tried to jump clear, but his back feet tangled in the scrolling wood detail that rimmed the top edge. The wobbling table and awkward, scrambling cat crashed to the ground while Isabella smugly looked on from the top of the bookcase.

It was Friday morning. The cats and I had spent another night in the flat above the Green Vase. My apartment had begun to feel more and more alien to me—the last vestige of my quiet, predictable, pre-Monty life.

He strode through the front door of the Green Vase just after breakfast, for no apparent reason other than to recline on the stool by the cash register, wingtipped feet propped up on the counter, mining the morning's paper for tidbits of the latest local gossip.

"Let's see," Monty said, shaking the edges of the paper to stretch out the center fold. "What do we have in here today?"

Monty shifted so that he could cross one long leg over the other. The cuff of his gray trousers slipped up to reveal his skinny, black-socked ankles. His bony back curved against the nearby wall, so that his pink and gray bow tie rested pertly on the folds of his black cashmere vest. Cufflinks in the form of miniature pink flamingoes, each with one leg crooked up under its body, decorated his wrists.

"Ah, here's a bit on the Mayor. This should be good."

The paper crackled as Monty brought the sheet in closer to his face, and his head slipped from view behind the printed shield. "It's another dating debacle for the Mayor," he said, perusing the article. "Here, listen to this."

The Mayor dined last night at Ciao, a popular Italian restaurant in North Beach. He was accompanied by yet another starlet from that city to the south, a fetching girl with a bit part in an 'artsy' independent film coming out this summer.

Isabella hopped up on the counter, her attention fixed on Monty's right wrist. Her eyes zoomed in on the flamingo's gold leg as it flickered in the early morning light.

Upon arrival, the Mayor took a seat at a table near the front window while the starlet pushed her way through the packed restaurant to the unisex powder room near the kitchen.

Isabella stretched out her neck and curiously nudged the metal bird, the pink of her nose the same shade as its painted feathers. Unaware of Isabella's attentions, Monty shook his hand as if shooing away a fly. Isabella ducked under the flying fingers, her hunting instincts piqued by the sudden movement. Her tail began to swing back and forth as Monty continued.

The Mayor scanned his menu, running a careful hand over his thick hair, swept back, as usual, with a shellacking coat of hair gel. He'd read halfway through the list of offerings when an elderly admirer approached his table.

The lovely lady was an inspirational barrage of color—with a disposition to match. She insisted on toasting the Honorable M. with a glass of the house red.

"Dilla," Monty gasped as he turned the page to pick up the rest of the article. Isabella's head swung back and forth, following his arm, her eyes never leaving the dangling flamingo.

Those of you who have frequented this establishment will remember that the house wine is served in signature ceramic carafes, fashioned into the shape of a chicken, with the spout decorated as the bird's beak.

To the surprise of the wait staff and nearby tables, our engaging spinster clucked loudly as the celebratory beverage glugged out of the container and into her glass.

Monty gulped, his eyes bulging. He shifted his arms up to read the bottom half of the paper. Isabella raised a tentative paw towards the nearest cufflink and gently swatted it. The bird's gold leg teetered as Isabella rose up on her hind legs to nose it. Monty, engrossed in the article, failed to notice.

All eyes in the cozy, family style dining room were soon on the Mayor's colorful companion as she urged him to cluck reciprocally while the waiter filled his glass.

A growing crowd of diners moved in to cheer on this heretofore unreported Tuscan tradition. In short order, the entire restaurant began calling for the Mayor's best chicken impersonation.

At long last, the Honorable M. succumbed to the pleadings of the people, stood up and let out the kind of clucking cackle this proud city expects of its fear-

less leaders—just as the stunned starlet emerged from
the powder room.

Representatives from the Mayor's office have so far
declined to comment.

"Oh, Dilla," Monty sighed, suddenly lowering the paper, startled to find Isabella's unblinking, ice-blue eyes
inches from the tip of his nose. He jumped back, nearly
falling off the stool in the process.

"Are you sure it was Dilla?" I asked from the other side
of the room. I'd been sifting through another open box
while Monty read.

"I'd bet my favorite pair of shoes on it," he said, easing
cautiously away from Isabella as Ivan's truck pulled up
outside.

IVAN MADE A quick job of demolishing the old brick
exterior of the Green Vase. By early afternoon, the deteriorated fronting had been stripped away leaving the wood
framing exposed like a skeleton.

Monty returned after lunch, allegedly to help super-
vise, and resumed his accumbent position on the stool
behind the cashier counter. Rupert joined him, sprawling
out on the counter as the two of them watched Ivan work.

"I know what you're thinking," Monty said loftily.

Rupert, busy grooming stray pieces of litter from the
fine, feathery hairs of his tail, snorkeled encouragingly.

"I think you're quite right, Rupert." Monty's fingers
reached up to his thick, frizzy curls as he stared out the
window to where Ivan's long, golden-brown waves shone
in the sun. "The mullet is definitely making a comeback.
What would you think if I grew mine out a bit longer in
the back. Maybe down to my shoulders?"

I looked up from the latest box, my hands on my hips,
shaking my head.

Rupert paused his grooming and stared at Monty as if

he were imagining the transition. His whiskers twitched critically.

"Well, yes, I suppose it might get a bit woolly," Monty said defensively, tugging on the short hairs at the nape of his neck.

Rupert's blue eyes swept pointedly from the curly top of Monty's head to his own feathery tail, spread out in a semi-circle on the counter.

"That's not a mullet. It's a tail," Monty spat bitterly. A Cheshire grin spread across Rupert's face.

The front door swung open, and we all turned to look at the entrant. The sun blazed behind the woman as she crossed the threshold, momentarily obliterating her features, but I had no doubt who she was.

The fetidly floral scent that horripilated down my spine unmistakably announced the arrival of Miranda C. Richards, Esquire.

Chapter 23

MIRANDA RICHARDS SURGED into the room, the putrid cloud of her perfume swilling around her.

She wore a flowing, salmon pink pants suit made of long, billowing sheets of fabric that flapped like gills as it swam around her. An emerald green broach sparkled on her right lapel; earrings made out of clumps of pea-sized, pea-colored, glass balls clung to each earlobe.

"Good afternoon," she greeted me briskly.

"Hello, Miranda," Monty bleated from behind the cash register, his face blanching as his feet hit the floor.

Her noxious perfume shocked me speechless. I could almost see the vile odor seeping into the recesses of the room, contaminating it with its brutal, nose-assaulting aura.

For the moment, mercifully, Miranda's focus had turned to Monty. She approached the cashier counter, each footstep echoing through the room like a brick falling off a building and slamming down onto concrete.

"Mr. Carmichael," she said, dismantling him with her cutting stare. "I didn't expect to find you here." The wide cuff of her pants swished as she walked, kicking up to reveal three-inch, taupe-colored heels. "To what do we owe your *inauspicious* presence here in the Green Vase?"

Monty slid away from the counter until his back hit the wall. "I've been helping with the remodel," he replied, straightening his bow tie, struggling vainly to sound important. "I presented the proposal at the last board meeting—perhaps you heard?"

Her painted lips curled menacingly as she placed a manicured hand on the counter next to Rupert. "Yes, I heard it was quite a *lengthy* oration."

Rupert sat frozen on the counter, his delicate pink nose overwhelmed by the floral onslaught of the perfume. He shook his head, his nose twitching with the same presneeze itch tormenting my own nasal passages.

Monty squirmed uncomfortably as Miranda leaned over the counter towards him, planting her elbow dangerously close to Rupert's right paw. "What I don't understand is why you're here *now*."

Monty pointed desperately at the sidewalk where Ivan was pulling rusty nails out of a recently removed framing board. Even though Ivan's face was pointed downward, I could tell he was straining to hear every word.

"And you thought that you would be the most assistance to Mr. Batrachos on *this* side of the wall?" She eyed Monty's lanky figure like a grasshopper she was about to squash under the spike of her heel.

"Puh . . . puh . . . perhaps," Monty stuttered, shrinking under the forceful burn of her gaze, "I should go outside and check up on him."

"Yes," she said, her voice a gelid stake, "perhaps you should."

He leapt up and soared around the counter, his eyes squirreling as he scurried out the front door to join Ivan on the sidewalk. For once, I was not relieved to see him leave.

Miranda watched until the front door clicked shut; then she shifted her gaze down to a terrified Rupert, huddling on the counter by her right sleeve. The moist surface of his nose pulsed from the battery of her offensive perfume.

"What's this?" she asked appraisingly, waiving a long, hooked fingernail dangerously close to Rupert's head. "One of your feline friends?" Rupert squeaked as the nail poked his stomach. "A little plump don't you think?"

Rupert's nose could take no more. A violent trembling spread through his body, signaling the start of the eruption. It was followed by a high-pitched screech, part Rupert, part Miranda, as a wet, mucus spray splattered across the broad, salmon front of her suit.

Fearing for Rupert's life, I sprinted across the room to intercede. I snatched my disoriented cat off the counter and whisked him into my arms.

"Sorry," I said, hugging Rupert close to my chest. "I'm so sorry, Miranda."

A frightening rage swept across her face, telegraphing the tempest within. She drew in a deep, voluminous breath, as mine vanished inside me. I slid my left foot backwards, trying to ease away from her fuming pyre.

Outside, Monty and Ivan had plastered their faces to the dingy glass still held in place by the wooden framing. Monty cupped his hands around his lips and mouthed, *"Run Rupert!"*

Through the glass, I saw Ivan turn to look quizzically at Monty.

A cool calm coated down Miranda's face as she regained her composure. "It's not a problem," she said stiffly, brushing off the front of her suit. "I'm sure it will come off at the cleaners."

"Mmm," was about all I could muster, marveling at her staggering transformation, terrified by the strength of the inner force which had wrought it.

Rupert had seen enough. He crawled up over my shoulders and leapt off my back, hitting the ground behind me with a scraping thunk. I listened as his chunky feet raced up the stairs to the kitchen.

"Now," she said, fixing me with her mascara stare. "How are things going, dear?" There was a sickening sweetness in her voice that was almost more nauseating than the smell of her perfume.

"Just fine." I said meekly. "Thanks."

"I understand you've left your previous place of employment," Miranda said, unblinking in her stare.

I cleared my throat, nodding. "I'm working on setting up shop here." I felt as if I might crumble into a pile of dust at any moment.

"Yes—I can see that," she said shrewdly, glancing around at the cluttered disarray. "I had hoped you would reconsider my advice to sell this place." She began moving around the room, dragging her glassy, red nails across the dusty crates and furniture.

"Tell me," Miranda said, her back turned to me, "have any customers come by while you've been working on the renovations?"

"No, I haven't noticed any." I shrugged my shoulders. "We've been closed, of course."

She whipped around to face me, the broad sheets of fabric fluttering around her like the cape of a cobra. "Don't you find that odd?" she said evenly, the pits of her pupils glowing like embers.

"I . . . really . . . hadn't thought about it," I replied, wilting under the continued pressure of her perfume.

Miranda turned away from me again, her voice calculatingly casual. "Given the profits Oscar's racked up over the last couple of years, I would have thought this place had been teeming with customers."

"I had never been here during the day before," I said haltingly, feeling strangely queasy. "I only ever saw Oscar on Saturday nights—for dinner."

Miranda flicked open a lid flap on the nearest box with the tip end of a fingernail and peeked inside, her face expressionless. "And have you found anything *unusual* in your perusal of the merchandise?" She looked up at me sharply.

"Not . . . not really," I replied, shaking my head, nervously pulling my fingers through the back of my hair.

"I have the suspicion," she said slowly, grittingly, stamping the lid of the box closed with the flat of her hand, "that Oscar might have *left* something here for you."

My face flushed violet as I stuttered, "Uhh . . . hmm, about Oscar—a funny thing happened right after he died."

She stared at me, her face a heavily-painted stone, unreadable.

"Someone called me to report on Oscar's autopsy. I thought he was from the police." I gulped. "But it turns out he was an imposter."

Her face registered no reaction. The curved edge of the nail on her right index finger traced a circle on the surface of the box.

"I'm starting to think," I said, nearly breathless, "that something might have happened to Oscar—to cause his death."

Miranda glanced over my shoulder to the bookcase. Isabella sat on her perch, serenely surveying the proceedings with her unflinching blue eyes. Miranda walked over to her and raised a heavily scented hand towards Isabella's feet.

"My mother is over the moon about this event at the Palace," she said softly, incongruously ignoring my last statement. "This is the female of the pair, isn't it," she asked, scratching Isabella gently under the chin. "She'll have an easier time getting into her costume." Isabella rumbled with a regal purr.

Miranda paused and pursed her lips. "That other one will need a *bath* before you show up at the Palace Hotel with him."

An exasperated puff of air escaped me. "Did you hear what I . . ."

"I suspect that Oscar," Miranda said harshly, as the manicured hand left Isabella and turned, palm out, to stop me, "got in over his head."

Her curling lips crunched up derisively as her eyes raked

my rumpled clothes and puzzled expression. "You should be more careful about who you consort with," she said with a pointed glance towards the sidewalk as she turned towards the exit, "if you want to avoid the same fate."

I listened as the percussion of her footsteps faded away, leaving me in the pounding silence of my twisting, turbulent thoughts.

Chapter 24

MONTY AND IVAN nearly tripped over each other in their efforts to peel their faces off the window as Miranda breezed past, utterly ignoring them. I stood where Miranda had left me, in the center of the Green Vase, flummoxed in the fallout from her visit.

Isabella hopped down from her perch and sauntered over, obviously pleased by Miranda's attentions. I stroked her head absentmindedly as Rupert nosed cautiously around the corner of the stairs, every hair fluffed out as a precautionary sensor.

Ivan cracked open the front door and leaned inside, a sympathetic look on his face. Monty's head goosed over his right shoulder, his face cringing in mock horror. "We thought Rupert was a goner."

I looked down at my feet. Instantly recovered from his traumatic experience, Rupert had sprawled out on his back, flopping the fluffy, white pillow of his tummy up into the air. He swatted lazily at my shoelace.

"I think he'll live," Ivan said, smiling as he and Monty walked inside.

"Miranda Richards in the Green Vase," Monty whistled. "I'll bet that's never happened before."

My head was still spinning from Miranda's barely veiled accusations. I looked at Monty, my expression troubled.

"Did Oscar have a lot of customers?" I asked. "I mean, you see everything that goes on around here. Were there many people coming and going to the Green Vase?"

"*Customers?*" Monty responded with an incredulous expression. "Come on, look at this place—no self-respecting patron of Jackson Square would set foot in here." He smiled cynically. "And even if they had, Oscar would have sent them away. He wasn't much into *customers.*"

My forehead crinkled, puzzling.

"The only regular visitor was Gordon Bosco," Monty offered. "He stopped by from time to time. I figured he and Oscar were buddies, and that's what kept Oscar out of trouble with the board." Monty tapped the tip of his nose knowingly. "That's why I wanted to get your presentation through before Bosco retired."

"Hmm," I responded vaguely. My thoughts trailed back five years ago—to the first time I'd visited the Green Vase.

I had just arrived in San Francisco, having landed a position with the accounting firm from an interview at a job fair on the East Coast. I'd never met my Uncle Oscar, but I'd received a note from an elderly aunt suggesting that I look him up.

I'd carried his address around with me for a couple of months until one weekend, while wandering through the city streets, I happened to end up in Jackson Square.

Having lost touch with most of my relatives over the years, I didn't have high expectations for Oscar. One by one, family members had gradually fallen out of my life, like leaves dropping silently off a tree. I'd hardly noticed they were gone until I woke up one day and saw that the limbs were bare.

But an ounce of curiosity, a spurious inclination that I couldn't quite let go of, had drawn me to the entrance of the Green Vase.

It was late afternoon on a sunny Saturday. The bright rays of the setting sun highlighted the decrepit condition of the store. The place looked deserted. I stood on the sidewalk, scanning the broken glass and darkened interior, suspecting that the building had long been abandoned.

A shadow moved inside as I was about to leave, and a short, rounded figure limped towards the door. Transfixed, I watched as his features came into view, a broad smile breaking across his weathered face.

"Can I help you?" he asked in a scratchy voice as the door creaked open. He squinted at me, studying my face. "You're my niece, aren't you?"

"Yes," I managed to get out, amazed at the instant recognition.

"I'm your Uncle Oscar then," he said, nodding his head towards the showroom. "Come on in."

I stepped into the dusky room, scanning the disorganized contents as my eyes adjusted to the dim light.

"Gold Rush," he said, stroking the rough stubble on the tip of his chin.

I raised an uneasy eyebrow towards him.

He cleared his throat and leaned against the cashier counter. "That's what my store's about—antiques from the Gold Rush."

I took a tentative step forward, studying the antique cash register on the counter. Oscar stared at me, gumming his dentures assessingly.

"You hungry?" he asked. "I'm about to start cooking." He gave me a sharp look. "You like fried chicken, don't you?"

Monty's voice broke through my memory. "It's like she zapped you with a life-sucking ray."

"Wha . . . what?" I asked, dragging myself back to the present.

"Miranda did a real number on you," he said, shaking his head. "You've been drooling like a zombie for the last couple of minutes."

"I was just thinking about something," I said absent-mindedly.

"So, what did Miranda want?" Monty asked persistently.

"Good question," I thought to myself, remembering her parting comments. My face twisted, reflecting the thoughts within as I looked at my tall, stringy neighbor.

"I think," I said slowly, "that she was trying to warn me."

IVAN RETURNED TO his work outside, and Monty skittered across the street to his studio. I shut the door behind them and collapsed into the dental chair.

My hand found the lever on the backside of the chair, and the recliner kicked back into its flattest horizontal position. The worn, aging leather crunched comfortably behind my head as the afternoon sun bathed my face in its soft warmth. Rupert bounded into my lap and curled up, rapidly dozing off into a deep sleep.

I concentrated on a spiderweb that stretched across the ceiling as numbers clicked in my head, not individually, but as a group, sifting faces and data, trying to sort them into a logical arrangement. The musty smells of the Green Vase showroom swirled around me, occasionally spiked with a rancid remnant whiff from Miranda's skunky perfume.

How could Oscar have run an antiques store with no customers? I knew, of course, that Oscar had hated that aspect of the business. And, certainly, he was known to be irascible with the hoity-toity clientele that frequented the Jackson Square neighborhood, but—*no* customers? That just wasn't possible. According to Miranda, Oscar's business had been booming in recent years.

For the last six months, every time I'd come to visit, it seemed that more and more shipping containers had been crammed into the store. I glanced around the room at the bulky wooden crates and cardboard boxes stacked up against the walls, an uncomfortable realization gnawing at my stomach.

I slipped deeper into the cushions of the dental chair, my forehead pounding, desperately missing the quiet predictability that had been my life just two weeks earlier. It felt like everything that meant anything had been turned upside down. My previous identity, the careful security of the life that I'd constructed—it had all been stripped away. All of those long, quiet hours of solitude glazed over in my memory as if they'd been lived by someone else. I thought wistfully of my old, dark cubicle with its cloth covered, sensory depriving, Monty-proof walls.

Monty, I thought irritably, muttering in my half-asleep state. Miranda seemed to think that I should distance myself from him. She must know, I mused, about his break-in to the Green Vase the week before Oscar died.

I sighed heavily. That was easier said than done. Monty was everywhere, at every moment; there was no way to avoid him. Any minute now, I expected to hear the rap of his knuckles on the front door. I clenched my eyelids firmly shut. I would simply pretend not to hear him.

But Monty's inescapable voice wormed its way into my head. He was giving the Green Vase renovation presentation to the board. His flat-pitched monologue droned in the deep background of my consciousness as the flat face and protruding, beaked nose of Gordon Bosco came into focus.

Gordon was seated at the front of the boardroom, a thin smile on his vanishing lips, his beady, black eyes staring at me. He leaned forward on the table, resting his weight on his right elbow as his wrist raised up so that he could prop up his chin on the palm of his hand. The cuff of his dark suit jacket slid down and a flickering flash of gold glimmered at his wrist.

Suddenly, Gordon stood up and walked across the room. He was no longer at the board meeting; he was in the Green Vase showroom, leaning over a wooden shipping crate, rummaging through it—looking for something.

I blinked and the vision changed. The rounded shoulders were no longer clothed by a double-breasted suit. A stained, navy blue collared shirt had taken its place.

I walked closer, my feet leadening. I struggled to lift each foot in front of the other, the foggy atmosphere of the room murking thick around my head. I knew those bent and sagging shoulders, that stale cooking smell, the guttural grunts the man made as he sifted through the contents of the crate. He stood up, as if to stretch a sore joint in his back.

"Oscar?" I called out questioningly. My voice echoed through the ether, waking me from the dream.

I reached back and pushed in the recline lever, righting the dental chair. Turfing a disgruntled Rupert to the floor, I got up and walked over to the nearest wooden shipping crate.

Grabbing the same crowbar Monty had so inexpertly used on the kangaroo's wooden housing, I tilted the crate on its side and slid the bar between the shipping brads. They popped off easily, as if they had only been superficially fastened. I pulled up the lid and looked inside.

A sea of cedar shavings spread across the surface of the crate. I dove my hand in, searching for the packaged contents. Up and down the interior I searched, sending more and more shavings out onto the floor.

Rupert chased a couple of cedar chips across the floor and then peeked over into the box, trying to figure out the new game I appeared to be playing. His back end wiggled for a preparatory moment; then he leapt in, disappearing beneath the surface of the chips.

A snowstorm of shavings exploded in the Green Vase as a submerged Rupert attempted to swim his way to the surface. I jumped into the box, chasing his whirlwind with my flailing arms. In short order, at least half of the crate's volume of cedar shavings had spilled out on the floor. By the time I hoisted Rupert out of the crate, I was certain that it had held nothing but packing materials.

I sat in the open crate for a moment, itchy shavings clinging to my hair and sliding down the inside of my shirt. Another sealed crate loomed a couple of feet away.

Rupert bounced behind me as I climbed out of the crate and crossed the room to the new target. He hopped excitedly at my feet as I opened it. This time, he dove in as soon as I cracked the lid.

Rupert rooted like a pig through the cedar shavings as I ran my hand back and forth inside the crate. This one was also empty.

I dragged an exhausted Rupert out of the crate and sat down on the lid, my eyes searching the Green Vase, studying the room as if I'd never seen it before. Standing next to the cashier counter near the front door, the stuffed kangaroo seemed to smile at me, the corners of its stitched-together mouth tilting upward in an inquiring, needling manner.

I got up and strode purposefully over to it. The faint scraping sounds of Ivan's construction work ground subtly outside as I stared into the dead animal's glass eyes, pondering its inquisitively smug grin.

The lips of the mouth were stitched together with a straining black thread—not the clear, nearly invisible fiber that had been used to sew up the rest of the body, but a heavy black sewing thread—like the kind Oscar had used to mend loose buttons and small tears in his clothing.

The shaft of every hair pimpling, I walked around the cashier counter, pulled open a drawer, and fished out a pair of scissors. Retracing my steps to the front of the kangaroo, I carefully began snipping away the black threads.

Snip. Snip. Snip. The mouth softened its expression as the lips began to part. I reached the last black thread, and the jaw dropped open. Easing up on the balls of my feet, I looked inside.

A wadded up piece of cloth seemed to be wedged in the oral cavity of the beast.

I reached cautiously into the gaping mouth and pulled

out one of Oscar's threadbare handkerchiefs. It was wadded up into a ball. Something had been wrapped inside.

The tulip embossed handle on the front door to the Green Vase creaked as it began to turn. I tilted the kangaroo's jaw back up, shoved the cloth and its contents into my pocket, and spun around as Ivan leaned in through the opening door.

Chapter 25

"I THINK I'M about done for today," Ivan said, poking his head into the shop. His face was covered with the residue of the day's work, every inch of skin smudged with grime. A dark mixture of soot and sweat blackened his baseball cap.

"Great," I said, surreptitiously trying to smooth down the bulge from the package I'd stuffed into my pocket. I stepped away from the kangaroo, hoping Ivan wouldn't notice the missing stitches. The mouth looked a lot more natural now that its cargo had been removed.

"I don't think we're expecting rain this weekend, but I've tarped up the exposed portion just in case." Ivan wiped his forehead with his wrist; he looked tired and spent from his efforts tearing out the brick wall. "I should be able to start laying the new brick on Monday."

I nodded encouragingly, holding my breath, waiting for Ivan to leave, but instead he stepped towards me, his hand brushing a stray cedar chip from the top of my head. "What have you been up to?" he asked, chuckling.

"Just going through some of those shipping crates," I

replied nervously, glancing quickly at the kangaroo's mouth. It looked as if it might fall open at any second.

"Oh, find anything interesting?" Ivan asked casually as he leaned against the cashier counter.

I couldn't help feeling as if there was an underlying urgency to his relaxed tone. I shrugged my shoulders, trying to shake my suspicions. "Not really."

It's what *wasn't* in the crates that was interesting, I thought to myself.

"There's something I've been meaning to talk to you about," Ivan said, his eyes uncharacteristically averting mine.

I waited, every nerve tensing. A sliver of space had opened up between the kangaroo's lips.

"I don't know if you were aware," Ivan continued, looking more and more uncomfortable, "but your uncle had a . . ." He paused, seeming to search for a delicate phrasing. ". . . *discreet* relationship with the construction industry here in San Francisco."

"Yes," I replied hurriedly, a sigh of relief whooshing through me. "I knew about that." I slid further into the middle of the room, hoping to draw Ivan's line of sight away from the quivering mouth of the kangaroo.

Ivan smiled as he rested a soiled elbow on the cashier counter, his right shoulder now dangerously close to the parting lips of the kangaroo. "That makes this much easier."

"Wait," I said, catching on. "*You* were his contact?"

Ivan nodded. "It was Harold, actually. I only recently started helping out."

"Mmm," I said encouragingly. I watched, horrified, as the kangaroo's top row of teeth became visible. "Is that why Harold was here that Thursday night when he caught Monty in the kitchen?" I asked quickly.

Ivan shrugged. "I guess so." He pursed his lips as if there were more words to come out. "I brought it up because I thought you should know—Harold took Oscar to a construction site that night, the Thursday right before he died." Ivan looked down at his feet as the kangaroo's jaw cracked open a full half-inch.

I held my breath, afraid that any other action would cause the mouth to drop completely.

Ivan shuffled his feet uncomfortably and then looked up at me. "I don't know what Oscar was looking for, but I can sneak you in there Monday night if you'd like to take a look around."

"Sure," I said tensely, trying to make as little motion as possible.

"Great," Ivan replied, finally turning towards the door. "I'll be off then."

The mouth fell open as Ivan's hand turned the gold-plated handle. I swooped in behind him and stood on my tiptoes, trying to block as much of the front of the kangaroo as possible with my head and shoulders. "I'll see you Monday night then," I said stiffly, a smile plastered on my paralyzed face.

"Well, I'll be here Monday morning to start laying down bricks," Ivan said, looking over his shoulder, a flicker of a question lighting the back of his eyes.

"Of course," I said, my voice squeaking from the pain in my toes.

"Are you all right?" Ivan asked, looking concerned.

I vibrated my head affirmatively, trying to maintain both my balance and the extra height.

"All right then," Ivan said, touching the brim of his baseball cap as he stepped out the door. "Have a good weekend."

I nearly tripped over my numbed feet as Ivan's truck pulled away from the curb. I checked to make sure Monty wasn't about to bound across the street; then I reached into my pocket to retrieve the rolled up handkerchief.

It was a traditional red and white design, one of a collection that Oscar had always carried around with him. The crumpled fabric had been worn threadbare from repeated washing. I held it in the palm of my hand, slowly, carefully, unfolding the edges, exposing the object inside.

It was a wire cage, roughly two inches square, that looked as if someone had unfolded an extra-large paperclip and re-bent it into the shape of a box.

A small scrap of paper had been fed into the wire cage. I pulled it out and unfolded it on the counter. Oscar's handwriting scrawled a single line of text.

It's in the tulips.

I looked up at the silently smiling kangaroo. "What in the world is that supposed to mean?"

I SPENT THE weekend packing up my apartment and ferrying loads of belongings over to the flat above the Green Vase.

In between trips, I'd re-sewn the kangaroo's mouth with a black, cord-like thread I'd found in a drawer in the kitchen. The effort had been clumsy and awkward. Even though the animal had clearly been dead for ages, I'd cringed each time I'd stuck the needle through the thick skin of its lips. Whatever the future focus of the Green Vase turned out to be, taxidermy was not in the cards.

By Sunday night, I was completely exhausted from the move. I took a hot shower and curled up in bed with a soothing cup of herbal tea and the Ralston book I'd checked out from the library.

It was a clear night, as Ivan had predicted. A nearly full moon shone through the flimsy curtains in the bedroom. Rupert and Isabella curled up together at the foot of the bed, sleeping peacefully as I turned the pages, my mind wandering drowsily. My mouth was half-open in a yawn when I heard the first bump.

At first I thought it was someone driving by on the street outside, probably a cab bottoming out on a pothole, and I didn't think much of it. I took another sip of tea and returned to my book.

The second bump seemed nearer, as if it were inside

the building. Isabella jerked up with intruder-alert eyes, jumped to the floor, and headed down the stairs to the kitchen. I sat bolt upright, tensely listening.

The third bump brought me out of the bed. I grabbed my robe and quietly crept down the stairs to the kitchen, my insides churning with terror.

A crashing sound came next, followed closely by the tinkling of breaking glass. Now, I was both terrified and angry. I pulled out my cell phone and was about to dial the police when Rupert sped happily past me, his fluffed-up tail flag-poled in a greeting stance.

Still gripping my phone in my hand, I slid noiselessly down the stairs to the first floor. Skulking around the corner of the stairs, I grabbed the gold-headed cane from its display case and hurdled silently over the open hatch to the basement.

Someone had apparently come up from the tunnel and was trying to flee out the front door of the Green Vase. That someone was now bent over the padlock I'd hooked into the framing of the front door.

It was pitch-black in the back corner of the store where I stood. Near the front, moonlight streamed in through the clear plastic covering Ivan had stretched across the windows. It was just enough light to illuminate the shadow of the curly-headed intruder who was desperately fumbling with the latch to the door while a joyful, bunny-hopping Rupert danced circles around his feet.

I raised the cane over my head like a baseball bat and snuck closer, hoping to instill a serious fright in my obnoxious neighbor, before he had a chance to explain away his second break-in to the Green Vase.

Monty continued to struggle with the lock as I crept up behind him. I lowered the head of the cane to tap him on the shoulder—just as his left hand reached up to scratch his head. The two objects collided in the vicinity of Monty's left ear.

Apparently under the impression that he was being attacked by the dreaded, ear-biting spider, Monty yelped and jerked his hand back.

Unfortunately, his hand caught the hook of the cane, whipping it out of my hands. It flipped through the air, as if in slow motion. I watched the inevitable path of the cane's trajectory as Monty spun around in time to be beamed across the nose.

His painful howl echoed through the Green Vase.

"Monty," I had to yell to be heard over his scream. "What are you doing here?"

He glared at me through his hands, which were plastered up against his bleeding nose. I flipped on a light switch and helped him into the dental chair.

"Here," I said, handing him a paper towel, "tilt your head back."

The bleeding stopped a couple of minutes later, and he started to explain, his voice muffled by the paper towel clamped down on his throbbing nose.

Chapter 26

"DO YOU THINK I need to see a doctor?" Monty mumbled thickly from his prone position on the fully reclined dental chair.

"Not yet, you don't," I replied testily, brandishing the cane over his head.

"Hey," he said defensively, gently palpating his bloodied nose. "There's no need for violence."

"What are you doing in here?" I demanded, looking pointedly at the open hatch to the basement.

He raised himself up on an elbow, still holding the paper towel against his nose. "Please, let me explain."

Sighing, I crossed my arms in front of me, hooking the curved head of the cane around my forearm.

"It all started when . . ."

"It's late, Monty," I interrupted wearily. "Let's make this the abbreviated version of the story."

"Fine," he said huffily, vigorously blotting his nose with the paper towel. He swung his feet to the floor, strolled over to the cashier counter, and dropped the mottled paper into a trash can. "The condensed version then."

Monty leaned up against the counter, slowly tapping his toe against the floor, his mouth twitching in time with his shoe. Finally, he stretched his hands out in front of his face, thumbs touching to form a square viewing portal. "I was working late in my studio this evening, and I saw someone leaving Frank Napis's store."

"Who?" I prompted.

Monty bypassed the question. He strode around the back of the dental chair, his arms churning circles in the air above his head as if he were pulling down thoughts from the ceiling.

"I've had the sense all week that someone was sneaking in and out of there." Monty swung back towards me, a long, bony forefinger raised to the rafters. "You know me—a keen eye for detail." He vamped his eyebrows and smiled demurely.

I gripped the gold-headed cane in my hands, intensely wishing I'd walloped him over the head with it. Eying the cane warily, Monty resumed his pacing, taking care to trace a wide arc around me.

"So, I finally caught sight of him leaving Frank's store." Monty's head shuddered with the image. "It didn't seem right. He had no business being there." Monty swallowed as a clot of blood ran down the back of his throat.

"Wait—who?" I demanded.

"I only saw his back," Monty replied evasively, "as he was locking the door to the shop."

One of Monty's pale, lanky hands stroked the pointed cone of his chin as his eyes gazed, unseeingly, at the floor. I waited, bouncing the end of the cane against my palm. Monty's head jerked up nervously, and he continued.

"I tracked him down Jackson Street to the corner— under the radar, if you know what I mean." Monty doubled over and bounced along the floor in a motion that made him look like a long-limbed duck.

I sighed skeptically.

"That's right, sister," Monty confirmed, straightening and thumping his chest proudly. "He never saw me coming."

I thumped my forehead against the curved end of the cane.

"I had to maintain a safe distance," Monty said in a hushed voice, weaving his head back and forth, "so that I wouldn't be discovered. I tailed him to Wang's flower shop."

I looked up at him sharply. "Wang's?"

"Yes," Monty nodded importantly. "Wang's. I watched him open the door and step inside. It seems it wasn't locked—although the store is generally closed on Sundays."

Monty had reached the back of the Green Vase showroom. He drummed his fingers on the empty carcass of the kangaroo's crate. "I waited on the sidewalk for a moment, trying to decide what to do." Monty turned towards me, his posture questioning. "Should I follow him inside?"

Monty's long, flat feet slapped against the wooden floorboards as he paced towards me with an intensely inquisitive expression. He drew up his breath, his narrow chest expanding; then he vented it out in a splurt of air. "Yes! Of course I should!" His voice dropped in tone and tenor. "So I followed him inside."

"How did you keep this *person* from seeing you?" I asked suspiciously, unmoved by Monty's dramatics.

Monty cleared his throat importantly. "It did get a bit trickier—what with the close quarters." He leapt over the open hatch to the basement. "I had to come up with a disguise."

"What kind of disguise?" I asked dubiously.

A superior smile spread across Monty's face. "As luck would have it, Wang had left a stack of empty flowerpots near one of the front flower racks." Monty brushed his hand over the top of his head and scratched loose a few grains of potting soil from his scalp.

"This—suspect—I was following. He kind of lurked around the flower stall for a couple of minutes; then he slunk to the back, behind a rack of tulips." Monty crept towards me, his shoulders hunched up and his voice once again lowered.

"The store was empty except for the two of us. I peeked out from under my flowerpot and watched him sneak into the broom closet on the back wall."

Monty had moved to within inches of my face. Dried specks of blood freckled his pale, tremulous skin. "I couldn't figure out what he could be doing in there, so I waited . . . and waited . . . and waited. He didn't come out." Monty threw both hands up in the air. "I finally gave up and followed him into the broom closet."

I glanced at the open hatch to the basement, anticipating where this story was headed.

"You'll never believe it," Monty said, an intensity rising in his voice. "When I opened the door to the broom closet . . ."

I cut in. "He wasn't there."

Monty whipped his long bony finger at my face. "What—how did you know?" he demanded.

I bit my bottom lip, contemplating how much to share with him about my own trip through the tunnel. "Finish your bit first," I said, meeting his finger with my cane. "How did you wind up in here?"

Monty spun himself back into the room, determined to regain the suspense of his narrative. Striding slowly past Isabella's bookshelf, he ran his fingers along its facing, retracting them quickly as she reached over the edge to swat at them.

"I noticed the floor of the closet was uneven," he said in a conspiratorial tone. "It threw me for a moment—but then I realized that there was a trap door in the floor, just like this one." Monty thumped the edge of the open hatch. "I found the handle and pulled it open. I figured there must be a storage area of some sort beneath the store, so I decided to go down and check it out. I thought for sure I was about to have a nasty run-in with . . ." Monty paused, gulping.

I studied him, trying to fill in the gap he was so tenaciously avoiding. "The person that you were following?" I asked. "Monty, who was it?"

Monty's whole upper body convulsed, as if his torso had been dunked in icy water. He pointed the palms of his hands at me, indicating his refusal to answer. His pursed lips parted, and he whispered, "but I climbed down into the hatch anyway."

Monty had once again traveled to the front of the store and now stood facing me, on the other side of the still extended dental chair. He leaned towards me, crawling over the back of the chair as he spoke. "Do you know what I found?" he said, nearly squeaking in his excitement. "Guess, guess, you'll never guess! It was the . . ."

"The tunnel," I sighed.

Monty collapsed facedown on the chair, pounding it with his fists. "The tunnel! The tunnel!" he cried plaintively, curling himself up like a wounded animal.

Monty raised himself up on his elbows, his face reddened from his exertions. He ran his tongue over his top lip, pondering me for a moment. "And do you know where I came out?" he asked fiercely.

"My basement," I said placidly.

"You knew!" he cried out indignantly. "You knew, and you didn't tell me!"

"I didn't tell anyone," I replied honestly.

Monty slid his feet to the floor, sitting himself up on the flattened dental chair. "This whole business with Oscar is a bit strange," he said quietly, his pale face somber as he looked up at me. "You think something happened to him, don't you? That his death wasn't—natural."

I leaned back against the cash register counter. Monty took my silence as an affirmative response.

"You're not the only one," he said as he stood up and walked towards the counter. I held my breath as he sidled up to the kangaroo and wrapped his right arm over its shoulders. He looked at the kangaroo's face as he said softly, "I've been asking around about your tulip buddy

Leidesdorff. Someone told me a very odd story about him. I didn't know whether to believe it—until tonight."

"What story?" I asked, cringing as Monty stroked the kangaroo's head.

Monty raised one eyebrow suggestively. "That Leidesdorff used some crazy potion to fake his death. He assumed a new identity and lived on for many years—here, in San Francisco."

I left the counter and walked towards the dental chair, desperately wishing Monty would step away from the kangaroo.

"I have a theory," he said, scratching the animal's chin absentmindedly.

"Let's hear it," I sighed resignedly, tucking my robe more tightly around my waist. I turned towards the back of the room, feeling Monty's stare on my back.

"Oscar figured it out," he said flatly.

"Figured out what?" I snapped, whipping around to face him.

Monty beamed a triumphant smile as he raised his overused forefinger in front of my face. "How he did it— Leidesdorff, that is. Oscar must have figured out how Leidesdorff faked his death."

"I guess that's possible," I said tersely. I'd had enough of Monty for one evening. "What ever happened to this guy you followed into the tunnel?" I asked tiredly.

"Still alive, as far as I know," Monty replied evasively.

I poked him in the stomach with the cane. "You followed him into the tunnel. Where did he go from there?"

Monty googled his eyes around the room, searching for the man he had followed into the flower shop. He made as if to turn back towards the kangaroo, but I grabbed his long face in my hands and wrenched it towards me.

"Monty," I said firmly. "Who was it? Who did you follow into the tunnel?"

He swallowed hard, and I released him. He pushed past me, ambling to the back of the room. "I only ever saw him from behind, but—from that angle—he looked like . . ."

Monty's face skewed up so that when he spoke, the name squeaked out of him. "Oscar."

I rubbed my forehead, covering my face with my hands. "Out!" I said forcefully.

Monty's fingers shook as he fumbled with the still open hatch. "You really should put a lock on this," he advised.

"Out!" I reiterated, swinging my arm towards the door. I marched over to it and unhooked the padlock.

"Right," he replied. He paused on the threshold to point at me one last time. "Shouldn't you at least consider the possibility . . ."

I slammed the door shut on him, squashing his wing-tipped toes with the metal frame.

I TURNED OFF the lights in the store and climbed the stairs to the kitchen. Sleep, which had earlier seemed so close, had fled a million miles away. I placed my hands against the edge of the kitchen table and leaned over it, my eyes pouring into the swirling grooves on its surface as my head spun with images of Oscar.

Oscar cooking in his kitchen . . . commandeering a dozen chicken legs simmering in a wrought iron pot . . . preparing chicken broth for the cats . . . estimating the appropriate amounts of the ingredients as he siphoned them off into small bowls.

I looked up at the wall across from the kitchen table that held the shelf lined with cookbooks. Never, in all of the dinners I'd watched him prepare, had Oscar ever referenced a written recipe.

My eyes scanned the titles as my fingers danced along the spines. "The Art of Chicken" was particularly worn. I hooked the end of my finger into the top edge of the book's binder and pulled it out. Isabella watched closely as I carried it back to the table.

"Wrao," she said encouragingly, hopping up onto the chair beside me.

The cover creaked as I lifted it open. A faded sheet of paper had been tucked into the front flap. I pulled it out, my hands trembling as I examined the document. The ink was barely legible from watermarks and age, but I knew exactly what I was looking at.

It was an army death certificate—presumably the one mistakenly issued by the nurse when she had been about to send Oscar's body to the morgue.

My eyes traveled down to the bottom of the page to the slot allotted for the cause of death.

One word had been typed in—encephalitis. The same brain swelling diagnosis that had been given to a comatose William Leidesdorff almost a hundred years earlier.

Chapter 27

LATE AFTERNOON MONDAY, I sat on the curb outside my apartment, waiting for the local moving company that was scheduled to transport the last of the larger items of furniture from my apartment over to the Green Vase.

Before long, a bulky, green moving truck with a large, Irish shamrock painted on the side double-parked in front of my apartment building, and an eclectic mixture of Spanish and Irish accents tumbled out of the crowded cab.

I bade goodbye to the empty shell of my apartment as the last of my belongings were hefted into the truck. I'd been sleeping over at the Green Vase for less than a week, but in the short span of that absence, my apartment had grown cold and foreign. With all of the furniture gone, the scuffed, dingy walls seemed harsh and unwelcoming; the previously unnoticed noise of the traffic below my window grated on my nerves. I climbed into my car to follow the moving truck to Jackson Square and didn't look back.

Ivan's bricklaying project was in full swing as we pulled up to the Green Vase. Already, the transformation was amazing. Bright red, neatly square, un-crumbled bricks formed the crisp outlines of the windows and door. Freshly smeared mortar oozed thickly between each brick, like the rich, creamy center of an Oreo cookie.

Ivan stood up from his stooped position near the front door to greet me. "Your neighbor's looking for you," he said as he helped one of the movers through the entrance.

"I'm sure he is," I replied, ducking as my chest of drawers soared past. I had somehow managed to avoid Monty on my way out the door earlier that morning.

Twenty minutes later, most of the contents of my apartment had been squeezed into the flat above the Green Vase. What wouldn't fit upstairs had been left in the show-room. I leaned against the cashier counter, surveying the crowded chaos, numbed by the magnitude of the mess.

Ivan cracked open the front door and called inside, "I should be able to finish up the brickwork tomorrow morning." His tool belt jingled from the assortment of hammers and other implements hanging in its loops. "I'll swing by to pick you up in about half an hour to go to the construction site."

"Okay," I said. "I'll see you then."

He waved and turned to leave. "Full Monty, incoming, twelve o'clock," he warned.

Smiling weakly, I braced myself for Monty's entrance. I peeked through the glass sections of the door as it swung shut behind Ivan.

Monty was chugging across the street in high gear, the purple and green silk tie he'd cinched around his neck flapping in the breeze. A freshly cut, violet-colored tulip clung to his lapel as he vaulted up the steps to the Green Vase and barged through the front door.

"It looks like you've moved out of your old place," he said, snooping through the piles of my belongings.

I nodded, wiping a film of grit from my forehead. "This is the last of it."

Monty strode over to the closed hatch to the basement and began to hop up and down on it. "So, I was wondering," he said, the floor squeaking as he bounced up and down. "Who else knows about the tunnel?"

Rupert peeked around the corner of the stairs, investigating the source of the commotion. His furry head jiggled as he followed Monty's jack-hammering legs.

"Rupert and Isabella," I replied, opting to leave Mr. Wang out of the picture for the time being.

Rupert decided to join in on the hop. He trotted up to Monty and began to bounce beside him.

"Ivan?" Monty asked, his gaze focused on Rupert, who was struggling to catch up to Monty's energetic tempo.

"No," I replied, shaking my head at the sight of them.

Monty stopped hopping and bent down towards Rupert's panting fluff of fur. "I can't believe *you* didn't tell me about the tunnel, either. I thought we were mates!"

Monty walked back towards the front of the store; Rupert paced amicably behind him. "I want to show you something in my studio," he said. "It's a painting I've borrowed from Dilla."

"What kind of painting?" I asked skeptically. I felt exhausted from the effort of the move.

"One of a warehouse," Monty said with an air of exaggerated nonchalance. "With a line of tulips across the front."

He leaned back against the cashier counter as I stared at him, a recognition triggering somewhere in the recesses of my memory.

Monty yawned into his hand and then stretched his long fingers out in front of his face, as if examining his manicure. "It's the warehouse that was owned by that Leidesdorff fellow."

"I saw that painting in Miranda's office!" I exclaimed as the canvas on Miranda's wall suddenly flashed into focus.

The corners of Monty's mouth pushed down, an impressed look on his face. "Yes, I suppose Miranda had it in her office for a while. She doesn't keep anything in there for long. Always looking to trade up."

Monty slapped the side of his neck with the inside of his hand, releasing a whiff of his citrus aftershave. "So are you coming or what?"

WE CROSSED THE darkening street to Monty's brightly lit studio. He unlocked the door and held it open, ushering me inside.

In stark contrast to the dusty, cramped, and disorganized Green Vase showroom, the smaller square footage of Monty's studio felt spacious. Paintings were artfully spaced throughout the room on creamy, off-white walls. Four-inch spotlights had been carefully aimed to highlight each frame. Partitions crisscrossed the room to provide additional wall space.

Monty glided across the polished tile floor and led me to an easel at the back of the room. An arrangement of fresh flowers, mostly pink roses, perched on the corner of his desk, near a rounded divot that marked the spot where Monty propped up his feet when he leaned back in his chair.

Monty picked up the corner of a sheet hanging over the easel and, with a grand flourish, flipped it up.

It was the painting I'd studied in Miranda's office. The same large, barn-like structure dominated the picture. It was situated on the edge of the water. I now realized that the lush row of purple flowers along the front of the building were tulips. Each tulip head was represented by three upward swinging brush strokes, creating the familiar three-petaled design I now immediately associated with Leidesdorff.

"How do you know this is Leidesdorff's warehouse?" I asked, my eyes scanning the canvas.

Monty pumped his eyebrows. "Because it matches this." He pulled out an ink sketch matching the building in the painting. "I copied this out of a book at the library."

"And the writing in the bottom corner?" I asked, indicating the smudge I'd been unable to make out in Miranda's office. "Who's the painter?"

Monty raised a finger and pulled out a magnifying glass from his desk drawer. He walked around to the front of the painting and leaned over the writing. "It's hard to say," he said, squinting as he rotated the lens back and forth. "The name is kind of hard to read."

Monty slid the magnifying glass towards the middle of the painting, running it along the stretch of tulips fronting the warehouse. Suddenly he stopped. His pale green eyes narrowed, and his small mouth puckered.

He shook his head back and forth as if to clear it and refocused the lens of the magnifying glass. A disturbed, shuffling sound bubbled up from where he had plastered himself against the painting.

"There's a flashlight in the top drawer," he said, his eyes not leaving their position inches away from the row of tulips. "Toss it over, would you?"

I fished the light out of the drawer and handed it to him. "What is it?" I asked. "What do you see?"

Monty grumbled bitterly under his breath. Finally, he leaned back from the easel and stretched his back, a sour expression on his face. "Someone's having a go with us," he said, handing me the magnifying glass.

I took up Monty's position near the bottom of the painting. With the flashlight in one hand and the magnifying glass in the other, I leaned in to the spot he'd been studying.

There was something in the leaves, lurking just below the purple heads of the three-petaled tulips. Something white and round and fluffy—with orange-tipped ears and a pleasant, sleepy smile on his face.

"Rupert?" I asked, incredulous.

Monty sighed. "And Isabella. She's a couple of inches to the left."

I slid the magnifying glass down to the signature on the bottom corner that Monty had been unable to decipher.

As the writing expanded under the lens, I bit down on

my lip to stifle the exclamation that nearly leapt out of my mouth.

The painting had been signed with a sloppy, looping "O," trailed by a long, squiggling paraph.

Chapter 28

I'D BECOME SO engrossed in the painting, I'd nearly forgotten about Ivan. As Monty bent back over the canvas with the magnifying glass, I saw Ivan's figure ambling up the street towards the Green Vase. If Monty caught sight of Ivan, there would be no way to keep him from joining us at the construction site.

"Well, that's very interesting," I said, stepping back from the easel.

Monty remained crouched over the canvas, absorbed in the rendering of the two white cats hiding in the tulip leaves.

"I, uh, hmm," I said, scrambling for an excuse to leave. "I need to get back to the store to, uh, feed the cats."

I began backing away towards the door, but something on the corner of Monty's desk caught my eye. It was a small wire cage—just like the one I'd found in the mouth of the kangaroo.

"What's this?" I asked, reaching for the wire object.

Monty glanced up, still distracted by the painting. "Oh, funny story," he said, returning his face to the magnifying glass. "My dry cleaner said he found that in the front pocket of one of my shirts. I figure he got me mixed up with someone else."

I turned the cage over in my hands, letting the light reflect off of the metal wires. It was the perfect shape for an acquisitive cat to have carried off in her mouth as she ran down the stairs from the kitchen to the Green Vase showroom—and leapt up onto Monty's shoulders.

"Thanks for showing me the painting," I said. My hand turned the knob behind my back as I slipped the second wire cage into my pocket. Out of the corner of my eye, I could see that Ivan had almost reached the Green Vase. "See you tomorrow, Monty."

Monty mumbled something from behind the easel, but I didn't wait for a clarification. I eased out the front door and scooted across the street to where Ivan was walking up the steps to the Green Vase. I scampered up behind him and swept him inside as quickly as possible.

"Get down," I insisted. "Monty might see you."

"Wha—," was all he got out before I squashed his head down behind the counter.

Carefully, cautiously, I peeped over the edge and peered back across to the studio. Monty was still studying the painting.

"I was over at Monty's," I hissed to the crouching Ivan. "He almost saw you coming down the street."

Ivan looked up, amused. "And you'd prefer not to bring him along?"

"I don't want the entire population of Jackson Square to know about it by noon tomorrow," I replied. Ivan chuckled.

My eyes were still focused on Monty. I watched as he stood up and raised his index finger into the air, as if an idea had suddenly occurred to him. He strode briskly across the studio to the stairs that led to the second floor.

"He's going upstairs to get something," I reported down to Ivan. "This is our chance."

"Great," Ivan grunted from underneath the counter, "just give me the word."

"Now," I whispered urgently, swinging open the front door and whisking him through it. I quickly turned the tulip key in the lock, and the two of us sprinted down the street. We pulled up as soon as we rounded the corner, both of us breathing hard.

"I think we made it," I said, peeking around the side of a building as I grabbed the stitch in my side.

IVAN LED ME into the financial district and its forest of dark, dozing office buildings. The closed eyelids of the unlit windows snored in a deep, restful silence, undisturbed by the blinking electronic signs persistently flashing time, temperature, and market measurements to the vacant streets.

A last, lawyer-looking type straggled wearily down stone steps to the sidewalk, lugging a pile of briefs that would steal half of tonight's much needed sleep. His crisp, legal uniform had wilted from the day's endeavors; it was crumpled with perspiration and mental fatigue. He fell in line behind us as we approached Market Street's bright, wide-awake glare.

Ahead of us, a homeless man pushed a rusting, metal shopping cart, piled high with a pathetic collection of crinkling plastic bags and discarded cardboard. He turned onto Market's main drag, filled, on such a clear tepid night, with a number of similarly bedraggled figures, shuffling to position themselves on the best piece of concrete. The rotting human forms huddled on the grimy sidewalk underneath filthy, lice-infested blankets, their bodies almost unrecognizable from the toll of poverty's accelerated decay.

We walked past an uncountable number of these downtrodden shadows, carefully shading our eyes from their pleading faces and handwritten cardboard signs. A swirling wind whistled through the whole of us, stirring up an odorous stench of stale body odor and callous inhumanity.

Despite all of her fantastic, overblown stories of instant

success and rapidly acquired wealth, San Francisco has not been kind to many, if not most, who have washed up on her shore. But that reality has never seemed to slow the relentless, ever-incoming tide chasing her illusion.

WE STOPPED AT the corner of Market and Montgomery, waiting for a traffic light to change. I looked down at my feet, noticing a bronze flagstone set into the sidewalk. It was a marker commemorating the city's original shoreline. The rectangular inset included a map depicting the original delineation of the city's boundaries. I stooped down over the marker, mentally comparing it to Oscar's parchment until a laughing Ivan grabbed my hand and pulled me into the street.

"You're turning into your uncle," he yelled over the noise of the traffic. "He used to spend hours staring at that stone."

Our feet found the curb on the opposite side of the street, and we headed down New Montgomery, past the Palace Hotel where Dilla's cat costume auction would be held at the end of the week.

According to Mr. Wang, the far end of the tunnel surfaced somewhere within this lavish building.

The Palace Hotel had been one of William Ralston's last projects, one he zealously pursued despite the infamous diamond fiasco. Ralston had dreamed of building one of the finest hotels in the world as a tribute to his beloved San Francisco, a city he credited as the inspiration for his phenomenal run of luck—Ralston's stubborn belief in his predestined prosperity had apparently been undiminished by the diamond deal meltdown.

Ralston spared no cost or extravagance on his new hotel, nearly bankrupting the project in the process. As the over-budget venture neared completion, Ralston's bank succumbed to a run on its reserves. After temporarily closing its doors to recuperate, the bank's board of director's moved to oust him.

Ralston was last seen alive the afternoon following his ouster, jumping into the bay at Aquatic Park for his daily swim. Onlookers from the shore saw him struggling and mounted a rescue effort, but Ralston could not be resuscitated. Ralston's business partner, William Sharon, pushed the Palace project to completion, and the hotel opened a few months after Ralston's death.

I stared up at the building as Ivan whisked me past.

It was solid and stately, but the current rendition lacked some of the whimsical grandeur of the original structure, destroyed by fire in the aftermath of the 1906 earthquake. Sketches of the earlier building depicted a magnificent, palace-like edifice bulging with column after column of gleaming bay windows, so that each guest had the perfect place to watch—and be watched by—the citizens of San Francisco.

A couple of blocks past the Palace, a seedier side of San Francisco filled in around us. We were headed deeper into the South of Market district where the city's rising rental rates had inspired the rapid construction of several high-rise condominiums. Flocks of yuppies had nested in these pricey, elevated cubbies, lured by lower rents and birdhouse views of the city's skyline.

The street level where we walked was home to the neighborhood's edgier inhabitants. I moved closer to Ivan as a dark, disheveled man drinking out of a paper sack–covered bottle stopped to leer at me.

"It's up here on the right," Ivan said as we approached a lot enclosed by a ten-foot high chain-link fence. A sign announced the imminent arrival of yet another luxury apartment building.

The immense building site had previously served as a twenty-dollar a day parking lot. The cracked asphalt had been scalped away, along with several underlying tons of dirt, sand, and muck.

A fleet of voracious bulldozers and other menacing excavation equipment was parked for the night on a landing, fifteen feet below the street level. Beyond this midway staging area, the depths of the mammoth pit sank into a murky darkness, illuminated only by a small halo of light focused on a twenty-foot high pile driver that had been halted midway through one of its head-splitting poundings.

A few forlorn streetlamps hung over the sidewalk where Ivan and I stood. He scanned up and down the deserted street before pulling a key out of his pocket and prizing open a padlock hooked through a gate in the fence.

"There's a ladder over on the right," he said briskly, as if he were ushering me into an amusement park and not this treacherous, chthonic sinkhole. "I'll keep watch up here."

I nodded nervously, biting down on my lip as he handed me his flashlight. I had forgotten mine in the rush to escape the Green Vase without being seen by Monty.

The rains from the previous week had pooled in this sub-sea level hole. The weekend's clear weather hadn't done much to dry the thick, gooey mud that quickly layered the soles of my tennis shoes, adding at least three slippery inches to my height. I struggled to keep my balance as I slid across the sloped staging area to the ladder.

Gripping the top rung, I panned the flashlight's beam across the bottom of the pit. Nothing in the churned up mud suggested the presence of a recently uncovered antique.

I tucked the flashlight into my coat pocket so that I could hold on to the ladder with both hands. In near darkness, I carefully began my descent, each foot blindly feeling for the next rung.

The pit quickly swallowed up the sounds of the city, creating a suffocating silence that was interrupted only by the squishing of my shoes. I was hardly visible to myself, much less to anyone else, but I had the eerie sensation of being watched by someone other than Ivan.

My feet finally found the slimy floor of the pit, and I

steadied myself with the ladder while I pulled out the flashlight. Just as I clicked the lever to turn it back on, a surprised gasp sounded above my head.

I swung the flashlight up towards the source of a slipping, sliding slurp—in time to illuminate a mud-covered Monty somersaulting over the edge of the pit, his purple and green silk tie flapping in his shocked face.

Chapter 29

MONTY'S LONG, LANKY arms flailed against the oozing, earthen wall of the pit as he pummeled to the bottom. His feet dug into the wall of mud, the pointed tips of his shoes carving out two parallel grooves as he slid to the bottom. He landed with a squelching thud, spread-eagled on the floor of the pit.

I sighed resignedly and then called out, "Are you okay?"

A muddy paw rose up out of the mud and waved in my direction. "Fine, thanks."

Monty sat up gingerly, looking mildly disgruntled, but he didn't appear to have broken any bones. I walked over and helped him up, shining the light over his mud-dappled suit.

"You're covered in mud," I said. "Otherwise, you appear to be okay."

"So," Monty said, grinning as he scraped a glob of mud off his face. "What are you kids up to?" He pointed a knobby finger at me. "I had quite a job keeping up with you two after the sprint down Jackson Street." He wagged the finger reproachfully. "How am I supposed to protect you if you keep sneaking off like this?"

I returned his point with the direct beam of the flashlight. Mud had caked his curly hair and slimed over his eyebrows. He was lucky he hadn't broken his neck falling over the side of the pit.

"Protect me? What makes you think you need to protect me?" I asked, incredulous. "Have you lost your mind?"

Monty cleared his throat as he straightened his soiled tie. "I have a theory . . ."

I couldn't take another theory. "Oh, for the love of—where's Ivan?"

Monty pointed up towards the street as Ivan's concerned face peeked over the edge.

Ivan called out, "You all right, Carmichael?"

Monty waved back, throwing his right arm up into a mock salute. The gesture knocked him off kilter, causing him to stagger backwards. His left foot slipped on the slick floor of the pit. He wobbled for a long moment, desperately trying to regain his balance, but both feet flew out from under him. He landed like a flipped pancake, smacking against the gelatinous surface of the mud.

Ivan grimaced as he pulled back from the ledge to his surveillance post.

Monty righted himself and began to stroll a circle around me. "So, what are we doing down here anyway? What's the story?"

With each step, his feet sunk further into the gloppy mire. His mud-soaked pants flapped against his bony legs as he tried to shake his feet free of the mud. Monty looked more stork-like than ever.

I threw my hands up in the air, relenting. "Oscar came here the Thursday before he died—the night Harold Wombler caught you in the kitchen above the Green Vase."

Monty stroked his chin, the wheels in his head spinning. "Ah," he said, raising a soiled forefinger. "And you're wondering if Oscar found something down here related to Leidesdorff. Something that shed light on how

Leidesdorff managed to give everyone the slip back in 1848." He crept up behind my right ear and lowered his voice to a loud whisper. "Something that showed Oscar how to perform the same trick."

I whipped around, nearly knocking Monty over. "Oscar's dead, okay? I saw him with my own eyes. I watched his casket being buried into the ground. You're way off base."

"Whatever you say, dear," Monty said in a patronizing falsetto.

"You have to keep all of this under your hat, do you understand?" I said sternly. "You can't tell anyone about my visit here tonight."

"Cross my heart," he replied, solemnly smearing the front of his suit jacket to make the mark. "Now then," he asked eagerly, straightening the battered tulip still pinned limply to his lapel. "What are we looking for?"

"I'm not sure really," I said, tracking the light towards the back corner of the pit.

The wet ground glistened. Water had collected in the lowest corner, swamping the mud into a black, putrid-swilling soup.

Monty crinkled up his nose as I slid towards the make-shift pond. "Oh, surely not in there," he said as I shone the flashlight into the murky water.

A film of mossy-green algae skimmed the surface of the standing water and clung to a collection of decomposing leaves, broken twigs, and blown away trash that poked out of the muck. Monty grabbed one of the larger twigs and stirred the brew. The motion disrupted the stringy arms of the algae, causing chunks to break off and swarm around the stick.

"Yeck," he said, as I circled the flashlight's beam over the water, searching for any evidence of the uncovered antique that had drawn Oscar to the construction site.

This location, I thought uneasily, was all wrong. It was too far inland for Oscar's interests. This part of the city had originally been covered in the sand dunes that had been scraped down to fill in the bay. It wasn't part of the landfill area.

"I don't think there's anything down here," I said, playing the light over the water one more time.

"Sounds good to me," Monty said, turning towards the ladder he'd missed on his way down.

Something flickered in the beam of my flashlight. "Hold on a minute," I called back to him, bending down towards the water. I could have sworn I'd seen something shining just beneath the surface.

I stepped tentatively into the edge of the pond. The water seeped through my tennis shoes, causing my toes to recoil and curl up under the balls of my feet.

Gritting my teeth, I willed myself forward into the water, quickly sinking in halfway up to my shins as my feet disappeared beneath the black surface. The mud wrapped its slithering tentacles around my shoes, threatening to pull me down into its limicolous lair.

Water slopped over my knees as the pond rippled from a movement other than my own. I froze. "Monty," I said slowly, "is that you?"

There was no answer—only the fishy aroma rising up from the stagnant water. My chest thumping, I turned to look behind me.

I found myself face to face with a Frankenstein-impersonating Monty.

"Wha-ah-ah . . . ," he cackled in a deep throated voice, quickly followed by a wind-sucking "whump" as I slugged him squarely, satisfyingly, in the stomach.

I pushed forward into the water. Monty waded after me, flapping noisily.

"This is worse than the tunnel," I muttered.

"Couldn't agree with you more," Monty replied, disturbingly close to my ear. I swatted my right hand behind my head but didn't make contact.

The longer we spent on the bottom of the construction pit, the more curious its thriving insect population became of us. The inquisitive shuffling of thousands of insect legs ringed the bank of the pond. The more intrepid observers began to skitter across the surface of the water towards us.

Then we heard the rustle of a slightly larger being at the edge of the dank water.

Monty whispered tensely, "Tell me that wasn't a rat."

I panned the beam of the flashlight around the shadowy periphery. The glassy pits of several pairs of pupils reflected back. We'd attracted quite a crowd.

"Okay," I said grimly, "it wasn't *a* rat—more like *many* rats."

"I don't do rats," Monty whimpered. Gulping palely, he turned and sprinted out of the pond, splashing loudly as he hollered at the rats to make way.

"I thought you were here to protect me?" I called out as I turned to follow him.

Something sparkled in the water near my feet. The wake of Monty's departure had disturbed the bottom surface of the pond. A turbulence of slimy debris floated to the surface.

I trained my flashlight down into the soupy water and finally found the object that had drawn me in to begin with. I shoved the sleeves of my sweater up my arms as far as they would go and reached down into the muck. The thick sludge closed in around my hands like a pair of gloves, melding into every groove on the surface of my fingers. I grabbed on to the shiny object and pulled it up to the surface. A feathering layer of slime trailed behind it.

I could hear Monty clambering up the rungs of the ladder as I held the object under the flashlight to inspect it.

Smoothing my hands over the curling metal shape, I wondered how one of Leidesdorff's tulip-shaped cufflinks could have made its way to the bottom of this construction pit.

This one felt somehow different—lighter—than the one I'd inspected in Oscar's kitchen. I flipped it over.

The back read, "Made in Japan."

Chapter 30

IVAN GREETED US as we topped the ladder and headed for the gate. "Find anything useful?" he asked, grinning as he surveyed our mud-covered condition.

"Nope, not a thing," Monty muttered bitterly. "Nada. Zip. Nothing."

"You were certainly thorough," Ivan said wryly. "Did you take a swim in the pond at the bottom corner?"

"*That one* forced me in," Monty said churlishly, jerking his head in my direction.

"Thank you for letting me check it out," I said, shrugging my shoulders. I looked back down at the steep sides of the pit. "That would have been quite a climb for Oscar. His knees were giving out."

"Oh, he got around pretty good for an old guy," Ivan said, a slight edge in his voice as he cinched the padlock around the gate.

"You're sure it was *this* lot?" I asked, still perplexed. The fake cufflink had only heightened my suspicions.

Ivan looked up from the lock. The curve of his face seemed to harden. "I'm sure," he replied curtly. He shook his head at our disheveled appearance. "I'll let Monty walk you home if that's all right. I need to head off in the opposite direction."

MONTY AND I trudged through the empty downtown streets, a muddy, earthy-smelling pair.

I turned my head to look at Monty. A slide of packed brown goop covered his charcoal gray slacks from the top of his angular hip to the edge of his tailored cuff. Another smear of mud sheathed the back of his shoulders. Drying flakes fell to the ground with every scraping step.

"What do you think?" Monty asked, elbowing me with a crusting sleeve. He slapped a bolus of damp dirt under his chin, creating a mud-brown beard. He worked the tip with his fingers, shaping it into a cone, and turned towards me, running a primping hand along the side of his head.

I ignored him.

We rounded a corner, turning down the street towards Mr. Wang's flower stall. A faint glow burned in the window. "Probably sneaking another late night smoke," I thought.

Monty pointed to the lit window as we approached. "Looks like Wang's still up." He cupped his grimy hands around his eyes and peered in through the steamed glass. "Let's see what old Wang is up to."

Monty's back stiffened. "What's *he* doing in there?" he asked, his voice ilking repulsion.

"Who?" I demanded, trying to push my way up to the window. Rough, plywood boards had been cinched down over most of the stall to protect it at night from intruders. The portion of the window that remained unshielded was just wide enough for Monty's head, and I couldn't get him to budge.

"Look at *him*—chatting away with Wang." Monty suctioned his tongue against the roof of his mouth and released it with an imperious, smacking sound. The mud-soaked soles of his wingtips slapped against the sidewalk as he tapped the toe of his foot up and down. "What's he up to?"

I pushed up onto my tiptoes, trying to leverage an angle to see in, but it was impossible for me to top Monty's towering, mud-tipped curls. I returned to the flats of my feet as the door creaked open. Mr. Wang's pale, balding head turtled out through the opening.

"Ah, there you are," he said genially, as if he had been expecting us. "Please," he beckoned with a gnarled hand, "come inside."

The door swung open, but, before we could pass through, a hunched figure pushed his way out. His spitting, gravelly voice ground back towards Mr. Wang's slight shadow. "That'll do it for me, Wang."

Harold Wombler wore the same pair of baggy, disintegrating overalls he'd worn the first day I met him. The loose, flapping jowls of his cheeks were carpeted with scratchy patches of grisly stubble. His sunken, blood-shot eyes surveyed Monty's mud-crusted appearance in a single, shifty motion.

"Nice outfit, Carmichael," he sneered as he barreled past us and lurched down the street, gimping along on his game leg.

Monty sputtered at Harold's retreating figure, struggling for a response. He turned to me, flabbergasted, "Did you see that?"

I shrugged sympathetically. Monty glanced down at his mud-soaked suit and blew out a heavy, frustrated sigh. His lips rolled inward, flattening his mouth out like a frog's. He drew himself up, pushed the flat of his hand against the door that had swung shut behind Harold, and strolled resolutely into the flower stall.

"Good evening, Wang," Monty said in a grand, pompous tone.

I followed him through the entrance. The warm, muggy atmosphere inside the flower stall fogged up my glasses.

Mr. Wang patted me fondly on the back. "You always

bring the most interesting guests," he said, glancing at Monty's unusually un-fastidious attire.

I found a clean spot on the inside of my shirt and wiped my lenses while the scents of freshly cut flowers and stale tobacco filtered through my sinuses.

"I gather Ivan's taken you to the construction site," Mr. Wang said calmly as he gangled back to his metal folding stool. He slid into it and pulled a cigar out of a side pocket in his jacket. His yellowed fingernails flicked on a lighter and held it, shakily, in front of his face.

Mr. Wang's narrow, nicotine-plundered chest emitted a suffocating wheeze as it pulled in air and heat through the tobacco leaves. He sunk back into his chair, his body relaxing as the drug permeated through his weak, anemic body. His bony fingers crawled up to his smooth, balding head, thoughtfully tufting its few remaining follicles.

Monty's right arm strutted against a wall; his left leg crooked jauntily into a triangle. The leather creases in his wingtips oozed out a slimy, black sludge.

Monty's long, pasty face carried a cynical expression. "What makes you think we've come from a construction site?" he queried, as if there were multiple locations within walking distance where a person could manage to cover himself with this much mud.

"Call it an educated hunch," Mr. Wang said, his eyes sweeping over Monty's mud-rumpled clothes. His gray eyes narrowed inquisitively. "Did you find anything?"

Monty stared at Mr. Wang suspiciously. "What's it to you, Wang? What's your angle in all of this?"

Mr. Wang reached into his front pocket, pulled out the black wallet, and flashed his badge at Monty. "I've been investigating the circumstances surrounding the death of the lady's uncle." He flipped the badge shut and slid it back into the pocket behind the crumpled cigarette pack. "I'm retired from the force, you see."

"Whoa, whoa, whoa, there mister," Monty said, striding boldly up to Mr. Wang and snatching the badge out of his pocket. A trail of drying dirt shattered on the floor behind him. "Let me take a look at that."

Mr. Wang raised his thin eyebrows, but did not object. He winked at me as he took another puff on the cigar. The smoke circled above his head and percolated up to Monty's careful scrutiny of the badge.

Monty held the badge up to a bare light bulb strung from the rafters of the flower stall. He made a strange earthy statue in the lambent light; smears of mud flattened the hair on the sides of his head making its shape even more conical than usual.

"Hmnh," Monty grunted shortly, handing back the badge. "Seems authentic."

Mr. Wang grinned wanly. "Thank you for your stamp of approval, Mr. Carmichael." Another puff of smoke eased its way out of the pinprick holes of his nostrils. "Now, please tell me about your excursion to the construction pit."

Monty's eyes swept down to his clothes. "All we came up with is lots and lots of mud."

I nodded, confirming, not wishing to discuss my discovery of the counterfeit tulip cufflink until I'd had a chance to study it more closely.

Another puff smoked out of Mr. Wang's head, obscuring his expression. "That's disappointing," he said quietly. "I had hoped we might get a hint to the last artifact Oscar unearthed before his death."

"Well, Wang, here's the way I see it." Monty stepped out from the wall, stroking his crusty eyebrows as he began to pace the meager confines of the flower stall. "We know that Oscar was well on his way to sorting out this Leidesdorff fellow—how he managed to fake his death back in 1848. Oscar found the entrance to the tunnel and unearthed that tulip-shaped key." Monty paused and swung around to give me a pointed look. "I'd say it's a pretty good guess that Oscar got his hands on Leidesdorff's sleeping potion."

A faint smile formed on Mr. Wang's colorless face as Monty began to lollop through the room.

"Let's go back to Leidesdorff and what happened in 1848." Monty paused and raised his bony index finger to the rafters. "I have a theory."

I groaned loudly, but he ignored me.

"I've been doing some research on this Leidesdorff character. It turns out he was quite a gambler. He'd bet on anything. If two ants were crossing the sidewalk, he'd ante up a position on the one he thought would make it to the other side first."

Monty reached a corner of the room and continued his march behind the rack of tulips, the top of his head bouncing just above its horizontal edge.

"Right before his death, Leidesdorff organized a horse race—the first one in Northern California. It was held out by the Mission Dolores chapel. The same chapel where he was allegedly buried a few days later."

Monty came to an abrupt halt as his walking space ran up against a wall. He spun around in a military style turn and resumed his purposeful strut along the back side of the tulip rack.

"Leidesdorff must have made all kinds of bets before that race. Imagine the temptation for a guy like him."

Monty snapped smartly around the corner of the tulip rack and stepped back into the center of the room, clicking his heels together as he crossed his arms in front of his chest.

"I think he got himself into a pickle betting on that race." Monty paused, then asserted, "I think our friend Leidesdorff faked his death to get out from under his gambling debt."

"But then, why didn't he leave town?" I asked. "Why did he stay in San Francisco afterwards?"

And how, I thought to myself, did he get mixed up with Ralston and the expansion of the tunnel through the new landfill towards the Green Vase?

Monty stood with his hands on his hips, his face contorting with thought.

Mr. Wang cut in with a clarifying wheeze. "I think Lei-

desdorff stayed because he was looking for something—
something he lost." He pointed the burnt ember tip of his
cigar towards me. "Or, should I say, *someone*."

My brow furrowed, trying to follow his nuance.

Mr. Wang tapped the cigar, knocking a ring of ashes
off the end. "Do you remember what I told you about
Leidesdorff's maid—the one who came with him from
New Orleans?"

Monty interjected, "New Orleans? Oh, I've got you
there, Wang. I read that she was Russian—came down
from Alaska."

Mr. Wang smiled indulgently. "I believe that was part
of her cover. It provided an excuse so that she wouldn't
have to talk to anyone. It allowed her to conceal her
French accent."

"Hortense?" I asked. "His maid was Hortense?"

"Leidesdorff's fiancée!" Monty exclaimed, slamming
his fist into his forehead. "Of course!"

Mr. Wang nodded. "Oscar always thought there was
more to the maid than historical references let on." He
shifted back into the metal chair, crossing one knobby
knee over the other. "Oscar didn't buy the story that Leidesdorff left New Orleans to soothe his broken heart. He
thought it was a bit too convenient that Leidesdorff's
fiancée was said to have died the night he left town."

Mr. Wang's right hand drifted slowly to the floor where
he dropped the spent cigar. "Oscar didn't think Leidesdorff was the type to give up so easily on something he
cared so much about. He speculated that Leidesdorff
figured out a way to secret his fiancée out of town with
him."

"That was Leidesdorff's big secret," I guessed. "What
he didn't want anyone to find out."

Mr. Wang uncrossed his legs and ground the cigar butt
with the heel of his shoe. He smiled wisely. "Leidesdorff
knew what the discovery of gold would do to this area.
What had once been a perfect hiding place was about to
fall under the spotlight of the world—and he would be at

the focus of it. His land up in the Sierra foothills ran right alongside Sutter's, where the first nuggets were discovered."

Monty stared avidly at Mr. Wang. "So what happened to her?" he demanded. "What happened to Hortense?"

"The last anyone saw of her was at Leidesdorff's funeral," I murmured.

Mr. Wang's voice rasped hoarsely. "Oscar guessed that the two of them had planned to slip out to sea and sail away, probably to an island in the Pacific. Leidesdorff traded with steamers that made regular trips to Hawaii to pick up sugar cane."

He tapped his thin lips with a cracked, nicotine-stained finger and said solemnly, "But something intervened, kept them from leaving. Something—went terribly wrong. I think that's what Oscar uncovered right before his death. That's the last clue we're looking for."

Chapter 31

MONTY AND I walked back towards Jackson Square without talking, our flaking footsteps the only conversation. Monty's favorite wingtips, I noted, would have to be retired.

The lights from Monty's studio shone ahead as we turned the last corner. I glanced over at him nervously. He had the disturbing look of a pending comment on his face, as if he had captured a thought that had been buzzing around in his brain and might, at any moment, expel it.

I sized up the distance to the front steps of the Green Vase. Thirty yards. Twenty yards.

I held my breath as we passed Frank Napis's darkened store. My right foot had broken even with the first crenelated column on the edge of the new brick front of the Green Vase—when Monty cleared his throat.

"Boy, am I tired," I said, yawning pointedly over the sound.

"Have you been thinking about my theory?" Monty asked, undeterred by the yawn.

I paused, ruefully eying the five remaining feet to the

front door. I edged slowly towards it, my hand searching my pocket for the tulip key.

"Which one?" I replied, gritting my teeth. My left foot slid backwards feeling for the first raised step.

"The Oscar theory," he said, and then annotated, "that he pulled a Leidesdorff."

Monty gulped as I glared at him, my eyes fuming, but he pressed on. "That he faked his death."

"No, Monty, I haven't," I said, my tired voice echoing the exhaustion within. I pulled out my key and engaged it in the lock. "I told you. That's ridiculous."

He swooped his index finger in front of my nose. "He's out there—I know it!"

"Good night, Monty," I muttered bitterly. I turned and walked inside, slamming the door shut behind me.

Something felt amiss in the darkened interior of the Green Vase. In my rush out the front door earlier that evening, I'd only managed to turn the tulip key in the lock. There hadn't been time to hook the extra padlock over the handle.

I had the uneasy feeling that someone had paid a visit while I'd been gone.

My eyes searched the showroom, panning over the dusty bookcases and looming wooden crates. And then I saw it—next to the slender green vase glowing in the dim light entering the room through the plastic-tarped windows.

Sitting suggestively on the cashier counter was a brand-new, unopened bottle of cat shampoo.

"Dilla," I thought with exasperation. "All right, all right," I mumbled. "I'll give him a bath."

I WOKE UP early the next morning, unsettled and out of sorts from a night of tossing and turning, still trying to ignore Monty's parting comments.

A bright sun hit the street outside, promising a gorgeous day ahead. I dug my running shoes out of a box of my belongings and headed out the front door, leaving a note for Ivan in case he came by to resume his brickwork before I returned.

Jackson Square was vacant, not surprising for such an early hour on a Tuesday morning. But as soon as I turned up Columbus, the fresh, clean sidewalks became tangled with energetic dog walkers, briskly rolling baby strollers, and sleepy waiters sucking down espressos out of steaming paper cups.

The city's network of electrically powered buses charged through the streets, menacing at any vehicle or pedestrian that dared to step into their path. Plucky taxicabs darted in and out behind the battered bumpers of the buses, taunting the metallic beasts. Overlooking this honking, hollering chaos, several wizened residents of Chinatown practiced tai chi on grassy stepped terraces cut into the housing-packed hillside, their peaceful meditations unheard by the snarl of traffic below.

I jogged along the sidewalk, winding through the melee of breakfast tables tumbling out of the tiny Italian bistros. The traffic became less aggressive as Columbus skirted down towards the edge of Fisherman's Wharf, and I peeled off to the swimming cove where William Ralston had taken his last, waterlogged breaths.

This bright, sunny morning, the area was already crowded with a screaming, squawking mix of kids and seagulls—wild legs running in all directions. I climbed halfway up the concrete steps to ensure a safe distance from both creatures and sat down for a rest.

The bay stretched out before me in a beautiful, lazy smile, its deep, blue surface reflecting the cornflower expanse of the sky. The sun baked down on the concrete steps, caressing my forehead with its soothing warmth.

The markers of a swimming lane bobbed in the water in front of me, but there were no takers this morning. I knew without testing that the beguiling water in the bay would be a frigid, wet-suit-requiring temperature.

I couldn't help but wonder about William Ralston and

his daily swims in this protected cove. What kind of person would subject himself, over and over again, to a dunking in that numbing, life-sucking cold? It seemed more a form of penitent self-flagellation than a health regimen.

I tried to imagine his short, tubby figure charging bravely into the chilly water, pushing it out in front of him as he waded in up to his waist. I watched him dive under, the paralyzing freeze of the water blanketing around his torpedo-shaped body, curling its cold, icy fingers around his heart, clamping down on the straining muscles as they struggled to keep pace with the pounding waves.

Ralston had been out near the edge of the cordoned swimming area, almost past the last buoy, when he'd seized up. A crowd of people had collected on the shore, shouting for the lifeguard, speculating on the identity of the victim, watching as a rescuer pulled the lifeless, barrel-chested body up into a small boat.

In the days that followed, the city had run wild with rumors on the cause of Ralston's death: suicide, poison, the unrelenting pressure of the scandal-seeking press. The findings of the coroner's jury that his death was due to natural causes did little to stem the speculation.

For all of his success, Ralston had been a troubled, isolated figure. The ouster from his failing bank was but the last tragedy of his fortune-filled life.

Early on in his career, he had fallen madly in love with the granddaughter of shipping magnate Cornelius Vanderbilt, a young woman named Louisa Thorne. Ralston succeeded in obtaining her family's approval of their courtship, and the happy couple giddily began to plan their wedding. But not long after their engagement, Louisa fell gravely ill and, after several bed-ridden months, died days before the scheduled betrothal.

Ralston never recovered from the loss; he carried a miniature portrait of Louisa in the front breast pocket of his suit—every day for the rest of his life. When he eventually married, his consolation bride was the niece of a close friend. Built on this foundation, the marriage was destined for strife. His wife's feelings of neglect and abandonment were only compounded by the christening of several of the Ralston children as namesakes for the long-deceased Louisa.

Ralston's other passion—second only to the ever-present ghost of Louisa—was his beloved city of San Francisco. Even as his bank began to founder, he decided to finance the construction of a five-star hotel that would cement her standing in the world as a first class city.

Ralston obsessed over every detail of the aptly named Palace Hotel, bedecking the windows with silk hangings and the marble floors with finely woven carpets. He mined far-flung forests for the best teak and mahogany panelling. No detail was too small; no expense too extravagant.

But now, as the icy water swirled around him, even that dream was slipping through his manacled fingertips. His pending bankruptcy threatened not only his bank, but the yet to be completed Palace Hotel as well.

In my mind's eye, I saw him drop further and further into the deep silence of the circling, scavenging water, sinking under the weight of his own despair.

A scrum of screaming children scaled the stairs, racing towards my seated position. I stood up and continued my jog.

My running shoes followed the edge of the bay, treading on an asphalt trail that took me up a heart-pounding hill into an abandoned army base that had been turned into a public reserve. Towards the crest of the hill, the asphalt path ducked under a dark tunnel of cypress trees. For several strides, I was hidden beneath a canopy of leafy, sea-infused green.

As I hit the downward slope on the opposite side, the trail broke out into an open field. I rolled down the path, tracking along the water's edge as my route skirted the long line of the Marina Green.

The wind swept across the dandelion-infested field, buffeting a stone head that stared out from a concrete obelisk. I cut across the weedy grass to inspect it more closely.

William Ralston's round, bearded face protruded from a relief set in the base of the skyward-pointing monument. The discolorations of the stone made his wide, balding forehead look sunburnt and wind-chapped.

Ralston's memorial marker had been positioned with his back to the scenic bay—so that he faced the skyline of his beloved city. Underneath his portrait, the glowing tribute read:

HE BLAZED THE PATH FOR SAN FRANCISCO'S
ONWARD MARCH TO ACHIEVEMENT AND RENOWN.

I left Ralston's proud gaze and crossed over into Crissy Field, a public park fronting the famed Presidio.

The wind picked up in intensity as I headed closer and closer to the foot of the Golden Gate Bridge, my feet crunching rhythmically on the cinder pathway. The whipping air streamed around me, lifting up the damp, sweaty roots on the underside of my head, softly cooling my overheating skin. A thousand troubled thoughts soared out of my head, numbed by the constant caresses of the wind.

The path turned to pavement as I started the last stretch to my destination. Waves crashed along the rocky embankment, foaming up, licking at my heels.

I approached the gaping mouth of the bay, and the city slipped from consciousness. The wild periphery of the Pacific roared around me, a mystical, untamed force. A voice made of wind and crashing water pealed across the span, pummeling me with its unwavering certainty, its overbearing confidence.

I remembered a line from Oscar's Leidesdorff story. "This is a place where anything is possible. You can do, or become, whatever or *whoever* you want."

I dug my feet into the pavement, desperately resisting the seductive coaxing of the wind.

But I was too weak to repel it.

The mirrored surface of the bay winked mischievously as my thoughts plunged down into the mire of Monty's persistent theory.

Chapter 32

MONTY'S RIGHT FOOT kicked out from under the red brick archway in front of the entrance to the Green Vase as I turned the corner into Jackson Square. His foot was encased in a brand-new, brown leather wingtip. The rest of Monty followed the foot.

I nearly turned and ran the other way when I saw him.

"Ah, there you are," he greeted me, a look of relief on his face.

"Don't you ever work in your studio?" I asked, wondering how long he had been standing in my doorway.

He didn't answer my question.

"I was thinking," he said, touching a long finger to his forehead. "We should make a visit to Mission Dolores, the chapel where your friend Leidesdorff was supposed to have been buried. Come on, I've got to be back in a couple of hours."

I threw my hands up and looked down at my sweaty running gear.

"All right," he conceded. "I'll give you ten minutes for a shower."

"Gee, thanks," I said, brushing past him. I un-hitched the padlock and turned the tulip key in the door.

FORTY-FIVE MINUTES later, Monty and I stood at the corner of 16th and Dolores, staring up at a towering church.

"Not bad digs for a final resting place," Monty said, standing on the sidewalk, gawking up at the stately building. "Maybe I should get on their waiting list."

Cream-colored walls rose up in a cluster of dome-capped turrets. Each dome formed a smooth onion shape, embossed around the bulb with bright, turquoise tiles.

Spanning across the turrets, the stone figure of a penitent priest presided over an ornamented façade. The priest's head bent down towards the pavement, positioned so that he could whisper his benediction to the congregation as they exited the church. The statue perched fearlessly on its parapet, several stories above the street, bathed in sunlight.

"They're not accepting any new applicants," I informed a disappointed Monty. "There aren't any active cemeteries within the city limits. Most people are buried in Colma, a couple of miles to the south."

Monty eyed me curiously.

I bit my lip, staring up at the haloed priest. "That's where Oscar is."

Monty cleared his throat and asked tentatively, "Did you have to pick out his plot?"

I shook my head. Still looking skyward, I replied, "Oscar had already purchased one."

I set off briskly down the street before Monty could start in on another Oscar death theory.

"Anyway, that isn't the location of Leidesdorff's grave," I called out over my shoulder as I pointed to a smaller building next to the turreted church we'd been admiring. "This is the original Mission."

"A little more humble," Monty said. He followed me

down the block to the entrance of the second structure. "You sure I couldn't even get in here?"

We stood in front of a demure, two-story building. Wide round columns of white-washed adobe supported a red tile roof. A simple cross rose from the apogee of the narrow pitch. Underneath, a line of cream-colored bells hung serenely in the shadowed belfry.

Monty tripped along at my heels as I mounted the steps to the entrance.

The visitor's center was manned by a harried-looking priest who was trying to organize a boisterous group of second-graders for a tour.

The priest's graying hair was clipped short, close to his scalp. He wore iron-rimmed spectacles on his clean-shaven, lightly tanned face. His trim physique had been carefully packaged in belted slacks and a button-down oxford.

As Monty and I walked up, it was clear that this very controlled, very respectable figure was on the verge of becoming completely unglued by the unruly tangle of children in the staging area.

"Children! Children!" he began, a pinched expression on his face as he tried to speak over the din of chatter. "Good morning, children, I'm Father Alfonso . . ."

I tried to catch the priest's eye to see if we could join the tour he was trying to start. I pulled out the ten dollar entrance fee for two adults and waved it inquiringly in the air. "Can we add on?" I asked.

"I suppose," he said wearily, reaching for the bill.

The priest opened a pair of heavy, wooden doors, and a waist-high tide of children swarmed through the opening. Monty and I followed the rowdy crowd inside.

We were standing at the back of the original Mission chapel, a long hall of a space with cream walls and a wooden ceiling. At the far opposite end, beyond the rows of roughly hewn pews, an altar of brightly-painted saints looked down upon a roped-off section of the sanctuary.

The school children were anxious to explore the color-

ful display at the front of the chapel, but the priest strad-
dled the open space between the pews, fending off their
forward progress.

Hurriedly, he began to sketch over the Mission's historical highlights. "Now, then. This is one of the few remaining
intact missions within the state of California. Quiet, please.
The ceiling is made up of the original redwood beams,
strapped together with rawhide strips . . ."

Monty and I scanned the ceiling as he spoke. The redwood beams had been painted in sharp, repeating, geomet-
ric shapes with a jarring combination of scarlet red, burnt
orange, and mint green. The mesmerizing effect of the roof
drew attention away from the simple clay tiles of the floor,
and it was a moment before I noticed the small, rectangular
inlay tucked up against the wall, almost hidden by a dingy
display case holding a scattering of religious artifacts and
an oil painting of the Virgin Mary.

Text had been etched into the gravestone:

WILLIAM ALEXANDER
LEIDESDORFF
DIED MAY 18, 1848

I stared at the worn concrete marker, wondering what,
if anything, lay beneath.

Monty apparently spied it a second later, evidenced by
the poking joust I received in the small of my back. I turned
to administer a reproaching scowl, but found myself staring
instead at the back wall of the chapel.

Monty had kneeled down to engage in a silent but animated conversation with a chubby, curly-haired boy.
Monty pointed his long finger towards the front of the
chapel, and the child's bulging cheeks grinned enthusiastically.

The priest glared primly at Monty as he continued, the
prickling in his voice registering his consternation. "The
Mission has one of only two remaining cemeteries within
the city of San Francisco . . ."

"Pssst," Monty hissed at me.

The irritated priest sped faster and faster through his mandatory list of facts. "Buried within the chapel is early civic leader William Leidesdorff, the Noe family . . ."

I never heard who else was buried underneath the chapel, because Monty began to buzz in my right ear. "I have a cunning plan—just wait for the signal."

I looked back over my shoulder, this time with alarm. Monty had shuffled to the back of the group, next to a spiraling metal staircase that led to a small choir loft in the belfry above us. Thick, hemp-like ropes hung down from the ceiling next to Monty's right hand. They were presumably attached to the bells we'd seen from the street outside.

The priest turned to indicate towards the altar at the front of the chapel, and Monty nodded to the chubby second-grader standing next to me. Monty reached over and yanked down on the hemp rope, setting off an ear-splitting, tintinnabular explosion.

The tightly wound priest uncoiled several inches into the air as the entire squadron of energized second-graders, led by Monty's pudgy accomplice, charged down the aisle to the front of the church.

The priest's horrified shriek echoed through the chamber. Monty poked me in the side of the stomach and smirked, "That's the signal."

I knelt down and ran my hands over the smooth, concrete stone marking Leidesdorff's grave, wondering how much time Monty's little caper was going to buy us.

As my fingers felt along the edges of the headstone, I realized that a narrow, almost undetectable gap ran along its edge with the clay floor tiles. The stone was loose in its fittings, I noted, wiggling it back and forth.

From the noise at the front of the room, it appeared that the children were demanding all of the priest's attention. "Keep an eye up front," I instructed Monty as I searched my shoulder bag for a nail file.

Monty's face broke into an impish, schoolboy's grin.

He murmured to me out of the corner of his mouth as he
kept his eyes fixed on the front of the chapel. "All clear at
the moment. The father is pulling one of the blessed cher-
ubs out of the baptismal enclosure. It looks like the kid is
about to receive a holy dunking."

Monty glanced quickly down at me. "How's it going?"

I found my file and fed it into the tiny crevice between
the stone marker and the floor tiles. I began sawing it back
and forth, trying to free the stone enough to pick it up.
Despite its small size, it was heavier than I had realized.

Monty returned to his watch. "Pull it out. Pull it out!"
he whispered urgently. "The whole gang's coming back
this way."

I slipped the file back into my shoulder bag and
straightened up, pretending to study one of the tarnished
gold objects inside the display case. A laughing line of
children charged down the center aisle of pews, closely
followed by the frazzled priest. We watched as they sped
out through a side door in the chapel and raced down the
path to the cemetery. The priest paused long enough to
grab a small bullhorn off of a counter before continuing
his pursuit.

I dropped back down to the floor and quickly reinserted the nail file as Father Alfonso's frayed voice began squawking out of the bullhorn. The concrete marker
shifted upwards about half an inch, and I gripped my
fingers around the raised edge. Slowly, painfully, it began
to give. I winced as a distinctly audible grating sound knit
the air with the lifting stone.

"A little help here," I said bitingly to Monty.

He knelt down, and together we pulled the stone the
rest of the way out of its nesting place. Underneath was a
flat, metal surface. In the center sat a keyhole fashioned in
the same decorative detailing as the front door to the
Green Vase. I pulled the tulip key out of my pocket, slid it
into the hole, and turned. The key engaged, and I pulled
up on the hinged floor piece.

A cool, musty smell oozed up from the black space below. I had opened the lid to a small rectangular box that sunk lengthwise into the floor. I leaned over the hole, peering inside.

"What do you see?" Monty asked, his face taut with suspense. "What's in there?"

I grimaced, reached my hand in, and pulled out a tarnished set of gold teeth.

"Ugh!" Monty gulped.

The bullhorned voice grew louder. Father Alfonso had apparently circled through the cemetery and was back in the visitor's center where we'd come in.

"Get in there and distract him until I can get this put back together," I hissed as I slipped the gold teeth into my pocket and slammed the lid of the box shut.

Monty's face paled in panic. "How about *you* go distract him, and *I'll* put the grave back together?" he said, smiling weakly.

"Hurry up!" I replied, shoving him towards the door. I knelt back to the floor and pulled on the key, trying to release it from the lock.

Monty winced and slid reluctantly through the doors to the visitor center. His voice carried into the chapel as I continued to jiggle the key, trying to free it.

"Ah, Father Alfonso," Monty said nervously. "There you are. I was hoping to ask you a couple of questions . . ."

I waited through a long, awkward pause as Monty struggled to come up with a discussion topic to distract the priest. I shook my head as his strained voice filled the void with, "I've been considering a career in the church."

The lock finally spit the key out of its grasp, and I fell backwards onto the tile floor. I began heaving at the concrete marker, trying to position it over its recessed position in the floor.

Monty's singsong falsetto echoed through the door to the visitor's center. "It must be so inspirational, so peaceful, to spend your days in this beautiful environment . . . devoted to the betterment of our fellow brothers and sisters."

"Well," Father Alfonso replied in an irritated voice, "some days are more blessed than others."

The headstone grated against the clay tiles. My fingers burned as I eased it over the recess and slid it into place. Through the wooden doors, I heard the priest offer uneasily, "I could get you some informational brochures if you're serious about this."

I crept across the room and peeked through the vertical crack between the swinging doors. The priest had pulled open a drawer and was flipping through a stack of promotional material, looking for a suitable pamphlet for Monty's potential career change. Monty was slouched against the front wall of the office, as far away as possible from the counter, with one hand plastered over his face.

"Do you have anything in there on the chapel?" Monty asked tentatively. "How about—the people who are buried in it? Say, William Leidesdorff?"

Father Alfonso pushed his wire rimmed glasses up against his eyes. He looked suspiciously at Monty. "Why do you ask?"

"Just a casual interest," Monty stammered through his fingers.

Father Alfonso glared furiously at Monty. "It's you, isn't it?! I knew there was something familiar about your face!"

Monty began sliding along the wall towards the door that led to the street, his face blushing as he stammered, "I . . . I . . . I don't know what you're talking about."

The priest reached back into the drawer, pulled out a brown, furry object, and waved it tauntingly at Monty. "Did you come back for this? You dropped it Saturday night on your way out the door—running from the police!"

Monty flattened himself against the exit to the outside. His right hand flailed behind his back, looking for the door handle. "Father, you've got me confused with someone else," he squeaked.

Father Alfonso's face crunched up into a sneer. "No,

it's definitely you. What kind of a degenerate gets their kicks trying to dig up a hundred and fifty year old grave? I thought I'd seen everything, ministering in this town . . ."

Monty's hand found the handle, and the door swung open. He launched himself through it and leapt down the steps to the pavement.

Father Alfonso looked disgusted as he dropped the fake mustache on the counter, picked up the bullhorn, and walked out the back door to the cemetery to round up the school children. I slipped through the chapel doors and picked up the fake mustache on my way out of the visitor's center.

On the steps outside, I watched the back of Monty's fleeing figure as he sprinted down the street, his suit coat flapping out behind him.

Sighing, I pulled the tarnished gold teeth from my pocket and studied them in the brighter outdoor light.

Clenched between the upper and lower jaws was the dried petal of a tulip.

Chapter 33

I CAUGHT UP with Monty about ten minutes later in the subterranean waiting platform of the BART station. Grudgingly, I sat down on a circular stone bench next to him.

He stared at the grimy wall of the empty train tunnel, his thin face frozen, his pale green eyes immobile.

"So," I said conversationally, "you'd already made one attempt at Leidesdorff's grave."

Monty sighed heavily as he turned to look at me, his face imploring. "I got the headstone up, but I couldn't get into the box underneath. Not without the key." His eyes gleamed. "What do you think Oscar meant by the gold teeth?"

I tilted back my head and stared at the arched concrete ceiling. Nothing from Monty, I thought, would surprise me at this point. "You didn't think the priest would recognize you?" I asked wearily.

Monty leaned towards me, pumping his eyebrows. "I was testing a theory, of sorts."

I closed my eyes and gritted my teeth.

"Look, it all goes back to Leidesdorff," Monty said as

he stood up and began pacing around the circular bench. "After he faked his death, he remained here in San Francisco, in plain sight—but in disguise. Leidesdorff must have shaved off those lamb chop sideburns. People had never seen what his face looked like underneath. I studied his picture on that plaque in the financial district. He would have looked completely different clean shaven."

"Father Alfonso recognized *you*—without your mustache," I said critically.

"Ah," Monty acknowledged, still circling the bench. "Unfortunately, Father Alfonso caught a glimpse of me unmasked. It was in the dark, and there was a lot of running, so I thought it was possible he didn't get a clear look at my face." Monty waved his hands dismissively. "That's not the point. The theory still stands."

I sighed, irritated, as Monty bent down towards me and whispered loudly, "What if Oscar did it in reverse?" He nodded his head up and down emphatically. "What if Oscar *added* facial hair? What if he's walking around Jackson Square, right in front of us?"

"I would recognize my uncle," I replied testily. "Even if he were wearing lamb chop sideburns."

Monty smiled slyly. "Not lamb chops." He took the fake mustache out of my fingers and plastered it over his top lip. Vamping it up and down, he said, "What if he's wearing a mustache?" He winked mischievously. "And a hat."

THE LIGHTS WERE on in the antiques store next to the Green Vase when we rounded the corner into Jackson Square. Frank Napis, it seemed, had returned.

Monty bounded ahead to the steps of Frank's store. "Look at this, Frank's back!" he called out. "I'll introduce you." He glanced back at me, his eyes twinkling. "Unless you've already met."

I stumbled to a stop on the sidewalk. The accumulated weight of Monty's endless theories bore down on my shoulders, crunching me beneath.

My mind flew back to the cemetery and the deep gaping hole that had swallowed Oscar's casket. I sank with him into the dirt, until the mounds on either side blocked out the sun. Shovelfuls of earth pushed down on my chest as one by one the layers fell in around me. My fingernails clawed at the blackness, scratching, grasping for air—until someone grabbed my hand and pulled me up.

"Come on," Monty said, dragging me towards the store.

I bit my lip as I followed Monty up the steps and through the shining glass entrance.

The entire front of Napis's boutique was constructed out of seamless, floor-to-ceiling glass panels that were so sparkling clear, it felt like you could walk straight through them. But as the door swung shut behind me, closing off the crisp spring air of the sidewalk, the impermeable integrity of the glass became immediately apparent. The swarmy atmosphere of the store was heavy with the slithering scents of sandalwood and hibiscus. Incense sticks burned on a pedestal next to the door, enhancing the smoky, stifling aura of the room.

I stepped tentatively forward onto a red and gold braided rug as the lonely whine of a sitar floated eerily through the open rafters.

Monty disappeared into the store, ducking behind a free-standing wall and into a maze of partitions that branched throughout the showroom. I stayed put, nervously staring at the floor, my head swimming from the heavily scented room.

"Frank," Monty called out from somewhere behind the wall. "There you are. Come on out. There's someone here I want you to meet."

There was a startling familiarity to the grunt that sounded in response.

My stomach swirled with tension as the sounds of Monty's slick-soled shoes were followed by a heavy shuffling. Reluctantly, I looked up from the floor, waiting for Frank Napis to emerge from the back of the store.

A decorative chunk of plaster hung on the wall in front

of me. Track lighting shone down on a ceramic relief full of frenetic, multi-armed deities. A riot of wildly gesturing limbs poked out of the surface, as if they might grab onto my collar and drag me into the chaos of their twisting melee.

Monty cleared his throat, and I slowly turned around, my eyes sucking in the sight of the man standing next to him. Nothing in what I saw quelled the questions circling my stomach.

The physical features of the man could best be described as nondescript. His eyes, nose, and mouth were all unremarkably bland. His face was like the surface of sand on a beach—worn down by years of erosion into a soft mold that reflected not its own content but only that of the most recent wave.

Fluttering on this bleak landscape was an enormous carrot-colored creature, stretching at least four inches across. Each strand of hair had been precisely waxed, combed, and wound into place. The mustache seemed to exist independent of the face it was attached to. It quivered as its owner walked over to greet me, as if it might take flight at any moment.

The voice of Frank Napis cut through the silence. It was stilted, halting, and yet—I felt certain I had heard it somewhere before. "You must be my new neighbor."

I reached out to shake his offered hand, studying his eccentric attire. He wore a linen safari suit with sturdy, knee-high boots—the sort, I imagined, a British colonial might have worn while hunting wild game in Africa. A thick leather bullwhip hung at his belted waist, and a blue silk scarf tufted out of the neck opening of his shirt. Around his head, the mysterious folds of a turban swirled towards the ceiling, dramatically increasing the man's height.

It wasn't Oscar, I kept repeating to myself, trying to drown out the questioning voice wiggling through my inner ear. It couldn't be.

"So, Frank," Monty bellowed awkwardly, pounding the man on the back. "How was your trip?"

"Ah, Montgomery," the man said, rolling the word so that he came to a full stop between 'mont' and 'gomery'. I stared at the mustache, waiting for each syllable to be released. "It was beautiful in Bombay."

"Isn't it the monsoon season?" Monty asked pleasantly.

"No," the man replied, drawing out the two letters. His diction sharpened with the repeat. "No, no." I could barely see the lips underneath the broad mustache. He pursed them together in a narrow pucker and then continued. "It was just hitting the southern tip of the coast as I left." He paused, stroking the mustache as if calming an excitable pet. "Of course, a little bit of water never hurt anyone."

Frank Napis and his mustache turned to address me. "You're Oscar's niece, aren't you?" The mustache beamed, the waxen strands crinkling under the centripetal force of his smile.

"Yes," I said, shifting uncomfortably in the stifling atmosphere of the showroom, unable to focus on anything other than the man with the imposing mustache.

"Everyone in Jackson Square has been eagerly anticipating your taking over the Green Vase." He made as if to wink at me, but it came off more like a nervous twitch. "Perhaps no one more than me."

Frank Napis drummed his fingertips across his substantial stomach. The front buttons of his linen suit strained against the pressure of its interior contents. The mammoth mustache apparently provided little impediment to the influx of food.

"I was so relieved when I got home last night and saw that you'd already begun work on the renovations," he continued.

"Yes, it's coming right along," I replied nervously.

I searched desperately for a definitive characteristic that I could point to—one on which I could firmly plant a conclusion that this wasn't some alter-embodiment of my deceased uncle. But the figure of Frank Napis was a dissatisfying muddle.

I turned away from the strange man and stared down at a

dark wooden table displaying an army of elephants, lions, and peacocks. The humanized animals brandished knives and swords as they charged across their battlefield on gold-painted chariots. A highly polished, fat-bellied Buddha posed serenely in the midst of the chaotic scene, his wide, beaming smile sealing up the answer to the question I wouldn't let myself ask.

Monty's short attention span had run its course, and he'd begun perambulating around the showroom. His head weaved in and out of view as he threaded his way through the partitions.

"So, Frank," Monty's voice called out from a hidden position on the far side of the shop. "Have you heard about the event coming up at the Palace Hotel on Friday? Dilla's holding a charity auction."

"Yes," Frank replied evenly, his eyes wandering across the room, following the clicking sounds of Monty's shoes. "I'm familiar with the pieces she's putting up."

Monty's head swung around a nearby corner. He'd apparently latched onto some sort of ceremonial headdress. An odd collection of dyed feathers and dead animal skin hung over his ears, swaying as he spoke. "Oh? The cat jewelry?"

"Yes, of course. The Leidesdorff jewelry," Frank said calmly.

"The cat costumes?" I asked, my forehead crinkling as I tried to understand.

"Yes, they belonged to William Leidesdorff's maid," Frank replied, his mustache twitching.

The blue eyes brewed devilishly beneath the turban. "It seems she was very fond of her kitty cats. She used to dress them up in costumes."

Chapter 34

"LEIDESDORFF HAD CATS?" Monty exclaimed.

Frank Napis cleared his throat. "I believe they belonged to his maid," he said patiently. "The cats apparently sailed with them here from New Orleans."

The mustache flicked under the influence of a jarring facial tic. "They were an unusual looking pair—white with orange highlights. Some sort of Siamese/Tabby mix."

I felt my face freeze over as Frank Napis stood there, rubbing his protruding belly, studying me curiously. Monty hung off the nearest partition, his jaw dropped to the floor.

The scene was interrupted by the rumbling sound of Ivan's truck pulling up in front of the Green Vase.

"That'll be Ivan," I said, struggling to find my voice. "He's the contractor." I cleared my throat. "I should go check in with him." I began sliding towards the front door, dragging a still apoplectic Monty along with me.

Frank relieved Monty of the headdress as he followed us towards the exit. "It was a great pleasure to meet you," he said, his expression providing no insight into his emotions. "Thank you for stopping by."

A breath of fresh air hit my face as I pushed Monty through the front door. I was about to follow him to the sidewalk when Frank's voice called out, "Oh, did you have a chance to look into the gutter issue?"

I turned back to the showroom, my overloaded sinuses taking another blast of sandalwood. "No need to worry," I said assuringly. "Ivan will be putting new ones up later this week."

Frank Napis stared at me strangely, his mustache curling like a cashew as his blue eyes bored into me. "You might want to check behind us in the alley, dear, before he gets started. The building in the lot that backs up to ours is under renovation. There's a chance they might have dug something up to cause the leak."

I TUMBLED DOWN the steps to the sidewalk. A last puff of the heavy sandalwood aroma surged out as the door swung shut behind me.

Monty stood on the sidewalk, dazedly muttering over and over again, "Leidesdorff had cats."

Ivan waved a greeting, then lowered the tailgate to his truck and began pulling tools out of the back. I turned the tulip key in the lock on the front door and walked inside.

Monty followed me in, circling through the store like a buzzard. "Maybe it's the Leidesdorff cats in the painting."

Rupert hopped down the stairs, summoned by the sound of Monty's voice. Crumbs of cat food hung under his chin as he poked his head around the corner. Monty picked up the gold-headed cane and pointed it dramatically at Rupert.

"You!" Monty exclaimed. "You've got some explaining to do there, Mister." Monty bent down towards Rupert, who sat on the floor smiling up at him. "What are you doing in Dilla's picture—hiding in the tulips?"

Monty spun around and parried the cane in my direction. "Hey, where did you get Rupert and Isabella, anyway?" he demanded.

I leaned against the cashier counter, remembering back a year ago.

It was a dark, rainy Saturday. I'd arrived at Oscar's for one of our regularly scheduled dinners.

Shivering, I rang the bell at the front door. Oscar called grumpily down from the window above. "You've got a key don't you? You know my knees can't take those stairs!"

Grinning, I let myself in. I crossed the crowded, dusty storeroom and hiked up to the kitchen. Oscar was bent over his stove, concentrating on a pot of frying chicken. Without looking up, he raised a grease-splattered hand in the air to acknowledge my arrival.

I pulled out a seat at the kitchen table. As I leaned across to pour myself a glass of water, I noticed a small cardboard box in the corner of the room. The flaps to the lid had been cut off; something appeared to be moving inside.

Eyeing Oscar's still turned back, I eased up in my chair so that I could look inside the box. Two small, white cats blinked up at me.

"What have you got here, Oscar?" I asked, bemused.

Oscar grunted from his skillet. "Found them in the alley this afternoon. They must have been abandoned. Figure I'll drop 'em off at the pound on Monday."

I circled the table and knelt down at the box. The cats matched each other in coloring—white coats with peachy-orange highlights—but they were opposites in physique.

The female of the pair was slender and sleek with long, gangly legs. Her sharp, blue eyes looked up at me expectantly as she stood up on her hind legs, reaching for the top edge of the box. She pushed her head against my hand when I reached in to pet her.

The second one, a male, sat back on his wide, fluffy rump and gazed up at me curiously. I reached over to scratch his head, but he flopped over onto his back, exposing his plump, round belly.

"They're awfully cute, Oscar," I called out, still rubbing the offered belly. "Don't you need a couple of cats around the store?"

I could hardly hear his mussitating grumble over the sizzling skillet. "Scraggly, flea bitten creatures . . . look like overgrown rats . . ."

"They're awfully clean for having been in the alley," I said, holding the female in my arms.

She purred appreciatively as Oscar muttered, "I never would have thought it'd be that hard to wash a cat."

Monty tapped me on the shoulder with the gold-headed cane. "Where do you go when you enter these trances?" he asked.

"I got the cats from Oscar," I said, the implication dawning on me for the first time.

Chapter 35

THE JARRING *BLEEP-BLEEP* of my alarm clock woke me early the next morning. I leapt out of the bed and into the wee hours of Wednesday. Rupert cracked open a condemning eye before dropping his head back down into the heap of blankets.

Isabella followed as I shrugged on a sweatshirt and slipped down to the kitchen. Her sharp eyes interrogated me as I grabbed the wide beam flashlight and descended the next flight to the showroom.

"Wrao," she admonished.

"Don't worry. I'll be careful," I replied.

I creaked open the iron-framed door and peeked out into a dark, pre-dawn Jackson Square. The windows on the opposite side of the street were dark—ensuring, I hoped, that Monty wouldn't be following me this time.

I rounded the corner past Frank Napis's glass-fronted store and stepped into the narrow alley that angled behind it. My bleary eyes blinked in the darkness as I flicked on the flashlight and started down the narrow passage, flanked on either side by steep, brick walls.

A couple of steps into the alley, I raised the flashlight's beam to a historical marker. It was set into the wall of the building that housed the store belonging to Frank Napis's next door neighbor.

The plaque commemorated the liquor store that had occupied the premises during the Gold Rush era.

Built in 1866 and occupied by A.P. Hotaling & Co., this building housed the largest liquor repository on the West Coast. It survived the 1906 earthquake and fire due to a mile long fire hose laid from Fisherman's Wharf over Telegraph Hill by the U.S. Navy. This prompted the famous doggerel by Charles Field:

> If, as they say, God spanked the town
> for being over frisky,
> Why did he burn the churches down
> and save Hotaling's whisky?

All of the whisky had been drunk up long ago. The barrels had been replaced by a collection of fine Persian rugs, mahogany tea tables, and puffy, poodle-impersonating lamp fixtures.

I panned the light down the alley to a fork that branched off behind Frank Napis's store. Treading softly through the early morning darkness, I turned the corner leading to the back side of the Green Vase.

It was easy to see why Frank had blamed the leak on Oscar's gutters. Oscar had applied the same approach to maintenance of the outside of his building as he had to the inside. White plastic elbow joints connected an odd collection of metal piping materials that were pinned precariously to the side of the building.

Next door, strong, solid iron neatly lined the edge of the roof. Frank's gutters were aligned with flawless precision to the windows and eaves. Every inch of the building stood in stern rebuke to the crumbling exterior of the

Green Vase. Even the small dumpster outside was parked in perfect parallel with the back stoop.

Yawning, I turned to face the opposite side of the alley and the lot that Frank had suggested I check out as a potential source of the infamous water leak.

The scavenged building was still in the deconstruction stage of its renovation process. Large swaths of thick plastic and blue tarp covered its empty window slots. A breeze wheezed through the cracks, gently pushing the coverings in and out, as if the building were breathing on a ventilator, recovering from the trauma of its recent surgery.

"The work's been stopped for several weeks now," Monty had told me, speaking in his authoritative, renovation-expert voice. "I think they're hung up on some sort of permit issue."

Halfway around the far side of the building, I found a loose tarp and pulled it back, revealing the gutted interior. The building had been stripped to its framing. The flooring was carved out down to the concrete basement. A hollow shell was all that remained—a shadow of the previous self, patiently waiting to be remade.

The first edges of daylight were beginning to lift up the corners of the surrounding darkness. I glanced furtively up and down the alley; then I pulled the tarp back to its widest position and stepped gingerly inside.

Coilings of ripped out electrical wire and shards of broken pipe were strewn across the concrete floor. Rusted nails jutted out of splintery beams. I puzzled at the fresh bird droppings that seemed to spot every surface before craning my neck up to the scalped rafters. A ten-foot square opening gaped in the center of the roof.

This location seemed a much more likely spot for Oscar to have found a Leidesdorff-related relic than the construction site Ivan had taken me to across town. The landfill under this stretch of Jackson Square had been filled in soon after the Gold Rush started, in the years immediately following Leidesdorff's alleged death.

I walked across the concrete floor, hopping over shovels, jackhammers, and an empty lunchbox, and made my way towards the corner that ran parallel to Frank Napis's store.

The concrete basement in this section of the building had been torn up. Huge chunks of pummelled stone were piled next to a gaping hole, which was at least ten feet wide. I leaned over the gap, peering down into the damp dirt.

The morning's sun continued to roll up into the sky, but this back corner of the building was still darkened in shadow. Circling my flashlight around the dug-up opening in the concrete, something in the dirt below caught my eye. I crawled over the edge and eased myself down into the hole to get a better look.

As my feet sank into the soggy bottom of the small pit, I saw the likely cause of the seepage into Frank Napis's basement. A broken water main poked out of a small bubbling pool of water and mud. It looked as if the diggers of this hole had hit the pipe. They had been distracted, I suspected, by the sudden appearance of a ship's bow in the bottom of the pit.

I crouched down on my knees, running my hand along the three feet of exposed planking. The boards were rough and splintered—frangible from the years of underground decay.

I scanned back and forth along the stretch of planking, confused by the angle of the structure. The boat, I finally realized, was upside down. It must have capsized and sunk here back when this lot of land was still under water.

I slid my fingertips around the bulging edge of one of the boards and pulled gently upward. The board gave easily, falling away from the boat and into my hands. It was as if it had been previously removed and simply reinserted into the open seam. The boards on either side of it came up just as easily.

I piled the removed planking on the floor of the pit and crept up to the opening in the boat. The missing boards provided about a foot and a half wide gap along the exposed portion of the bow.

Someone had scraped away much of the dirt—now a wet, pasty mud—that had been packed in around the up-ended interior of the boat. I stared into the inky blackness, trying to make out the faint outline of the object that had been unearthed inside. Trembling, I raised my flashlight towards the opening.

The pale, nacreous gleam of a human skull leered up at me.

I jumped away from the boat, stifling a scream. My feet slid on the slippery mud, and I found myself sitting on the dark bottom of the hole, staring at the boat's hull and its long, rectangular opening.

I shook my head, trying to clear the terrifying image from my panicked vision. After several thirsting gulps of damp, earthy air, I steeled myself to take another look. Had *this* been the construction site that had lured Oscar's interest? Had the hull of this boat shielded the last vital clue that Oscar had unearthed prior to his death?

A tight clenching in my heart, I crept back towards the boat. Wincing, I aimed the flashlight down into the hole and willed myself to look inside.

Enough of the mud had been scraped away from the corpse so that I could tell that it lay on its back, stretched out along the length of the bow.

I'd never seen a human body in that state of decay before—the flesh rotted away leaving nothing but bone. I was amazed at how much expression could still be communicated by the skeletal form. The corpse conveyed a frantic, terrified expression. The jaws of the mouth gaped open as if struggling for air. The arms were thrown outward, pounding helplessly against the walls of the up-ended boat.

Shreds of a faded leather coat draped from the bones. At the neck, the frayed edge of a cloth shirt peeked out from underneath the deteriorated leather collar. I panned the flashlight over to the nearest bony wrist.

The slightest sliver of the cloth shirt lined the sleeve of the leather coat.

Biting down on my lip almost to the point of drawing blood, I slid my hand into the hole and reached towards the skeletal wrist. The fabric of the rotted leather coat rolled like felt in my fingers as I cautiously slid it back.

The cufflink that had been pinned into the shirt was missing—someone had removed it. But its imprint was still visible from the years of underground decay spent laying against the fabric.

The cufflink had stained a clearly visible watermark on the cloth—in the shape of a three-petaled tulip.

Chapter 36

ISABELLA CURLED PROTECTIVELY around my legs as I stepped inside the Green Vase, my mind swirling from the morning's excursion down the alley.

Something in the Leidesdorff story circulating Jackson Square was not adding up. If the corpse under the boat was Leidesdorff, he had not lived long past the fake funeral procession to the Mission Dolores chapel. The Jackson Square neighborhood sat on top of one of the first sections of the bay to be reclaimed by landfill. That pushed Leidesdorff's date of death back to the 1848–49 time frame.

I searched through my memory of Mr. Wang's comments from the night I traveled through the tunnel and found him smoking in his flower shop. There had been rumors and speculations about Leidesdorff for years, but what had convinced Oscar of the story?

I heard Mr. Wang's thin, reedy voice scratching through his cigarette smoke. Leidesdorff's grave had turned up empty during the restoration work on the Mission Dolores chapel—but that was almost a hundred years ago. Oscar's more recent research had focused in on the matching handwriting samples from Leidesdorff's accounts and the ledger at the Tehama Hotel.

I sat down on the dental chair, contemplating the image of the burly Leidesdorff in his warehouse, overseeing the transfer of raw materials and finished goods. It would have taken a diligent accountant to keep track of all of those in-kind exchanges.

Nothing in the materials I had read indicated that Leidesdorff had received a formal education. He had grown up on St. Croix, a Dutch colony populated by thousands of slaves who worked on the island's sugar cane plantations. Despite having a white Dutch father, Leidesdorff's educational opportunities on the island would have been limited by his mother's black skin. He'd left home at an early age, penniless, with only the shirt on his back. It seemed unlikely that he would have had the opportunity to learn how to read or write.

The handwriting on Leidesdorff's accounts—and on the Tehama ledger—must belong to someone else.

My fingers drummed the cashier counter as the image in the warehouse expanded. A shadow of a figure stood beside Leidesdorff. The ever present assistant, the only person he would have trusted with his finances, the silent maid—the writer must have been Hortense.

I strummed my fingers more and more rapidly on the counter. Maybe Hortense had stayed on in San Francisco after Leidesdorff's death. Could *she* have been the one who made Ralston's acquaintance at the Tehama Hotel? Was *she* the one responsible for the continued digging on the tunnel?

Sighing heavily, I looked over at the front door. The tulip shape embossed on its handle glinted in the morning light. "And what's the deal with all of the tulips?" I muttered to myself.

I set my thoughts aside as Ivan's truck pulled up to the curb. On cue, Monty stepped jauntily out the door of his studio and danced across the street, a fresh application of citrus aftershave glistening on his face.

I opened the door and walked out to the sidewalk where Ivan had begun to unload the special glass panels inlaid with the Green Vase icon.

I began to yawn a greeting to Ivan and Monty, but it caught in my throat as a short, rounded figure stepped out from behind Ivan's truck.

"Gordon," Monty said brightly. "Top of the morning to you!" He grabbed onto one of Gordon Bosco's pudgy white hands and began an energetic hand pump. Gordon smiled obligingly as he wrenched himself free from Monty's grasp.

"Good morning, dear," Gordon said, stroking the front buttons of his suit as he turned his attention towards me. "I was wondering if I might have a word with you? It's about your uncle and that business matter I mentioned the other night at the dominoes game." He ushered me towards the front door. "Perhaps we could step inside?"

"Okay," I said timidly.

I glanced nervously back at Monty and Ivan as Gordon mounted the steps to the Green Vase. He turned the handle, his thumb rubbing the tulip embossing on the doorknob. Sucking in my breath, I followed him inside.

Gordon strolled into the crowded showroom, his eyes sweeping over the dusty piles and cardboard boxes. Slowly, he rounded the dental chair and turned to face me, his confidence and authority undiminished by the dusty surroundings. I shuffled to a stop in front of the cashier counter, feeling much smaller than the short-statured man in front of me.

Gordon's thin lips stretched into a smile. He tilted his head at the stuffed kangaroo standing next to me. "That's an interesting addition."

I smiled meekly, gulping. "I found it in one of the shipping crates."

"I see." The pale skin above Gordon's lips twitched as he rubbed his stubby fingers together. "Have you found anything else—unusual—in the shipping crates?"

"No." There was barely enough air in my lungs to squeeze the word out.

Gordon ran a hand along the back edge of the dental chair. "Oscar was a good business partner," he said, his voice slow and measured. "One of the best I ever had."

Gordon stepped around the chair, edging closer to the cashier counter. "But, a couple of months ago, I began to think he might have changed his mind about our partnership . . . I began to suspect that Oscar was hiding something from me."

My back stiffened against the edge of the counter.

Gordon stared at me intently. "So I had to proceed with *alternative* means to keep the pressure on Oscar—to ensure the success of the operation."

I shifted uncomfortably against the counter as Gordon turned away from me and strode, Monty-like, through the Green Vase showroom.

"You see, a couple of years ago, I bought a small biotech company. They were foundering, about to go under, but I had a lead on a new drug that could turn it all around for them."

Gordon's eyes jumped in and out of the open crates as he circled through the room.

"I'd been sitting on the board here in Jackson Square long enough to hear the Leidesdorff rumors. How he faked his death, hooked up with Ralston, maybe even made off with those missing diamonds."

My breath shortened as Gordon's tiny feet turned back towards the front of the store. His turnip-shaped figure advanced through the room, twisting deftly around cardboard boxes and display cases until he stood, once again, behind the dental chair—only a few feet away from me.

"As the story goes, somewhere in his travels, Leidesdorff came across a recipe for a sleeping drought that would put a person into a trance—slow down their body functions—so much so that they looked as if they were . . ." Gordon's hands crunched down on the head cushion of the chair as he leaned towards me and said squarely, "dead."

Gordon's keen eyes squinted together as if he were trying to look inside my head. "I hired Oscar to track down the recipe. He knew everything about the Gold Rush era. I was sure that he was the man to find it."

Gordon took two swift steps towards the counter, his dark eyes curdling with his suspicions. "That Sunday morning, I came by the Green Vase to get the formula from him." He paused and pursed his thin lips. "But he was already . . . gone when I got here."

I looked down at the short man glaring up at me, now no more than six inches away from my chin. There was a faint reddishness on his upper lip, just beneath his enormous, strangely immobile nose.

"That formula is worth a great deal to me. I've banked everything on it. We're already in licensing negotiations to partner the development of the drug with several large pharmaceutical companies. This could revolutionize the treatment for traumatic injuries, replace anesthesia for surgeries. The potential applications—and revenue streams—are endless."

I turned my head towards the stuffed kangaroo, trying to avoid the flecks of spit issuing from Gordon's hardening lips. "What about the brain swelling?" I asked, remembering the description of Leidesdorff's symptoms. "It sounds like there were some pretty gruesome side effects."

"Don't worry your pretty head about that, dear." Gordon's thin lips curled up, as if they held a valuable secret. "All I need is the information that Oscar uncovered about the formula. I'm quite certain that it—and whatever else he might have found—are hidden here, in the Green Vase."

The sound of breaking glass crashed against the sidewalk outside; Ivan had dropped one of the glass-containing cartons.

Gordon stepped back from me. As he turned towards

the door, he tugged down on the cuffs of his sleeves, which, for once, appeared to be missing their tulip-shaped cufflinks.

"I would appreciate it," he said, his voice flattening to a more business-like tone, "if you would let me know as soon as you find it—the formula that is. The diamonds are yours to keep. That was my agreement with Oscar."

I watched Gordon exit out to Jackson Street. He breezed past Monty and Ivan, who were both bent over the dropped container, picking up shards of glass from the pavement.

I chewed on my lip, pondering Gordon's business plan and wondering how William Leidesdorff had found his way to the bottom of the bay so soon after taking the potion Gordon was so desperate to get his hands on.

Chapter 37

BY NOON, IVAN had finished with the installation of all but the broken pane of glass. He left only after issuing numerous apologies for the breakage. Shortly after his departure, Monty sped off for an appointment.

I decided it was time to pay a visit to Mr. Wang.

I slipped in among the lunch crowds as I approached the flower stall. Mrs. Wang and her daughter were swamped with customers, but Mr. Wang was nowhere to be seen.

Just then, the slight figure of Harold Wombler emerged from behind an enormously wide man contemplating the begonia rack. I watched as Harold lumbered jerkily inside the store.

"Does he not own another pair of overalls?" I thought as the breeze caught one of the flaps of material and flashed the pale skin of his knobby knees.

Harold Wombler swung behind the tulip rack, nimble despite his gimping leg. The top edge of the broom closet door opened and closed. No one else in the crowd of shoppers seemed to have noticed.

I glanced over to where Mrs. Wang had begun to interrogate the overweight begonia shopper. Her daughter was busy counting out change at the register. I slid behind the tulip rack and turned the knob on the broom closet door.

I waited for a moment inside the closet, wanting to make sure Harold got far enough ahead, so that he wouldn't hear me open the hatch. A discarded flowerpot had been tossed into the corner. I counted slowly to ten, imagining what Monty must have looked like with the pot on his head, then I eased open the hatch.

The iron bars of the ladder disappeared into the darkness of the tunnel. I had no flashlight, I sighed ruefully as I stared down into the abyss. Grimacing away my hesitation, I swung my foot out to catch the first iron bar of the ladder and started down, silently closing the hatch above me.

My feet struggled to find each rung in the darkness. I waited, hanging against the wall, hoping that my eyes would adjust to the absence of light. Slowly, the shadowy margins of the ladder emerged in front of my face. I gripped the metal bars tightly as I continued down the ladder, feeling a great relief when my right foot hit the solid surface of the floor of the tunnel.

Damp, clammy air sunk in around me as I looked up and down the dark passageway. A buzzing murmur of insects percolated beneath my feet, up the walls, and over my head.

To my left, heading away from the direction of the Green Vase, a dim light bobbed in time with Harold's unmistakable limp. I headed off after him, struggling to keep my footing on the slippery concrete floor.

With each step, the walls that I could sense more than see crept closer and closer towards me. The tunnel's width collapsed down, feeding the claustrophobic frenzy building in my brain. I tried not to think of the corpse I'd seen earlier that morning, buried for a hundred and fifty years, submerged first in water, then in yards and yards of sand and mud.

Finally, I drew near enough to the glimmer from Harold's light to see more of my surroundings. The constricting sides of the tunnel were wetter than I remembered, undulating with a myriad of insect inhabitants, each of them ogling me with their antennaed eyes. I wrapped my arms about my waist, trying not to touch the pulsing, suppurating wall.

The corners of the tunnel rustled resentfully as I edged forward. I gripped my sides tighter, hunching over as legions of insect legs scrambled across the low ceiling. Armored plates of black, shiny chitin clicked at me in a menacing, threatening undertone. My presence in this subterranean domain was clearly unwelcome.

I had to force myself to slow my pace. Every screaming instinct demanded that I hurtle pell-mell to the nearest exit. I crunched myself up into a walking ball and tried to focus on the straggling glimmer of Harold's dim light.

The tunnel became rougher and more unstable. The damp draft of air funneling through it carried the feculent tang of raw sewage. A slimy, glutinous coating layered the floor and the walls. I stared desperately at Harold's light, still bumping along about twenty feet in front of me.

To my over-hyped imagination, the grumbling, discordant chant of the tunnel's insects seemed to be taking on more of a hungry tenor. I clamped my hands down over my ears, trying to dampen the voice shrieking inside my head, warning that the bugs were preparing to eat me. My pulse quickened as an unmistakable whirl of ravenous cravings suddenly raced down the tunnel towards me and swarmed around my head, boring into my ears with its deafening roar.

I dropped to the floor, my voice screeching in terror. The rippling surface of the ceiling erupted into a frenzied, flying foment. A multitude of creatures pelted down on top of me, clattering like pecans as they landed and chivied across the concrete. My fingers frantically scraped at my scalp. Every inch of skin shivered in a retching effort to dislodge the scattering hoards.

Hoping that my scream had been masked by the thundering passage of the BART train, I slowly pulled my head up from its fetal position and glanced down the tunnel towards Harold's light. My breath caught in my throat as the beam stopped and swung upwards.

Each second dragged out until I realized that Harold and his flashlight were moving up a ladder. A loud sigh escaped my petrified lungs. I was finally getting out of this wretched tunnel.

I watched Harold's costive movements as he slowly scaled the ladder. My initial relief was quickly muted by the dimming of his disappearing light. A few moments later, I stood in the darkness, listening as Harold clambered through the hatch and snapped it shut.

A narrow shaft of light filtered through the tunnel, lifting the cloak of blackness enough for me to see my hands if I held them in front of my face. As I did so, a delicate, tickling sensation scurried up my arm, launched over my shoulder, and disappeared down my back.

My whole body shook violently as I tried to dislodge the interloping insect. Trembling, I brought my hand back up, scanning its surface.

Tears began streaming down my face as a quivering cockroach blinked back at me, tittering conversationally, inquisitively twitching his long, sinuous antennae. I slung my hand up and down, trying to dislodge him. But when I dared to look back down at my hand, he was still there— amorously batting his beady eyes at me, whirring his wings in a proud, preening fashion.

I cringed as the roach began to pace back and forth on my palm, chattering away in a foppish manner. Then he paused, one antennae hovering pointedly in the air as his angling eyes studied me. "I have a theory."

"Surely, I've lost my mind," I replied.

But the convivial bug wasn't finished. He resumed his discourse, fluttering his wings as he circled my palm. "What if Oscar pulled a Leidesdorff? What if he faked his death? Shouldn't you at least consider the possibility?"

A swirling of half-Oscar images appeared in the darkness, each of them clothed in his stained, navy blue shirt.

One of them took on Gordon Bosco's large beaking nose; another, Harold Wombler's loose, hanging skin. A third marched up wearing Frank Napis's mustache and turban. I shook my head, trying to rid myself of the vision.

It couldn't be—it wasn't possible. Uncle Oscar wouldn't have done this to me.

One by one, each of the Oscars faded back into the tunnel. I was alone in the darkness, surrounded by the pre-fab walls of my office cubicle.

An oppressive silence closed in on me. My grasping fingers scraped at the cloth-covered walls. My mouth gasped for air as my lungs constricted, straining for oxygen.

And then, a sound I never thought I'd be so happy to hear cut through my delusional rantings.

"I think we should go with the pink taffeta bolster, Dilla," Monty's muffled voice permeated through the ceiling above my head. "It'll match the tint in the icing on the cupcakes."

Chapter 38

I CHARGED UP the ladder, momentarily forgetting about Harold Wombler as I burst through the hatch. Monty's voice droned somewhere nearby as I stood up in a dark closet.

"Don't worry, Dilla, I'm going to go check with the caterer right now."

I slid forward, holding my hands out in front of me, my feet blindly searching the space ahead. My left toe stubbed up against a vertical surface, and my fingers found the soft, painted panel of a door. Without thinking, I pulled the tulip key out of my pocket and fumbled it into the smooth, tulip-embossed door handle. A clicking sound broke through my pounding breathing as the key turned, and the door creaked open.

I peeked out into a forest of stainless steel appliances. I appeared to be in a kitchen at the Palace Hotel. The train that had run over the top of the tunnel must have been the BART line on Market Street.

To my right, an industrial-sized dishwasher arduously steamed rows of white china plates. Pots and pans of every size hung from racks on the ceiling. Stacks of wide-mouthed aluminum bowls were crammed onto every available shelf.

There was no sign of Monty—or, for that matter, Harold.

"Monty?" I called out softly, creeping around the back side of the dishwasher down a narrow hallway lined with mammoth-sized walk-in freezers.

"Monty?" I whispered a little louder, my voice bouncing off of the sterile, stainless steel walls.

"Good grief woman, put a sock in it!" Monty's voice scratched hoarsely as one of his Jell-O-like arms snaked out from the closest walk-in and yanked me inside. "She's going to hear you."

"Oh, thank goodness," I said, expelling a sigh of relief. "You're not a roach."

Monty's jaw squinched out of alignment as he responded with a half-quizical, half-offended look.

I stared at him, puzzled. Perhaps it was the dim, fluorescent lighting and the refrigerated air of the walk-in freezer, but Monty looked truly distraught. Gray hollows sunk under his green eyes, further accentuating his clammy, chalk-white cheeks. His pale, anemic countenance was a drab contrast to his cheerful, daisy-shaped cufflinks and matching sunny-yellow bow tie. The curls that usually bounced along on the top of his head had been stretched beyond their natural elasticity. He had the rough, haggard look of a hunted animal.

"What are you doing here?" he whispered crankily, fretfully peeking around the edge of the door to the walk-in freezer.

"I was following Harold Wombler," I said simply, omitting for the moment a retelling of my tunnel-tracking expedition.

Monty jumped as if I'd snapped his last frayed nerve. "What's *he* doing here?" he demanded. "As if there weren't enough people here already," he muttered under his breath.

He pressed his finger to his lips, silently shushing me. From the other side of the room, I heard the heavy, thunking sound of footsteps.

"Montgomery Carmichael," a female voice called out huskily, as if she were trying to lure an escaped pet. Fingernails clicked against the surface of the metal tables in the next room. Monty pulled the freezer door completely shut and flicked off the interior light. We stood together in the refrigerated darkness as footsteps echoed on the tile hallway and clunked out of the room.

I poked Monty as he cracked open the door. "Oh, come on. It can't be that bad."

"You have no idea," he replied grimly. He poked his head out the door and swiveled it to look up and down the hallway.

"You can't hide from her forever," I said, rubbing my arms to keep warm.

"Who . . . what?" he asked distractedly, still casing the corridor.

"From Dilla," I said, exasperated. I was certain that it had been her voice calling for Monty. The pressure of planning the charity event, I figured, was getting to him.

"Right." Monty pulled his head back into the walk-in and gave me a weak, wan smile. "Dilla." He began pacing back and forth, his color returning as he picked up a cucumber and tossed it into the air. It somersaulted above his head and smacked down onto the palm of his hand.

He launched the cucumber back into the air. "You see, I've got a bit of a situation here . . ."

The cucumber took a sideways twist and came down awkwardly. Monty juggled it for a moment, trying to clasp his fingers around the slick surface of the tubular vegetable, but it slipped out and clanged into a stack of metal pans on the floor.

Monty's face blanched as the cucumber cascaded from one row of pans to the next. He grabbed my hand and pulled me out of the walk-in. "Come on, we've got to get out of here."

Monty led me out of the kitchen area and into a maze of hushed, hotel corridors. Plush carpeting muffled our footsteps. Smooth, caramel-colored walls lined with gilded mirrors streamed past as I struggled to keep up with his long strides.

We approached a wide corridor, the main artery on the first floor of the Palace Hotel. Sleepy, floating music tinkled in the background. Monty stayed hidden behind a recess in the hallway as I squirmed around him and peered out into the elegant arcade.

A group of suited men carrying briefcases flashed by, closely followed by a bellboy pushing a shiny chrome luggage cart. I was about to step out into the corridor when Monty's strong fingers yanked my shoulders backwards, jolting my feet off the floor. He pulled me into the side hall just as Dilla's bustling figure swept past in the main corridor.

She wore a bright, parrot-green suit accessorized with a colorful scarf and a hat plumed with an arching green feather. She smiled pleasantly at the gawking hotel guests, nodding as she passed them, occasionally pausing to glance down at the cell phone she clutched in her right hand.

Monty collapsed against the wall. "Whew," he breathed, staring at the ceiling.

I walked to the corner and peeked out into the corridor, watching as the feather bobbed into the ballroom at the opposite end.

"I think you're safe," I reported to an anxious Monty. "For now anyway."

On the other side of the corridor, across from our recessed position, gold lettering identified the entrance to "The Pied Piper Lounge." I double-checked for Dilla's feather, beckoned to Monty, and crossed to the heavy wooden doors.

I held the door open as Monty scampered across, crouching and dodging in and out behind the people passing by, antics which only succeeded in drawing attention to himself.

The heavy doors swished shut behind us, closing off the din of activity from the busy corridor. The dark-panelled room featured a gold-trimmed bar that spanned the length of the lounge, protecting a ten-foot painting mounted on the wall behind it. Monty began circling the room as I wandered in front of the room-filling canvas.

I'd seen the mural several times before. It was a famous Maxfield Parrish piece that had been commissioned by William Sharon, Ralston's business partner, who completed construction of the Palace Hotel and ran it for many years after Ralston's death.

The painting depicted a scene from the Pied Piper fairy tale. In the story, a small town becomes infested with rats. The townspeople try everything to get rid of the vermin, but they are unsuccessful. In desperation, they hire the Pied Piper. With one twirl of his flute, the rats are sent running, but the townspeople refuse to pay him. Feeling cheated, the Piper absconds with the town's children. The eventual fate of the children—whether they are thrown off the edge of a cliff or returned safely to their families—depends on which version of the tale you chose to read.

Monty circled back to me and leaned up against the bar. "Hmph," he said derisively. "*The Pied Piper*. It's never been one of my favorites. A bit pedantic for my tastes."

He turned away as his cell phone began ringing in his suit pocket. I remained fixated on the painting's depiction of the Piper and the kidnapped children scaling the rugged mountain terrain above the town. My eyes panned to the profile of the Piper and his prominent, hooking nose.

The nose was almost exactly the same shape as the hawk-like beak that fronted Gordon Bosco's otherwise flat face.

My confused, tumbling thoughts suddenly clarified.

"Monty," I murmured slowly as Miranda Richards walked into the lounge through the swinging wood doors, dragging an apologetic-looking Dilla behind her. "Have you ever considered wearing a turban?"

Chapter 39

FRIDAY MORNING, A damp—but clean—Rupert sat on the cashier counter by the window, slowly grooming through his rumpled, wet hairs. Isabella perched on top of the bookcase, her expression serene as the sun soaked her white, gleaming coat. I was still upstairs, cleaning up the mess from Rupert's mid-bath escape.

I let out a sad, pitiful sigh as I surveyed the scene.

Thanks to Rupert's wet romp through the litter box, dried clumps of litter now clung to every surface. The ubiquitous, sandy particles were splattered on the walls, sprinkled across the floorboards, and sifted into my sheets. It was a miracle there was any left in the box.

My knees ached from the hour spent crawling on the hardwood floor. Tiny pebbles of litter were imprinted into the palms of my hands and the soft covering of my kneecaps.

I finally cleaned my way to the bathroom—the site of the worst carnage. Litter lined the sides of both the tub and the sink. It had been artfully sprayed across the shower curtain in the form of an uninterpretable abstract image.

In the middle of the mess, the upended domed lid to the red, plastic litter box rocked silently back and forth. Rupert had knocked it completely off the bottom tray during his soapy rampage.

Rupert and Isabella sat down in the hallway just outside the bathroom, curiously watching as I bent down to pick up the lid.

"Awfully brave of you," I said testily to Rupert. "Returning to the scene of the crime. What—have you come to admire your handiwork . . ."

My voice trailed off as I stared at the underside of the litter box lid. A small package had been taped to the interior cavity that was meant to hold the charcoal filter.

Isabella clicked her vocal cords and chirped informatively.

I pulled the package off with difficulty. It was layered with excessive amounts of strapping tape.

Leaving the mess in the bathroom, I slowly carried Oscar's package downstairs to the kitchen. Rupert bounced along behind while Isabella wound between my feet, herding me down the steps.

I cut into the dusty package with a pair of scissors, carefully peeling back the layers of tape. Cautiously, I spread the contents out on the kitchen table.

An hour later, I'd unwound several industrial-sized paperclips and, following Oscar's detailed instructions, had begun to fold them into odd-shaped wire boxes.

Holding one up for inspection, I looked through the wire cage to the shelf on the wall opposite the table.

I set the cage on the table, stood up, and reached for Oscar's worn phone book.

After flipping through the yellowed pages, I found the marked entry under 'Eckles' and picked up the phone.

Chapter 40

A HARSH, CALLOUS wind ballooned against the black silk folds of my evening gown as I stepped out of a taxi in front of the Palace Hotel. A pair of porters jogged down the marble steps to help me unload the cats.

Monty followed the porters down the stairs, the long tails of his black velvet tuxedo flapping out behind him. "They're the stars of the show tonight, boys," he called out. "Take them right on into the ballroom."

Rupert and Isabella looked up through the grills in their crates at the gray, unsettled sky streaming above us. A smear of thick, bloated clouds barely restrained the wild wetness it had just whipped up from the sea. Tiny flecks of rain began to spatter onto the street as I followed Monty and the porters up the steps.

Inside, my high-heeled shoes slid awkwardly across the floor of the polished marble foyer. I wobbled past an over-sized flower display whose wide thicket of long, graceful stems almost touched the ceiling and crossed the central corridor to the entrance of the opulent ballroom, every edge and corner of which dripped with a swooping gold dressing.

Heavy drops of rain began to splinter against the stained glass ceiling. I glanced up, envisioning the tempest swirling above, thankful that, for once, I would be safely out of the water's reach.

Dilla spied me from across the room and raised her hand in a wave. She threaded her way through a sea of small, circular tables covered with sheets of almond pink taffeta, each one festooned with flowers and a heavy calorie count of cat-inspired confections.

Dilla was decked out in a low-waisted, flapper-style dress made from a shimmering silver fabric. A matching silver headband swept back the tight gray curls on her head while the tulip necklace hung around her neck. She bustled effortlessly through the growing crowd, acknowledging the guests as she swished by them.

"There you are, dear!" she said, smiling broadly. "They've taken the kitties to the dressing room. Here, I'll give you a tour on the way back."

Dilla led me into the ballroom, pointing at the elevated stage lining the back wall. "Monty will conduct the auction from the main stage," she said, her eyes sparkling with excitement, "while the kitty cats parade back and forth on the catwalk."

I shook my head, amused at the cat-sized runway that cut up through the center of the room, running perpendicular to the stage. Monty was nothing if not creative.

Waiters percolated through the taffeta tables with drinks and samplings from Monty's cat-shaped cupcakes. Monty himself bopped through the crowd, chatting and glad-handing with the guests, most of whom were connected in some way to Jackson Square. The curls on the top of his head bounced merrily up and down; his face flushed as he soaked up compliments.

"Well, thank you, thank you very much," I heard him gush to Etty Gabella. "Yes, the cupcakes were my idea. That frosting is delightful, don't you think?"

Across the room, I watched as the thickly mascaraed eyes of Miranda Richards honed in on Monty's giddy figure. Her long, blood-red nails clicked against the cat-walk platform, ominously transmitting her displeasure.

Miranda had chosen a hip-hugging, neck-plunging, red velvet gown for the night's event. Her hair was styled with a gleaming gold comb, the handle of which poked up out of her upswept hair. Her face was even more made-up than usual, enhancing the vampy effect of the outfit.

The gold fin of the comb sharked through the tables as she closed in on Monty. If he hadn't been so self-distracted, I would have tried to warn him. As it was, I could only shudder as Monty swung away from Etty and found himself face to face with Miranda's glowering Medusa.

Monty grimaced and instinctively lurched backwards, almost toppling a surprised, cupcake-carrying waiter. Monty spun sideways, trying to avoid the tumbling tray of pink frosting—and staggered straight into the arms of a nearly unrecognizable but clearly disgruntled Harold Wombler.

Harold had traded in his shredded overalls, for one night at least. The stiffly-pressed fabric of his tuxedo fell awkwardly onto his wrinkled frame. The pale skin of his scalp peeked out through the track marks of the brush that had combed through the greasy strands of his stringy black hair.

Monty smiled weakly into Harold's gruff, grisly glare as Miranda's long red nails cinched into the back of his collar.

Dilla tugged me towards the back of the stage and slid open a door that had been camouflaged in the wall panel-ing. I left Monty to his fate and followed her into a tiny dressing room where Rupert and Isabella waited impa-tiently in their crates.

Dilla shut the wall-panel door and pulled out the flat, wooden box that held the cat costumes. "Is everything ready on your end?" she whispered tensely.

I nodded solemnly as she handed me Isabella's chain mail costume.

Dilla picked up a silvery feather stole and looped it several times around her neck. She patted me on the shoulder, and, with a wink, whispered in my ear. "The rest of the pieces are in the box, dear. I'm heading back outside. I'll catch up with you later."

I waited for the door to shut behind her before I dug into the folds of the box, fished out the tulip necklace, and stashed it in the pocket of my dress.

I TURNED TO pull the rest of the cat costumes out of the box but jumped as a scraping bump sounded against the shared wall with the ballroom. A second later, the sword of Miranda's pungent perfume sliced into my nose.

The frostiness of her voice followed the perfume through the wall. "There'll be no shenanigans tonight, Mr. Carmichael. Do you understand me?"

Monty squeaked out a response. "Oh, no. No, of course not, Miranda."

"I'll be watching you," she replied threateningly. She must have turned away from the wall because her voice began to fade out as she muttered, "You *and* my mother."

Tentatively, I slid open the paneled door and found a pale-faced Monty cowering against the wall. Miranda's curvy, crimson figure marched towards the entrance of the ballroom where Dilla hovered, no doubt waiting for the Mayor to arrive.

Monty looked like he was about to faint. I pulled him into the dressing room.

"For the record," Monty hissed, "I *really* don't like this plan." The haggard look had returned to his eyes.

I gave him my sternest stare.

He threw his hands up in the air. "Miranda's going to *kill* me," he said, his whole body cringing.

"That's never slowed you down before," I replied caustically. "Don't worry," I smirked. "I'll protect you."

Grumbling under his breath, Monty picked up Rupert and carried him through the door to the ballroom.

I followed with Isabella. She leapt out of my arms as soon as I neared the catwalk, ready to begin her part in the evening's festivities.

Monty carried Rupert up the steps to the stage and gently set him down on the platform. Rupert walked a couple of paces up the catwalk, paused, and then wandered back to where Monty stood on the stage, fiddling with his microphone.

Rupert plopped his furry back end down next to Monty's feet. His bulging stomach poked jester-like out of his costume as he hungrily eyed a nearby table of cupcakes.

I glanced around the ballroom and found Frank Napis's turbaned head bobbing through the crowd. I shifted my position, trying to get a better look, but my view was blocked by a wave of neck turning that swept across the room. A chorus of gushy, female sighs confirmed that the Mayor had arrived.

A scuffle broke out in the hotel's main corridor as the Mayor's security personnel tackled a man in a bright yellow chicken suit. He had been showing up at the Mayor's public appearances ever since the newspaper report of the incident at the Italian restaurant.

Somewhat flustered by the loud clucking in the hallway, the Mayor hesitated at the entrance to the ballroom. He looked as if he was about to turn around, but a beaming Dilla quickly latched on to his arm and pulled him inside. Dilla began guiding the Mayor through the ballroom, her silver dress shimmering as she waltzed proudly beside him. Miranda trailed close behind them—intent on preventing Dilla from providing any further inspiration to the chicken imposter outside.

Sheets of rain curtained the domed, stained glass roof of the ballroom as a loud screech of feedback sounded from Monty's microphone. "Good evening everyone." He adjusted the sound down. "Good evening. Yes, that's better."

Monty's voice boomed over the pelting rain. "Welcome to tonight's charity event. We're so glad you could make it. I'm Montgomery Carmichael, and I'll be your auctioneer tonight. I'd like to thank our hostess for the evening, the lovely Dilla Eckles . . ."

Rupert remained seated on the podium, staring up with interest as Monty described the non-profit, no-kill shelter that would benefit from the evening's auction. As Monty spoke, Isabella began to saunter regally up and down the runway, glamorously blinking her long eyelashes at the crowd. Monty explained how the auction would be conducted, then invited the guests to approach the catwalk to inspect the cat costumes during the intermission.

I sat down at a taffeta table, watching as the crowd mingled towards the stage and catwalk.

Miranda must have been wearing an extra-strength version of her perfume, because a whiff of it hooked my nose from halfway across the room. I spent several seconds trying to stifle a perfume-induced sneeze before finally giving in.

"Ah . . . choo!"

"Bless you," Ivan said, appearing at my left shoulder.

He was dressed in a rented tuxedo that didn't quite fit his muscular frame. He tugged at the black tie circling his neck, looking as uncomfortable in his getup as I felt in mine.

"Cupcake?" he offered, holding up a small plate loaded with the tiny, pink-topped cakes.

"Thanks," I replied, trying to mask my unease. I took the nearest cupcake from Ivan's tray and carefully bit a corner off. "Mmm," I hummed nervously, attempting to make a show of appetite.

An even stronger surge of Miranda's perfume zoomed into my nostrils. My second sneeze nearly blew the icing off the cupcake.

"Gesundheit," Ivan said, laughing as I tried to wipe icing from my fingers. "Here, have something to wash it down."

He handed me a small cup of punch. The juice was a deep, berry red. It was a much darker color than the pink liquid in the cups I'd seen circulating on the waiters' trays. I looked back up at him, intending to decline the drink, but he was staring at me so intently, so eagerly, that I smiled back and took a sip.

I nearly choked on the tartness of the drink. That batch must have gotten a double dose of powder mix, I thought, still gagging as I set it down on the nearest table.

I scanned the room for a glass of water and found, instead, the beady eyes of Frank Napis—staring at me from underneath his blue silk turban. The strangest smile curved on the thin lips that lurked beneath his hulking mustache.

Monty shuffled up behind Frank and tapped him on the shoulder. Anxiously palming his microphone, Monty whispered something in Frank's ear.

Frank glanced up at the stage and began to walk towards it. Monty nodded grimly in my direction, indicating it was time for me to take up my position.

"Shall we take a look then?" I asked Ivan, the inside of my mouth still puckering. I ushered him towards the opposite side of the catwalk.

Rupert waddled up to me, licking a pink, frosty substance from his lips. I gently lifted him off of the platform and into my arms.

A beaming Dilla led the Mayor up to the catwalk. Miranda—a dark, suspicious look on her face—shadowed behind them.

I lost Ivan in the crowd gathering around the Mayor. Rupert and I slipped back towards the entrance to the kitchen as Dilla's carefully choreographed voice gushed, "Now, Mr. Mayor, I understand you're a bit of a diamond aficionado."

"Yes, well, I used to own a small shop on Union Street," he replied affably, his handsome face unaware of the trap Dilla was about to spring.

Dilla stroked his sleeve adoringly as the surrounding crowd leaned in. "These are pretend jewels of course, but you'll have to tell me what you think. They're from my late aunt's estate, you know."

Mr. Wang popped out of the doorway to the kitchen. "Good luck," he wheezed to me, patting Rupert on the head.

Over on the catwalk, Isabella strolled up to Dilla and the Mayor for an inspection. The lights from the ceiling above were focused on this stretch of the catwalk, so that the clear stones in Isabella's costume sparkled against her coat.

"Dilla," the Mayor gasped. "I thought you said this was costume jewelry."

The Mayor reached into his suit pocket for a monocle-sized eyepiece. He fitted it over his left eye and leaned towards the catwalk. Isabella paused, waiting, as he squinted at her costume.

Dilla nodded emphatically to a blanching Monty, who had edged up behind Napis's towering turban. Reluctantly, he pushed a button on his microphone, switching the device's input to a wire hidden in Dilla's silvery scarf.

The Mayor's voice echoed through the room. "In between the colored stones," he said, still studying Isabella's costume. "I'd swear those are *real* diamonds."

The room fell silent as the bewildered Mayor shook his head, trying to make sense of his inexplicably booming voice.

A faint, clicking sound ticked behind the wall. A second later, the lights went out.

The darkness was accompanied by a general sense of chaotic commotion. I ran into the kitchen with Rupert and raced down the corridor in the darkness, sliding on the slick tile floor in front of the line of walk-in refrigerators, desperately listening for the clinking sound of Isabella's costume. I let out a sigh of relief as she met us at the broom closet.

The lights came back on as I lifted up the hatch.

I tried to imagine the look on Miranda's face as Dilla swooned into the unfortunate Mayor's arms and sobbed convincingly, "My necklace! My necklace! It's gone!"

Chapter 41

PERCHED ON THE edge of the open hatch in the floor of the broom closet, I ripped off my high heels and crammed on the pair of running shoes I'd stashed earlier that evening.

Rupert hopped up and down impatiently as I slipped one handle of a wide-mouthed canvas bag over my head. I held the bag open for him, and he quickly clambered inside.

The bag bulged as Rupert scrambled to right himself. One of his back legs jabbed through the canvas into my stomach.

"We rehearsed this part, remember?" I said painfully as Rupert's head finally poked up out of the top of the bag.

I started down the ladder, pausing when my head sank even with the floor of the closet. Isabella climbed nimbly over my back and teetered on my shoulders as I continued my descent to the tunnel below. With all of this awkward cargo, the ladder seemed a lot longer than I remembered, but we finally made it to the bottom.

Isabella leapt from my shoulders as soon as my feet hit

the slick concrete floor. I reached into the bag, squeezed my arm around Rupert, and pulled out Oscar's trusty flashlight. I flicked it on and raced down the tunnel after Isabella, the black silk folds of my dress rippling out behind me.

The walls buzzed with a speculative chatter that propagated ahead of us, building up into a cheer as we sped through the dark passageway. The chain mail of Isabella's costume clinked in half time with my pounding feet. Rupert gripped his claws into the canvas bag as it bounced wildly off of my chest. An exhilarated thrill electrified every nerve of my perspiring body.

We passed the metal rungs that led up to Mr. Wang's flower shop. A few minutes later, the walls of the tunnel changed from slime-covered concrete to damp red bricks.

Nearly breathless, I pulled up at the entrance to the basement of the Green Vase. Panting heavily, I pulled the tulip key out of a zippered pocket in the canvas bag and engaged it in the lock. I followed Isabella into the basement, intentionally leaving the door ajar behind me.

I released Rupert from the canvas bag and climbed into one of the dusty wardrobes. The cats squashed in with me, Isabella keeping her keen blue eyes pasted on the opening in the brick wall.

I clicked off the flashlight, leaving us in the dim darkness of the single bare light bulb on the opposite side of the basement. Through the loose slats in the doors of the wardrobe, I could just make out the glossy black eyes of the stuffed kangaroo as it stared into the dark entrance of the tunnel.

WE DIDN'T HAVE long to wait. As soon as we settled into our spying position, the brick door creaked forward, pivoting on its interior hinge. I held my breath as a darkened figure in a black tuxedo emerged and stepped cautiously into the basement.

The furry fence of an imposing, red-haired mustache

covered the man's mouth. Generous amounts of wax had been applied to the fixture, particularly at its curling ends.

A blue silk turban was wrapped around the man's head—covering most of his tower of frizzy brown curls. His watery green eyes searched the darkness as he approached the kangaroo.

"I feel ridiculous," Monty said as he placed a hand on the kangaroo's shoulder. The pillow he'd stuffed under his cummerbund bulged out around his slender waist.

"You look great," I assured him from my camouflaged position in the wardrobe. "Very convincing."

Monty sent a nettled look in my direction and leaned in towards the kangaroo's face. Gingerly, he tipped open the mouth—free, once again, from the constraints of the thick black thread.

A tangible tension swept the air as the entrance to the tunnel creaked open a second time.

Chapter 42

"FRANK—I DIDN'T" think you could move that fast," a man whispered coldly out of the darkness.

I knew the voice, but it carried a harsh edge that twisted it into something strange and unfamiliar.

Monty's face was frozen, inches away from the kangaroo's gaping mouth. A bewildered expression muddled through his green eyes as they flickered briefly towards the location of my hiding place.

"I bet you thought you'd outsmarted me." One of the man's tanned, calloused hands clenched into a boulder-sized fist. "You and Dilla."

The fury of the speaker nearly strangled his voice. "But you see, it's very simple. Gordon wants the formula, and I want the diamonds."

The fake mustache bobbed up and down as Monty licked his lips and moved his fingers towards the open oral cavity.

"The gig's up." The voice grew louder, sneering, more irritated. "I know who you are—underneath that turban, behind that mustache."

A shadow stepped into the room. The faint light illuminated the strong bulky shoulders, the chiseled face . . . the red, knitted tissue of the scar that framed the rim of his jawbone.

"Step away from the kangaroo," Ivan paused, savoring the next word, "Oscar."

Monty's eyes bulged. A trickle of sweat slid down his face as Ivan lurched forward and grabbed his shoulder.

"Ivan, that's not Oscar."

It was a sharp, female voice we all instantly recognized. "Or Frank, for that matter. He's not that tall, even *with* that ridiculous turban."

Ivan whipped around as Miranda Richards stepped into the basement, her evening gown and heavy makeup seemingly unruffled by the trip through the tunnel.

Tucked inside the wardrobe, I shuddered as the floral fog of her perfume seeped through the crack between the doors. I put my hand over my nose, trying to form a barrier against the sticky sweet aroma, but its forceful fingers pried their way in. A faint trickle of irritation ran up and down my throat as the skin on the inside of my nose swelled in reaction to the offensive odor.

"Miranda? What are you doing here?" Ivan's hardened features rippled with uncertainty.

Monty shrunk out from under Ivan's loosened grip, dipping his shoulder as he rounded the kangaroo, careful to keep his face blocked by the animal's stuffed head.

"Following this ill-conceived circus, *obviously*," Miranda replied sharply.

She glowered at Ivan. "I warned Oscar about you. I knew what you were up to—but Oscar wanted to give you a chance." She glanced in Monty's direction, her eyes piercing through the stuffed kangaroo. "He always gave people a second chance."

Ivan wiped a thin layer of sweat from his brow as Miranda stepped into his face and poked a long, red fingernail into his chest. "I watched you work your way through Jackson Square on all of those renovation projects—looking for the entrance to the tunnel—looking for that wretched Ralston diamond. I knew you'd eventually worm your way into the Green Vase."

She sniffed, jabbing her nail at Ivan's ill-fitting suit. "But I didn't think you'd be stupid enough to fall for *this* little caper." She stepped around the kangaroo to glare at Monty. "I'll get to you in a minute, Mr. Carmichael."

Monty stepped sheepishly around the kangaroo, his narrow head comically balancing the wobbling turban. "Ah, Miranda, Ivan, good to see you," he said, his fingers nervously twiddling the fake mustache.

Miranda circled in front of the wardrobe. The intensity of her perfume surged around me. I began gulping in air through my mouth, desperately trying to avoid a sneeze.

"How can you think Oscar's still alive?" Miranda's scornful voice ilked accusingly at Ivan. "You were here the morning he died. Or, shall I say, *when* he died. You saw him go down, and you used the opportunity to search his basement. Then you left him on the floor and locked the door behind you."

"No," Ivan said, stepping back from Miranda's frightening glare. "No, he was perfectly fine when I left. It's your mother you should be talking to. Oscar kicked me out when Dilla arrived."

Miranda's eyes slanted into charcoal-colored slits as Ivan drew himself up, his lips firming resolutely. "Oscar's not dead. I'm sure of it. He found the recipe to Leidesdorff's sleeping potion. He used it to fake his death . . ." Ivan's face hardened again. ". . . after he found the diamond."

Miranda grabbed Ivan by the tie and bent him down towards her. "You fool. Leidesdorff didn't fake his death—he faked the symptoms leading up to it. Leidesdorff drowned the day after his fake funeral . . . just as the side effects from the toxin were about to kill him. Oscar found his body buried in the lot behind us."

Miranda shoved Ivan back towards the wall. "The potion doesn't work."

A feverish sweat dripped down my face as Miranda's perfume waged a second assault on the wardrobe. My nose blistered from the burning vapors. I couldn't hold back the sneeze much longer. I braced myself for the inevitable blast.

But the silence in the basement was broken by another sound—one that emanated at my feet.

Everyone turned towards the wardrobe as Rupert belched out a cupcake-smelling hiccup.

Chapter 43

"IT DOESN'T . . . WORK?" Ivan's voice murmured through the basement, dazed and disbelieving.

Three short footsteps slammed against the concrete. The door of the wardrobe flew open, and Miranda's furious face leaned in. "I tried to put you off this," she spit out at me as a gagging wave of perfume gushed into the wardrobe. "I tried to warn you."

But as I looked up and over Miranda's shoulder, the sneeze begging to be released from my nose was suddenly snuffed out—by the sight of the pale, de-turbaned man standing in the open door to the tunnel. Miranda read my stare and snapped her head out of the wardrobe.

The group of us stared in silence at the half-Frank Napis, half-Gordon Bosco figure who had just entered the basement.

Freed of the towering blue turban, his bare, balding head glistened in the dim light of the basement. The furry, orangish-red mustache hung lopsided from the flat plate of twitching skin above his thin, vanishing lips.

His demeanor was surprisingly unconcerned. "That's

very interesting, Miranda," he said, calmly removing the limp mustache from his lips. "But I disagree."

Minus the fuzzy Napis mustache and the protruding Bosco nose, the man's face faded almost into nothing, a soft lump of un-molded, shapeless clay.

Ivan shook his head, as if trying to clear his vision. Half-formed words sputtered out of Monty's mouth like water from a faulty sprinkler.

"Fra—? Gor—? Nooo . . ." The turban wobbled on Monty's head as he slapped a hand on one of his bony hips. "Well, I'll be a purple-legged hinky bird."

Miranda scowled. "Of course it doesn't work." Her thickly painted lips scrunched up derisively. "I should know. Leidesdorff's fiancée—the maid he brought here from New Orleans—is my great aunt, several times over."

I stumbled out of the wardrobe, my legs cramped and stiff. Rupert hopped out behind me and took a seat in front of Monty, curiously staring up at his wobbling turban and fake mustache. Isabella circled the room, her costume twinkling in the dim light as she paused to sniff at a small puddle of water collecting near the entrance of the tunnel.

Miranda glared callously at the un-masked man. Unfazed, he gazed steadily back at her.

"Did you really think I didn't know," she spat bitterly, "that it was *you* parading around in that turban, causing all of the trouble with the board?"

"To the contrary, Miranda" he replied, his voice calm and even. "I was counting on it."

She stepped back from him, shaking her head. "Oscar wouldn't let me confront you. He told me not to worry. He said that he had a plan."

Monty's right forefinger swung into action. "Aha!" he exclaimed, pointing at the ceiling. "I knew it. Oscar *did* fake his death!"

Monty dove behind the kangaroo, deflecting the blunt of Miranda's withering glare.

"I told you," she said, gritting her teeth, "all of you. The potion doesn't work."

Ivan gulped and tugged on his collar, his eyes nervously flitting back and forth between me and Miranda.

The short, featureless man stroked his chin thoughtfully. The pale skin above his thin lips twitched in the eerie glow of the basement. "Tell us then, Miranda," he said, his voice clear and deliberate. "Tell us what really happened to William Leidesdorff."

She glowered at him for a moment. Then, with a deprecating sigh, Miranda began to tell the story—the same one Dilla had relayed to me earlier that afternoon.

Chapter 44

"WILLIAM LEIDESDORFF MADE—and lost—his first fortune in New Orleans. It was the gambling. He couldn't walk away from a game of chance." Miranda swished through the basement as she spoke, filling it with her red velvet gown and swamping perfume.

"He was flamboyant and charismatic . . . worldly and charming . . . and, for a brief period, wildly rich. All of the women in New Orleans had their eye on him, but there was one French debutante who was particularly infatuated."

"Hortense," Monty and I said in unison.

Miranda nodded, her eyes registering a slight irritation from our interruption. "As Leidesdorff's gambling debts mounted and threatened to sink his business empire, he was quickly dropped from most social circles."

Miranda sighed sourly. "But Hortense was young and naive. She only became more obsessed with him. When her family rejected their proposed marriage, she ran away with him to California. The family told everyone that she had died to try to mitigate the resulting scandal."

The high heels on Miranda's feet stamped across the increasingly wet floor of the basement. The pool of water trickling into the basement from the tunnel seemed to be spreading.

"I suppose they were happy for a while, but the trouble that had started in New Orleans eventually followed them here. Leidesdorff never really kicked his gambling addiction. The seed of that sickness was always in him." Miranda shook her head. "Everything went downhill when Leidesdorff met Joseph Folsom."

"Ah," Monty interjected. He raised his forefinger as if he were about to contribute a thought, but Miranda silenced him with a throttling glare.

"Captain Folsom came to California to make a name for himself in the war with Mexico. But while there was plenty of fighting in other parts of the state, Northern California was relatively quiet. Folsom found himself stuck in an un-glamorous, low paying customs officer assignment. He grew frustrated standing by while everyone around him made fortunes buying and selling real estate. Even before the Gold Rush, the value of land in San Francisco had begun to dramatically appreciate—no one made more money off of that rise than William Leidesdorff."

Miranda's courtroom persona had taken over from her otherwise abrasive personality. For a moment, I found myself lost in the story, detached from the unpleasant harshness of the speaker.

"Folsom scraped together every penny of his meager earnings, trying to purchase a piece of land in the growing town, but he couldn't compete with the loads of money Leidesdorff could bring to the table. Folsom lost bid after bid."

Miranda paused to take a breath, and the silent room waited anxiously for her to continue. I brushed my fingers against my cheeks—they had begun to pulse with a faint inner heat. I must be coming down sick, I thought, swallowing thickly as Miranda resumed the story.

"When Folsom found out about Leidesdorff's gambling addiction, he knew he'd found his way in. It wasn't long before Leidesdorff lost his house, his warehouse, and most of his savings—all of it in games of chance."

A dull pounding began building inside my head. I thought wistfully of the aspirin bottle in the kitchen, two stories above.

"Hortense finally convinced Leidesdorff that they had to skip town. Leidesdorff collected a much gold as he could from his last piece of land up in the Sierras. They planned to sell it and hop aboard one of the sugar cane steamers en route to Hawaii. They'd have enough of a nest egg to start over somewhere new."

Miranda and her sweet, flowery perfume circled behind me, fueling the sickening wave of nausea in my stomach. My head swooned with lightness, and I grabbed on to the furry shoulder of the kangaroo.

"But Folsom was relentless. He organized a horse race and named Leidesdorff as the honorary sponsor. It was an historic event—the first one to be held in Northern California. Leidesdorff couldn't refuse.

"The race was held out by the Mission Dolores. Leidesdorff quickly got caught up in a bet on the main race. Despite the vast amount of gold sitting on it, Leidesdorff was about to ante up his land in the Sierras on a bet with Folsom when Hortense intervened."

Miranda drew up her breath, ran her tongue over the pasty coating of her lips, then continued. "Leidesdorff often wore a pair of tulip-shaped cufflinks. They were a present from Hortense. She'd bought them at a voodoo shop in New Orleans. You see, *she* was the one with the tulip fixation."

Miranda swung her curvy figure in front of the balding man standing in the corner of the basement. "The cufflinks had been specially designed, so that the interior of the stem was hollow. The head of each tulip could be twisted off to access a vial of sleeping potion inside the stem."

The balding man's pudgy fingers tugged on the tulip-free cuffs of his shirt. His thin lips curved up in a confident smile as Miranda pushed herself closer in towards his flat, featureless face.

"Leidesdorff never knew what hit him. His temperature jumped up; his face turned a bright, tomato red. He crumpled to the ground from the throbbing pain inside of his head. They carried him into the Mission to wait for a doctor, but he slipped into a coma before one could be summoned."

I was feeling more and more sympathy for the drugged Leidesdorff. My own head felt as if a dozen firefighters had pushed their way in to quench a five alarm blaze.

"Hortense confessed what she'd done to the Mission's priest, and he took pity on her. The priest pronounced Leidesdorff dead, and they hastily arranged the funeral. Hortense and the priest dug a rabbit hole under the wall of the church to feed ventilation into Leidesdorff's shallow grave. As soon as the funeral was over, the two of them hefted Leidesdorff's comatose body into a small dingy, and Hortense began rowing it through the bay."

Miranda's long, crunchy eyelashes were now only inches away from the balding head.

"She was a small woman. It took her all afternoon to get the boat back around to the small inlet cove near the entrance to the tunnel. She was planning on pulling in there for the night to let Leidesdorff recoup from the potion; then the two of them could row out to one of the steamer vessels the next morning."

Miranda's voice intensified sternly.

"Needless to say, the potion didn't perform as advertised. Leidesdorff did come out of the coma—but he was consumed by a delirious, drug-induced hallucination. The boat was just inside the cove, only about forty to fifty yards from the bank when all of Leidesdorff's thrashing about flipped it over. Hortense tried to save him . . . but it was all she could do to get to shore herself."

Miranda's sharply outlined eyes stared into the inky

blackness of the tunnel. "It was just as well. Leidesdorff drowned before the toxin could kill him."

Across the room, Ivan glanced uneasily at me, a flicker of emotion cluttering the strong lines of his face.

The sharp, eagle eyes of the de-turbaned, un-mustached man narrowed skeptically.

"Of course, Hortense blamed herself—but she never forgave Folsom for his role in Leidesdorff's demise. Hortense haunted him for the rest of his life. Folsom never understood why his luck took such a precipitous downward turn.

"Hortense sent Folsom on a wild-goose chase to the Virgin Islands to look for Anna Spark, the woman Hortense had paid to pose as Leidesdorff's mother. Folsom mortgaged everything he had to purchase the Leidesdorff land in the Sierras from the woman posing as Leidesdorff's mother, presumed to be his sole surviving heir.

"Hortense took on a disguise and obtained a position at the Tehama Hotel. She began spreading the rumor that Leidesdorff had faked his death—the mere thought of it nearly drove Folsom mad. Of course, the endless years of litigation over the Leidesdorff estate pushed him completely over the edge. By the time it finally concluded in Folsom's favor, he was bankrupt."

Miranda's dominating voice leveled the basement with its steely, shoveling tone.

"Folsom eventually died at the age of thirty-eight, the exact same age as Leidesdorff on his passing—from the sudden onset of a mysterious fever and unexplained brain swelling."

Chapter 45

"WHAT ABOUT THE tunnel?" Monty could stay quiet no longer. A squeaking peep piped out of his mouth as Miranda spun around at him and spiked the underside of his bouncing chin with one of her razor sharp nails. The turban teetered on his head as he stretched his long neck towards the ceiling. "Was Hortense responsible for that, too?"

"Yes," a deep, confident voice sounded through the basement before Miranda had a chance to respond. The balding man stepped forward into the center of our circle, his self-assurance apparently un-rattled by Miranda's revelations. Despite his altered appearance, I still thought of him as Gordon Bosco.

"Hortense never really accepted Leidesdorff's death. She always held on to the hope that the potion worked—that he might be revived—if only she could find him."

Monty collapsed against the wall of the basement as Miranda released him from her hooking fingernail.

"Hortense met William Ralston while she was working at the Tehama Hotel," Gordon continued. "She knew he could help her. He was one of the few people with the influence and capital to extend the tunnel through the landfill towards the area where Leidesdorff had drowned, where he was now buried."

My feverish vision blurred as I stared into the flat, rolling contours of Gordon's face. Dizzying, I glanced down at my feet where the icy pool of water seeping in from the tunnel had begun to soak my running shoes.

"Ralston was intrigued by Hortense's story—particularly when she told him about the underground tunnel. Ralston purchased the Tehama for the site of his new bank. He had the old building lifted up from its foundation and carted off, so that the substructure remained undisturbed."

The cool water crept up over my shoes, lapping frigid shackles around my ankles.

"Hortense pleaded with Ralston to extend the tunnel through the new landfill to the area where Leidesdorff had drowned. Ralston wanted to keep the tunnel a secret, so he agreed—in exchange for her silence."

A frigid tension crept up my legs, tightening the tendons that ran behind my knees.

"Ralston's workers finished the Green Vase end of the tunnel without any sign of Leidesdorff's corpse. Hortense tried to convince Ralston to dig further, but he had already set his sights on his new hotel—whose location would be on the other side of town. Ralston focused all of his resources on the tunnel's extension to the new construction site."

My shoulders scrunched up as the rising freeze of the water met the feverish heat of my head.

"Hortense didn't take his rejection well. The last Ralston saw of her was right before the diamonds went missing from the vault at his bank." Gordon stroked his thin lips thoughtfully. "Hortense used the smaller diamonds to make the cat costumes, but the larger one was too big to fit into the chain netting. Oscar was pretty sure she hid it here in the Green Vase."

"If you figured out all of this," Miranda sighed tiredly, "why are you so insistent that the potion works?" Her voice remained firm, but her darkened eyes had begun to betray her.

"Oh, it works." Gordon replied slyly. "Like you, Oscar tried to convince me that it didn't. But I didn't believe it then, and I don't believe it now." He strummed his substantial stomach. "Tell me, dear," he said, leaning towards me. "I'm so curious. What's hidden in the stuffed kangaroo?"

I stared back, unable to answer. The pounding in my head had become unbearable. I felt as if I might pass out at any moment.

Ivan pursed his lips and briskly approached the kangaroo. His roughened fingers reached into the open mouth and gingerly fished out Oscar's wadded up handkerchief. He unfolded the worn cloth and unwrapped a gleaming wire cage.

"Hey," Monty said, reaching over Ivan's right shoulder to pluck the cage out of Ivan's hands. "That's the thing my dry cleaner found in my shirt pocket."

I struggled to clear my throat. "It's a spider cage," I whispered hoarsely. "Oscar traveled all the way to New Orleans to track down the old voodoo recipe Hortense had picked up there. It uses venom from a spider that now lives in the Australian desert."

Monty turned the glinting wires over in his hands. "I can poke my fingers through the wires," he said nervously, holding the cage up to catch the dim light on the opposite end of the basement. "How does it keep them trapped inside?"

"It doesn't," Gordon replied, his eyes gleaming. "The spiders just like to spin their webs inside these wire structures. They're kind of small. If you look closely, I think there's one in there right now."

Monty began bobbling the cage in his fingers as Gordon continued softly. "You know, the venom from this spider has an extraordinary effect on human beings."

Monty gulped as Gordon crept a circle around him. "It causes a rapid swelling when injected into the skin.

I've seen it make a person's earlobe swell up like a grapefruit."

The wire cage flew up into the air as Monty screeched and grabbed onto both sides of the turban, frantically pulling it down over his ears.

Miranda caught the wire cage in her hand, apparently unconcerned with the spider riding inside of it. "You can't get hurt from just one," she said scornfully. "It takes hundreds and hundreds of spiders to make up a small amount of potion."

Gordon nodded as he pulled a gold, tulip-shaped cufflink out of his pocket. He held it in front of my face, so that I could read the 'Made in Japan' label on its back. "I think you're familiar with my new line of cufflinks. You found the empty one I'd tossed into the bottom of that construction site across town."

The rod-shaped gold piece flickered in the dim light as Gordon rolled it back and forth in his fingers. "I had a set of them made a couple of months ago. They're a lot like the ones William Leidesdorff used to wear—with a slight improvement."

Like a magician performing for an audience, Gordon flourished his fingers and wrapped them around the tulip head. Slowly, he unscrewed the lid on the small vial concealed within the stem. As he lifted the lid, I saw that it had been adapted to fit a narrow gauge needle. Hanging from the pointed tip of the needle was a drop of deep, berry red liquid.

It was the same red color as the juice Ivan had offered me earlier at the Palace Hotel.

"I ran a little experiment a while back. I injected a single drop of the toxin into the earlobe of our arachnophobic friend here," Gordon said casually. "Predictably, his ear swelled up like a balloon. Then, I sent him over to Oscar's for the antidote."

Still tugging desperately down on the blue silk turban, Monty's eyes bulged. "Oscar gave me a drink of water . . . I thought it was water . . ."

The red drop hanging from the tip of the needle let loose and fell to the floor. The drop of liquid formed a neat circle on the concrete. Slowly, the circle turned from berry red to a burnt reddish shade.

It was the same color as the stain on the floor of the Green Vase.

My face flushed with the heat burning under my forehead.

"If a larger dose is administered, the toxin causes the fever, encephalitis, and, finally, comatose state that William Leidesdorff experienced, sometimes interrupted by hallucinations. I am quite certain, however, that all of those nasty side effects can be prevented and a convincing comatose state still achieved—with use of the appropriate antidote. That's what Oscar was holding back from me. That's the last piece I need."

The voice fell away, as distant and blurry as Gordon Bosco's fading, nondescript face. "Are you feeling ill, dear. You look a bit feverish."

The freezing water bound itself around my knees, lashing frosted welts against my legs. I collapsed onto the floor, icy drops splashing and sizzling against my burning cheeks, as a great roaring rush echoed through the tunnel.

Chapter 46

A TOWERING WALL of water crashed through the entrance to the tunnel and pounded into the basement, submerging us all in a swirling vortex of upended shipping crates, streaking mascara, bobbing turbans, and fake mustaches.

The soggy, white lump of Rupert floated past me, the jewels in his chain jacket leaking a rainbow of color into the water. I tried to grab onto him, but he tumbled by, just out of reach.

Out of nowhere, one of Monty's long, stringy arms chased after Rupert's white blur, and his fingers latched onto the netting of the chain jacket. Monty's free arm looped around the kangaroo's neck and together he and Rupert rode up through the hatch on the shoulders of the inexplicably buoyant kangaroo.

A million thoughts swam through my bleary, waterlogged head as I sank deeper into the turbulent water.

William Leidesdorff's terrified, thrashing figure tumbled past me, the arms of his brown suede jacket flailing inches from my nose. Underneath his thick lamb chop sideburns, the swarthy skin of his handsome face contorted with confusion, struggling to understand the unseen force that had struck him down.

He was followed by Hortense, already exhausted from the hours of paddling the small, loaded dingy through the choppy waters of the bay. The thick folds of her dress pulled down on her as she fought to tread water, each ream of fabric a ballooning weight. Already, her face was scarred by the unthinkable awareness of Leidesdorff's lifeless body sinking through the depths below. As fewer and fewer bubbles percolated to the surface, her mind broke from the realization that her world had changed forever.

A moment later, the round, torpedo-shaped body of William Ralston flashed past me, his short, stubby arms making ineffectual cuts at the hard, unrelenting sea. The hungry waves slipped their drowning tentacles into his lungs, feasting on his denial, his refusal to acknowledge the failures that had drowned his business, his hopes, his dreams . . . his life.

The liquid weight of the water pushed up against my chest and bruised my back against the concrete floor. A numbing darkness circled around me, stifling all thought, all action. I found myself curtained in the deep, cloth-covered silence of my cubicle—filled only by a constant stream of colorless, meaningless numbers, slowly stealing seconds . . . minutes . . . hours . . . until there was no more time left.

Somehow, I sensed Oscar's presence in the basement, looming just beyond the boundaries of my limited vision. His voice carried through the water. "We're almost done. We can't turn back now."

I looked up through the layers of sparkling water to a perfect blue sky. Oscar's voice sounded again. "It's in the tulips."

I shook my head, flustered even in the depths of my delirium. "What does that mean?" I tried to shout, but the water had sealed my lips tightly shut.

Two white kitty cats sat by the side of the warehouse,

hiding in the leaves of the three petaled tulips. In the tulips . . .

My chest prickled as if punctured by a million cactus spines. My brain pounded against my skull. The hot feverish pressure swelled in my head. I couldn't take much more.

One of Miranda's sharp red nails circled around my neck. I looked up into her face, streaked with black smears of mascara, her eyes dark, glowing circles.

Gordon stood behind her, smiling serenely, watching as Miranda deftly prized open my mouth and poured in a sickeningly sweet liquid. My mouth was filled with the horrible taste of her highly concentrated, floral perfume.

Isabella chirped sharply as Harold Wombler bent down on the floor next to Miranda. His slippery, sliding fingers began to stuff tulip petals into my gaping mouth. Their silky smooth texture provided an instant comfort to my pulsing tongue.

Gordon Bosco beamed triumphantly and scampered to the other end of the basement, up the rickety stairs and through the hatch as a giant sucking sound pulled the water back into the tunnel and slammed the door shut.

Chapter 47

I OPENED MY eyes to the cold, antiseptic atmosphere of a hospital. The dark and quiet of the room was interrupted only by the regular beeping of the machines surrounding my bed. A remarkable sensation of antiseptically soaked oxygen passed freely in and out of my lungs.

I pushed myself up on my elbows to study the other occupants of the room. The turban still perched on his head, Monty slumped in a chair near the door, his long face smashed up against the wall, a slimy string of drool hanging from his bottom lip.

Miranda paced the far side of the room in one of her bright red, fitted suits. She forced her painted lips into a half-smile as she leaned over my bed and asked, "You've come through it then?"

I blinked, suddenly remembering the flood in the basement. "What happened?" I gasped as the words seared my parched throat. "Where are Rupert and Isabella?"

Miranda waved her manicured hand dismissively. "They're fine—staying with Mr. Wang until you're ready to pick them up."

I put my hand against my damp, clammy forehead. "Where did all of that water come from?"

"There wasn't any water," Miranda snapped. "Ivan hit you with the toxin. It can cause extreme delusions—of drowning." She smirked. "You're lucky I was there with the antidote."

"Antidote?" I murmured, my head still groggy.

Miranda let out a tired sigh. "A concentrated extract of tulip petals. I had the cupcake frosting laced with it, but I guess it wasn't enough to offset the dose you got. I've been carrying the stuff around with me for weeks—ever since Oscar . . ." She pursed her lips. "I'm surprised you haven't noticed—it has a pretty strong smell."

I rubbed my eyes, remembering the last scene from the basement. "You . . . poured it down my throat."

Miranda nodded. "It has to be administered orally, to be effective." She shook her head, as if disappointed in my performance. "Now Gordon Bosco has the antidote—although I'm sure he's dropped that name for good now."

"I thought he wanted it for his biotech company?" I asked, feeling bewildered.

Miranda's high heels stamped a semi-circle through the cramped space around my bed. "The company was a ruse, a shell with no employees—it gave him a legitimate excuse to pursue the potion. No, he's got some other purpose in mind, I'm afraid."

She pursed her lips. "Ivan, of course, has been arrested. He had already committed several violations of his parole, but the poisoning on top of that should put him back in prison for a while."

I gripped the sides of the bed, suddenly feeling the loss of time. "How long have I been . . . asleep?"

Miranda rolled her eyes, "Several days now. I didn't think you were ever going to wake up." She glanced over at Monty's snoring frame and wrinkled her powdered nose. "*Please* tell Mr. Carmichael to go home and take a shower."

Miranda leaned over my bed, her eyes harshly probing

my face. One of the red claws pressed into my arm. "My mother disappeared in all of the melee at the Palace Hotel," she said sharply, her eyes interrogating me. "I don't suppose you know where she's run off to?"

"Harold was there, too—in the basement," I murmured, now feigning my fogginess. "He put tulip petals . . . on my tongue."

"No. No, he wasn't." Miranda turned away from the bed, her voice lacking its usual conviction. "You must be mistaken."

I CHECKED OUT of the hospital two days later. Mrs. Wang dropped the cats off soon after I arrived back at the Green Vase. I released Rupert and Isabella from their cat carriers and shut the door behind us.

"Have you got it, then?" Mrs. Wang asked—in a voice that sounded an awful lot like Dilla Eckles.

I smiled, pulled the tulip necklace out of my pocket, and handed it to her.

She took the necklace from me, twisting its tulip chain links over in her hands. Turning back towards the door, she flipped open the locket. I watched over her shoulder as the faded photo of Leidesdorff honed in on the door handle.

Mrs. Wang carefully fed the edge of the locket lid into a flat, curling crevice carved into the sculpted tulips in the facing surrounding the handle. The slightest click sounded as the ridges engaged with a hidden fixture and a cavity behind the facing popped open.

Mrs. Wang reached inside and plucked out a package. She turned to me and pressed it into the palm of my right hand.

"Oh, no, honey, this is for you," she replied to my surprised expression.

"What am I going to do with . . ." I sputtered.

But she was already out the door, disappearing down the street.

A week later, my tires crunched on the gravel of the cemetery's parking lot. A light, misting rain began to fall as I stepped outside of the car and zipped up my rain jacket.

Monty babbled along beside me as we followed a group of mourners down a cinder path into the maze of stone markers. "It was so sudden—shocking really."

"He had chronic emphysema from all of that smoking," I replied, trying to hide my emotions. "He lived a lot longer than the doctors thought he would."

After Mr. Wang's funeral, Monty and I walked up the hill to Oscar's headstone. The falling moisture had collected on the shoots of fresh grass covering his grave, pooling into sparkling, jewel-like drops on the bending tips of the blades.

I stared down into the shimmering green, waiting for Monty's inevitable commentary.

"You could have him dug up," he said. "Exhumed, I believe, is the proper term. So that you would know, one way or the other, for certain."

I shook my head.

Monty raised his finger to the dark clouds above our head. "Shouldn't you at least consider . . . ," but his voice trailed off at my resolute expression.

I reached into my pocket and ran my fingers over the cold, cool surface of the stone resting inside.

"Well, are you up for dinner?" Monty asked energetically. "There's a new restaurant that just opened up. All of the critics are raving about it—it's radical San Francisco cuisine. They're serving fried chicken."

The rain began to fall harder as we walked out of the cemetery to the parking lot—the drops sliding harmlessly off of the firm outer layer of my skin.

"I've got a new idea for your store." Monty offered, undeterred by my silent pondering. "I've been discussing it with Rupert. He's quite keen on it—well, he will be once he gets used to the idea."

I rolled my eyes towards the dark sky above us.

"Forget about antiques and accounting. You need a break from all of that. It's time for a dramatic change." He swung his arms out grandly. "I think you should open up a salon—for cats! You know, where they can get bathed, blown dry, and manicured. People would definitely pay for that, here, in San Francisco."

I shook my head, trying not to laugh. "Monty," I said, finally speaking, "I really don't think . . ."

"I've got a friend over at the *Chronicle*. I bet we could get him to do an article on you. I can see the headline now:

FORMER ACCOUNTANT AND FELINE ENTHUSIAST REBECCA M. HALE SHARES HER INSIGHTS ON HOW TO WASH A CAT

> "[A] wild, refreshing
> over-the-top-of-Nob-Hill thriller."
>
> —*The Best Reviews*

THE *NEW YORK TIMES* BESTSELLING SERIES FROM

· Rebecca M. Hale ·

HOW TO MOON A CAT

A Cats and Curios Mystery

When Rupert the cat sniffs out a dusty green vase with a toy bear inside, his owner has no doubt this is another of her Uncle Oscar's infamous clues to one of his valuable hidden treasures. Eager to put together the pieces of the puzzle, she's soon heading to Nevada City with her two cats, having no idea that this road trip will put her life in danger.

facebook.com/TheCrimeSceneBooks
penguin.com
howtowashacat.com